BLOOD AND JUDGMENT

LARS WALKER

BLOOD AND JUDGMENT

This is a work of fiction. All the characters and events portrayed in this book are fictional, and any resemblance to real people or incidents is purely coincidental.

A Baen Books Original

Baen Publishing Enterprises
P.O. Box 1403
Riverdale, NY 10471
www.baen.com

ISBN: 0-7434-7173-3

Cover art by Gary Ruddell

First printing, December 2003

Distributed by Simon & Schuster
1230 Avenue of the Americas
New York, NY 10020

Production by Windhaven Press, Auburn, NH
Printed in the United States of America

For Mark and Patty

Many thanks are due to Prof. Dale Nelson of Mayville State University, North Dakota, and to Dave Alpern, for making time to read the manuscript of this book. Their comments and suggestions were insightful and invaluable.

❋ PROLOGUE ❋

"Who needs counselors?" asked Ben. His brother Frank stretched the blanket over the window while he smashed it in with a brick. The glass fell inside the building almost silently.

"Not us, man," said Frank. He folded the blanket over the frame to protect them from shards and they scrambled inside.

"Damn straight," said Ben. "We coulda spent thousands of bucks on some fancy-ass shrink, but we worked it out on our own."

"That's right, bro."

Inside, they stood facing each other in street light from the window, two men with ponytails. Ben was a large, fat, bearded man in jeans and a black leather jacket. Frank was a skinny bearded man in a tie-dyed T-shirt and cargo pants.

1

"You know what we got?" asked Ben.

"No?" asked Frank, who wasn't tracking very well.

"Common ground," said Ben. "I heard somebody say that on the radio once. Common ground."

"Common ground. Awesome, man."

"That's all we need, common ground. You got common ground, you can work anything out. Specially in a family."

"Hey, man, I'm really sorry for all that crap I said."

"And I'm sorry I set your van on fire."

"Hey, it's cool."

They shared a hug.

"So where're we gonna do this?" asked Ben.

Frank looked around vaguely, but the building was dark.

"Maybe up on the stage there, where the altar used to be," Ben suggested.

Frank set off down the center aisle, between the theater seats, and Ben followed him up the steps to the stage. They sat themselves facing each other, cross-legged in the dark.

"This musta been a real pretty little church, before those arts-farts turned it into a pansy theater," said Ben, looking around.

"I can still feel the church vibes," said Frank. "Gives me the heebie-jeebies."

"That's what I mean. Common ground. This is something we can—you know—share."

"Share, man—that's cool. Hey, I love you,

brother. I'm sorry I called you a fascist, redneck carrion-eater."

"Bygones will be bygones. I'm sorry I called you a rat's-ass Commie slacker."

"Water under the rainbow, man."

"Well, how we gonna do this?"

"We need, you know, some kind of fire, and something to make it spread. I got fire." Frank pulled a Bic lighter, some Zigzag papers and a baggy full of pot from the pockets of his cargo pants. He began to roll himself a joint with practiced fingers, the first smooth, efficient movement he'd made all evening.

"I've got the stuff to make it spread," said Ben, pulling a bottle of amber liquid in a paper bag from under his jacket. "You know, we won't need all of this. Sin to waste it." He twisted the cap off and took a pull as Frank lit up. "Ground don't get any commoner than this," Ben said.

It was at that moment that they both realized they were not alone.

The police report filed later that night said that the two men received the lacerations that put them in the hospital through trying to jump simultaneously through the same broken window.

❄ CHAPTER 1 ❄

Will Sverdrup picked his way between furniture and human legs in the crowded teachers' lounge, headed for the telephone. For luck, it wasn't in use. The worst part of the casting process was the handful of days you spent waiting between auditions and call-backs. He'd waited long enough. He wanted to know.

I won't be Hamlet, he told himself as he dialed Bess's number. *I'll get a good part, like Horatio or Laertes, but I won't get the big one. I can handle that.* The phone rang at the other end. Good. He'd tried to reach Bess twice before, but the line had been busy. She'd been using it, making call-backs.

"Check's in the mail," said the voice at the other end.

"Hi Bess. It's Will, returning your call."

"Hey, Will, I've been waiting to hear back

4

from you. I'm happy to inform you that you've been cast as Hamlet, if you're willing to accept the part."

Will nearly dropped the receiver.

"Hey, Will—you there?"

"Yeah—I don't know what to say."

"Say you'll take the part and work like hell to make us glad we cast you."

"I can't believe it. The part was Randy's. Everybody knew that. He's got the talent, he's got the moves—he even looks good in tights."

"Oh no it wasn't, my low-self-esteemed friend. The part was yours from the beginning."

"But Randy—"

"Randy's all flash. He's got great tricks. I'd cast him in a minute as Richard III, or Ariel, or Puck. But Hamlet is the greatest part in the greatest play in the English language—maybe the greatest play in the world. It calls for more than nice legs and ballet moves. You're wrong. Everybody knew the part was yours—everybody but you.

"And by the way, you don't look so bad in tights yourself."

Will accepted the part formally and hung the phone up. He announced the casting to the other teachers, who gave him a loud standing ovation, so that he was sorry he'd mentioned it.

Wanting time alone, he headed out into the hall and toward an exit. As he turned a corner he ran into Principal Hellstrom. Each of them took a short jump backwards.

"Still with the white shirt and tie, Will?" asked the principal. He was a large bald man with a goatee. He wore a black "NO FEAR" T-shirt, jeans and a reversed baseball cap. Will frankly didn't consider that appropriate attire for a school administrator, but he kept his mouth shut about it.

"The students'll never listen to you unless you get into their world," said Hellstrom.

Students were coming down the hall. No point in pursuing this in public. No point in pursuing it at all, when it came to that. Will said he'd think about it and went on his way again.

He made a detour for the nearest men's room. When he pushed the door open he found a large sophomore boy and a small junior boy inside. The large sophomore, a young man named Eric Smedhammer equipped with a shaved head, several tattoos and innumerable piercings, had the junior (a boy named Jason Something) up against the wall next to the paper towel dispenser, one big hand around his throat.

At the sight of a teacher, Eric let his victim go. He followed the victim out, walking straight forward so that Will had to move out of his way, a small smile on his face. Will found himself staring at the boy's black T-shirt, silk-screened with a picture of Yggxvthwul, the tentacled monster-antihero of a popular video game.

Will let him go. He should have talked to him, put him on report. But Eric had been through a terrible ordeal. Everyone was cutting him slack for the time being.

The face Will saw in the mirror as he washed his hands was one he'd never been able to categorize, though categorizing faces was a hobby of his. The brown hair was a little longer than the current fashion. The face was neither round nor long, and its nose could only be described as "average."

He thought it was a good kind of face for an actor.

He could be anyone.

Not entirely by coincidence, Will's sophomore English class was beginning a study of *Hamlet*.

"Will we have to go to your play?" asked Jason Nordquist, a red-haired boy.

"I suppose there might be some kind of extra credit if you wrote a report on it."

"And what happens if we give the star, like, a thumbs-down?" asked Jason Weber, a fat boy.

"You'd have to give a good reason, and demonstrate an understanding of the play that would justify your review."

"Hey, that's blackmail," said Jason Nordquist.

"No, extortion. Now let's look at the play itself. You've all read it, I hope—or at least started it. Who can give us a short synopsis—what's the plot of the play?"

After a silence in which students looked at each other nervously, Jason Weber said, "Hamlet's the prince of Denmark. His uncle killed his father and married his mother, and the uncle's the king now. His father's ghost tells Hamlet what happened. Hamlet pretends to be insane so his uncle won't look for any trouble from him. He kills an old man, Polonius, who was spying on him. The king sends him to England. Polonius' daughter Ophelia, who was Hamlet's girlfriend, goes nuts with grief. Her brother—what's the name?"

"Laertes," said Will. "Go on. You're doing great."

"Laertes plots with the king to kill Hamlet. Hamlet comes back quicker than expected, and fights a duel with Laertes. The king and Laertes poison the tip of Hamlet's sword, and also poison a cup of wine that they figure he'll drink from. But Hamlet's mother drinks the wine first and croaks, and Laertes gets stuck with the sword before Hamlet gets wounded with it. When Hamlet figures out what's happening, he kills the king before he dies himself, and by then the stage is full of dead bodies. Kinda like the Denmark Chainsaw Massacre."

"Good," said Will. "Concise and accurate. So why do we still read *Hamlet*, and perform it, after three hundred years? What is *Hamlet* about?"

"It's about a man who couldn't make up his mind?" hazarded Kimberly Olson, a good student.

"You've seen the Laurence Olivier movie, I take it?"

"My dad rented it once."

"I saw part of the Kenneth Branagh one," said Jason Weber. "I liked the part at the end where Norway conquered Denmark."

"That was an interesting way to do it," said Will. "It's something we Norwegians dreamed about for hundreds of years in real life, but never quite managed. It's not quite as good for me though, because I'm part Dane myself. My ancestors came from Norway, but some of *their* ancestors came from Denmark, and brought the name 'Sverdrup' with them.

"But back to Olivier. He's a bit out of fashion just now, but his is one point of view. Even so, to say Hamlet can't make up his mind begs the question. The real issue is, *why* does Hamlet hesitate? Why does he have trouble just going ahead and getting revenge for his father's murder?"

"Because it would be immoral?" asked a girl named Kimberly Engel.

"That's an interesting point." There were groans from the class. "All right, it's an interesting point to *me*. The original Hamlet, who may have been a genuine historical character, was a Viking, or maybe a pre-Viking.

"The oldest version of the story we have comes from a Danish historian named Saxo Grammaticus, who wrote in the early thirteenth century. It's impossible to date the story—assuming it actually happened—because Saxo was an incredibly sloppy historian. He threw every legend he could find in a hat and pulled them out in whatever order he grabbed them—"

"You mean Shakespeare stole the story? He was a—what do you call it—plagiarizer?" asked Jason Nordquist.

"No. Not at all. If you ever read Saxo—and don't worry, I'm not gonna put you through that—you'd see that Shakespeare made gold out of lead. Saxo's Hamlet story is a kind of Clever Jack fairy tale, and a bad one. Even on its own terms it doesn't hold together."

"But wasn't there a Hamlet play before Shakespeare's?" asked Kimberly Olson.

"There seems to have been. A playwright named Thomas Kyd may have written it, but we don't have that play, so we can't tell what, if anything, Shakespeare may have borrowed."

Somebody said something Will didn't catch, and there was giggling.

"Look," said Will. "Any writer will tell you that there are only about a half dozen basic plots. Nobody comes up with entirely new stories— not understandable stories, anyway. It's what you do with the material that counts. Was *The Magnificent Seven* a bad movie because it was based on *Seven Samurai*?"

The blank looks he got told him nobody had heard of *Seven Samurai*, so he let it go.

"I was talking about revenge. There was no taboo against it in the original Hamlet's culture. On the contrary, avenging a father's murder would have been a sacred obligation.

"And for Shakespeare, well, even though he lived in a nominally Christian culture, most Elizabethans made a moral exception for revenge. An Elizabethan gentleman who failed to avenge a murdered father would probably have ended up a social outcast.

"So where's the problem? Why can't Hamlet just kill the king?"

After a moment Jason Nordquist said, "Maybe he wants to go on living. Look what happened to John Wilkes Booth and Lee Harvey Oswald."

"Good point. This may be the real meaning of the most famous passage in the play. Any idea what passage I'm talking about?"

Kimberly Engel said, *"To be or not to be?"*

"Right, the soliloquy. Most people think he's contemplating suicide. That's how Olivier played it. But I think it's more complicated than that. Hamlet knows he will probably die if he kills the king. He's torn between his normal desire to survive and his ethical duty to get revenge. To get full price for his father's life, he has to discount his own life—throw it away.

"So he asks, *'what is a human life worth?'* What is a human being? Why do we put a high value on a human life? Again and again in the play, Hamlet talks about what's natural—*'foul and unnatural murder'*; *'this is most foul, strange, and unnatural.'*

"You've got to understand what *natural* means in the play. Nowadays we think about nature—animals, the environment, the rain forests. But for Shakespeare it meant *natural law*. Natural law is a concept that's so far out of fashion nowadays it's actually taboo. It holds that there is a universal moral law—constant in all times and places and cultures—which everyone understands, or ought to. A few years ago a Supreme Court nominee got in big trouble because he'd written opinions that defended the idea of natural law. What was ironic was that his biggest critic was a Roman Catholic, and Roman Catholics still believe in natural law, officially."

Will picked up his book.

"*'What a piece of work is man,'*" he read, "*'how noble in reason, how infinite in faculties; in form and moving how express and admirable, in action how like an angel, in apprehension how like a god: the beauty of the world, the paragon of animals! And yet to me what is this quintessence of dust?'*"

He turned a few pages. "*'Alas, poor Yorick! I knew him, Horatio, a fellow of infinite jest, of most excellent fancy. He hath borne me on his back a thousand times. And now how abhorred in my imagination it is! My gorge rises at it. Here hung those lips that I have kissed I know not how oft. . . . To what base uses may we return, Horatio! Why may not imagination trace the noble dust of Alexander till 'a find it stopping a bunghole? . . . Thus: Alexander died, Alexander was buried, Alexander returneth to dust; the dust is of earth; of earth we make loam;*

and why of that loam whereto he was converted
might they not stop up a beer barrel?'"

He put the book down. "Now you can groan
all afternoon about how irrelevant Hamlet is to
your lives, but if you think this is irrelevant
you're just not paying attention.

"Modern people live in a state of contradic-
tion, what the psychologists call 'cognitive dissonance.' That means we believe one thing in
our heads, and another in our hearts. On one
side we believe that human beings are the purely
accidental products of chance and evolution. On
the other hand, we believe that every human
being is infinitely valuable and endowed with
inalienable rights.

"These two ideas don't work together. One or
the other can be true, but not both. But we try
to believe in both of them at once."

He saw only blank looks on the students'
faces.

"Okay, look at it this way," he said. "Let's
imagine a scene we've all seen on the news.
There's a man standing on a lawn in the middle
of the night, and behind him his house is a
smoldering ruin, destroyed by fire. But his family
has been rescued.

"A news reporter, with all the legendary sen-
sitivity of his profession, asks the man how he
feels. What does he say?"

No response.

"Come on, you all know what he says."

"He says, 'Well, the house and all the stuff

inside, that's just stuff. The important thing is, we have our lives,'" said Kimberly Johnson, a star of the girls' basketball team.

"Exactly. But have you ever analyzed that statement scientifically? The house—the furniture—the belongings—they're all matter. What do scientists tell us about matter?"

"It's made up of energy?" asked Jason Weber.

"Yes, but I was thinking of how long it lasts."

"You can't destroy it, except with a nuclear reaction," said Kimberly Engel.

"Right. Scientifically, matter is the most eternal thing we know about. People, on the other hand, are personalities. When you love a person, it's the personality you care about, not the matter that makes up their body. But scientifically, you can't verify that personalities even exist. A lot of scientists believe that personality is a sheer illusion.

"So looking at it scientifically, what that man says to the reporter is silly. He's valuing an illusion that lasts maybe eighty or a hundred years over a substance that lasts from Big Bang to Big Bang."

"Wait a minute," said Kimberly Engel. "That's not exactly true. A house isn't just matter—it's a certain arrangement of matter. And people are another kind of arrangement of matter. We value some patterns over others. What's wrong with that?"

"That's exactly my point. On what basis do we value one random pattern over another? Break things down too far and matter doesn't matter anymore."

"Do you really believe that?" asked Kimberly Johnson.

"It doesn't matter what I believe. It's precisely this issue that Hamlet agonizes over in this play. And that's why Hamlet matters in the twenty-first century just as much as he did in the seventeenth. Hamlet says, '*What a piece of work is man—*' in other words, what a work of art—and then he describes Alexander the Great rotting into loam and being made into a clay barrel stopper, or a king being eaten by worms and ending up part of a beggar's lunch. How can both things be true? What is a human being? This is what the play is about."

"'T'stupid," said a voice from the back. Will looked and saw that it was Eric Smedhammer.

"What's stupid, Eric?"

"The question."

"Why?"

"I dunno."

"'*The rest is silence,*'" said Will.

"Huh?"

Will drove home later that afternoon. He lived in an old white frame farmhouse three miles from town. Like many small farms, the operation itself had been swallowed up by a corporate farmer, but the owner had saved the house and a shed, as well as their windbreak of pine trees, by renting them out as a dwelling and garage.

It was December, the sun declining on a cold, clear day. Will always had trouble with the essential paradox of winter days—sunny means cold, cloudy means (relatively) warm. He understood the meteorology of the thing, the blanket effect, but it still seemed fundamentally wrong. The snow lay in blue and white billows over the fields, but the straight grid of roads stretched black and clean and dry, tempting one and all to ignore the speed limit.

He parked his Jeep Cherokee in the shed and walked ten yards to the house. He unlocked the door (he always felt that locking doors shouldn't be necessary with a farmhouse, but he did it anyway) and let his cat Abelard out.

He got out of his down jacket and watch cap. There was a message on his answering machine. *"Will, this is Ginnie. I really need to talk to you. Don't shut me out, Will. I'm sorry if I offended you. Call me, please."*

Will erased the message. "Leave me alone, Ginnie," he said to the air. "It's not gonna work."

JUTLAND, DENMARK, 501 A.D.

Amlodd shivered himself awake. The woolen cloak he'd wrapped himself in had trailed off the hummock where he lay, into the water. Now it was soaked through. The sky paled in the east. He could see the light beyond the standing rushes.

For one moment he could not remember why he was here. He thought he still lived in a world where his father was alive. Then he remembered where he was and who he was.

There's a sound that comes before sound— a harbinger of noise that alerts the secret mind. It was this that had wakened him, and he sat very still until the true voice came. Dogs were barking. Men were marching. Captains called out orders. The jarl's men were yet a distance off, but they came. The way they had yet to come would be the measure of his life-span.

Amlodd had prepared himself for this. A man's life-thread was spun out at his birth by the Norns. His was a golden one, he was sure of that. But gold threads were famously short. He hadn't expected his own thread to be quite so short as this, but so it was.

What fretted him was that he would never get his revenge. The army would cut him down before he got near Feng.

A raven flapped down, a dead mouse in its beak, and attempted to light on a nearby rock. It slipped and tumbled into the water. It flapped up again, spraying wetness, and got its footing at last, but its mouse was gone and it was covered with yellow-green slime. It flapped off another spray of water, but lost its balance again doing it and fell in. When it had struggled up yet again, it stood with its wings spread to dry them. Amlodd laughed in spite of himself.

"You think that's funny, eh?" asked the raven.

"Yes, as a matter of fact." Amlodd was not greatly surprised to be addressed by a bird. In his mind he was dead already, and this raven could be the guide who would lead him to the next world. Ravens were the birds of Odin. To have such a guide was a great honor.

"What do you here?" the bird asked.

"I prepare myself to die."

"Why?"

"I rather thought you knew that already."

"Humor me."

"My father was Orvendil, jarl of Jutland. He was murdered by my uncle Feng, who is now jarl. His claim was that my father beat my mother—which was a lie. But he married my mother anyway."

"But surely you're in no danger, if your mother means so much to your uncle. No mother would stand for her son's murder."

"So I thought. Until I took the misstep of going hunting with him. I nearly got his spear in my back. I ran like a deer, but they're chasing me down. No doubt he'll say 'twas an accident. His bodyguard will back him up."

"So why don't you avenge your father?"

Amlodd shook his head. "I am one; they are many," he said. "I'll not see the sun ride to noon this day."

"You might if you walked wisely."

Amlodd hunched forward, all attention. "Of what wisdom do you speak?"

"You are the son of Orvendil—grandson,

through your mother, of Hrorek the king. A man such as you was born to feed the ravens. If I told you how to get vengeance and live to fight again, would you give me and my kin great feasts?"

"I'd fill the land with corpses from sky to sky."

"A feast to remember! Tongues, livers, hearts, but especially eyes! Eyes for me! The eye is the sweetest part of your whoreson dead body!"

"I'll give you eyes."

"Then learn the wisdom of the Raven."

"Yes?"

In response the raven fell again into the water and covered himself with slime.

Amlodd laughed. Then he went silent. The raven took wing with a clatter and a spray and flew off, crying.

Amlodd nodded slowly. He had to act quickly; he could hear the warriors coming. He stripped to the skin and slid into the biting cold water, stirring up the mire and covering himself with slime and mud. He crawled up the bank, shuddering. In a moment he would stand upright before all their eyes and face his enemies with naught but his defenselessness for a shield. Live or die, such a deed must be acceptable to the gods.

He glanced back at his discarded clothes. His sword—his inheritance from his father—lay there forlorn. He hated to leave it.

Why not take it? Not in the ordinary way, of course, but suppose he made it a token of his change?

He waded back to the hummock and unsheathed the thing. So beautiful! A long, straight blade, grooved down its length, with a pattern of writhing serpents etched in the steel. He took it in his hand by the blade, near its point. Cold as his hand was, he barely felt the two edges slice into his fingers, but he saw the blood well out.

Then he began to sing, rose, and set out naked to meet his foes.

❧ CHAPTER II ❧

Tuesday night at the Epsom Playhouse. Theater communities are incestuous groups anywhere, but nowhere more than in small college
towns. Epsom's wasn't an exclusive community—
the casting committee always gave extra points
to newcomers—but there was a solid core of
people who carried on from show to show, so
that these first-reading nights always combined
the excitement of a new project with the comfort of a reunion.

Will came up the steps and in through the
arched entry doors, and went downstairs to the
basement, where folding chairs and tables had
been arranged and Pat, the stage manager, had
set up a coffee urn on the counter between the
main room and the kitchen.

Diane Voss and Peter Nilsson were there
already. Diane was a slender red-haired woman

in her forties, sort of a Mary Astor type. Peter looked a little like the late Ed Flanders. Also present were Alan Johnson and Johnny Olson (Leonard Nimoy and Fred Gwynne), thirty-something, reliable bit players who had no great talent and knew it, but were dependable and enjoyed being part of the show.

At the end of the U-shaped formation of tables, behind a pile of scripts, sat Bess Borglum, the director. She looked like Glenn Close, but shorter. Will went over and sat down, taking the book she offered.

"Here you go, Hamlet," she said with a weary smile.

"I'm still adjusting to that," he said.

"Well, get used to it. We're depending on you, kid. There's a lot riding on this."

"Thanks for putting me at ease."

"Hey, this is the kitchen. Get used to the heat. You've got no idea how many asses I had to kiss to persuade the committee to schedule a classic. The way they figure it, you can never go wrong with another British sex farce. So if this isn't a big success, we probably won't see another one in this lifetime."

"You look tired."

"Yeah, well, you know—the same old thing."

"Minn?"

"I think I'm getting old, Will. I'm not keeping up like I used to."

"Hey, she loves you. It'll be okay."

"Your mouth to God's ear."

They heard footsteps coming down the stairway, and Randy Storm appeared. A David Copperfield (the illusionist) clone, he had the room's attention in a moment—that was one of his gifts. A girl hung on his arm. There was always a girl on his arm, and rarely the same one twice. Randy taught at the college, and was young enough to use the female students as a discreet dating pool.

Will was surprised by this one though. She didn't look like the general field of Randy's girls. Decidedly plain, she completely baffled Will's system of labeling people by actors they resembled. This girl didn't look like anybody he'd ever seen before. She was a blonde in good shape—she looked like a runner—but her face didn't impress. Her thinnish nose turned up at the end, and her mouth was wide and thin over a rather weak chin.

Then she smiled in response to something Randy said, and the stars came out for Will Sverdrup. That gauche mouth parted into a graceful curve, revealing perfect teeth. Her overbite was as elegant, in its way, as Gene Tierney's, but bigger—a Cinemascope smile.

Randy brought her over to the tables and introduced her as Rosemary Schmitt.

"This is our fabled director, Bess Borglum," he said, "and this is Will Sverdrup, who—unless I'm very much mistaken—will be our Hamlet."

Will started to say something, then stopped himself.

"That's okay," said Rosemary. "I've decided to allow each cast member one 'Rosemary for remembrance' joke. After that, I kill them."

They all laughed and Rosemary asked, "Is it true the theater has a ghost?"

"Oh, yes," said Bess. "I've seen him myself, working here late. He wears a clerical collar, so people think he's some pastor who hanged himself in the sacristy, back when this was a church. He'd been caught molesting a little girl, they say."

She picked up two scripts and handed one to each of them. They moved off, clearly wrapped up in each other.

"Rosemary has a part?" Will asked Bess.

"Yeah. Rosey will be Ophelia."

"She wasn't at the auditions."

"No, I made an executive decision. I originally cast Lori Nelson, but she came down with mono. Randy knew this girl, and said she was good, so I asked her to read for me."

Will suppressed his pleasure at this news. Lori was a nice girl, but a little overweight and prone to eye-batting. Working with Rosemary promised to be a lot more stimulating.

Next to arrive was Dr. Howard Smedhammer, Eric the big student's father. He was much smaller than his son, constructed along the lines of Claude Raines. Will seemed to recall that Eric had been adopted. He wanted to talk to Howie about his son, but he'd have to do it later, in private.

"I think this is pretty much everybody," said Bess, "except for Sean, and Sean will be along. Let's sit down and call the roll."

They pulled up folding chairs around the tables, with a clatter of steel and plastic on linoleum.

"Okay, speak up when your part is called. Hamlet—"

"Here," said Will.

"Gertrude."

"Here," said Diane.

"Claudius."

"*Present*," said a melodious voice from the staircase, and everyone turned to see Sean O'Reardon. There was no problem categorizing Sean. He lived a part, and lived it by choice. He looked like John Barrymore, talked like John Barrymore, and acted like John Barrymore. That Barrymore's style was long out of use in the theater bothered Sean not a whit. He had found a vehicle and he would drive it into the ground. As he reached the foot of the stairs, he paused a moment and half-turned to let everyone enjoy his profile.

"Good evening, Sean," said Bess. "Take a chair. Ophelia."

"Here," said Rosemary.

"Polonius."

"Here, said Peter.

"You'll also be the gravedigger. Laertes."

Randy said, "Here."

"Horatio."

"Here," said Howie.

"Rosencrantz and Guildenstern."

Alan and Johnny said, "Here." And "Here."

"Alan and Johnny, you'll be also be playing Antonio and Bernardo, and you'll be Players, and one of you will be the gravedigger's assistant, and the other one will be Osric, and there'll also be several extras, who'll come in when we start blocking—Thursday night."

"So how are we going to play it?" asked Randy. "Elizabethan dress? Modern? Kenneth Branagh?"

"We're planning on a modified Elizabethan. Subdued colors, lots of golds and blacks, and a dark, stylized set with moveable stage elements. We're making a virtue of necessity—the budget won't stretch to more, but I think it's probably the best approach anyway."

"I hope the men will have codpieces at least," said Diane.

"Sorry to disappoint you, Diane."

"Not the first time I've been disappointed in that area."

When the laughter died down, Bess said, "Okay, let's open the scripts. We've made quite a lot of cuts, so if anybody hasn't got a pencil, there's some in the box here. First of all we're cutting Scene 1, Act 1. . . ."

Will hated every cut. There wasn't one that didn't amputate some bit of poetry he adored, but he understood the purpose and agreed with it. No audience in Epsom would sit still for the whole thing, and no amateur company could hope to pull it off.

After the meeting broke up, he got his coat and followed Howie out to the parking lot. "Got a minute?" he asked.

"Sure," said Howie.

"I caught Eric in the washroom today. He was attacking another student."

"Attacking?"

"He had him pushed up against the wall, with his hand around his neck."

"I find that pretty hard to believe, Will. Who was this other student?"

"A junior."

"An upperclassman?"

"A small upperclassman."

Howie leaned against his car trunk, arms crossed. "Did it occur to you that maybe Eric was defending himself against this older boy?"

"This older boy is a wimp. He's in the chess club."

Howie shook his head. "You've got the wrong idea about Eric, Will. Sure he's big, but he's gentle. He's sensitive."

Will started to say something, but Howie went on.

"I have a very open relationship with my son, Will. I know him. I'm not saying he's not capable of violence, if he's pushed. Who isn't? But I'll bet, if you look into it closely, you'll find out that that older boy said something to hurt him. He's going through a hard stage, and with all this crap about his mother—can you blame him for being touchy?"

"No, I understand that. And what you're saying is exactly how I see it. I just wish you'd talk to him about this. If he should hurt somebody, it would be as bad for him as for the one he hurt."

"I'll talk to him, Will. I talk to him all the time."

"Okay. I'm sorry if I jumped to conclusions."

"Hey, I appreciate your concern."

Howie got in his Mercedes and drove off.

Will walked to his Jeep, past a tattered poster on a light pole that announced a reward for information concerning the whereabouts of Angela Smedhammer, wife to Howard and mother to Eric.

Back at the farm, Will checked his answering machine (another call from Ginnie, which he erased) and his e-mail. He fixed a snack in the microwave and watched the news on TV. Abelard seemed upset, so he let him out. A minute later he had to let him in again.

Will corrected some student papers he'd taken home, then sat in front of the TV for brain candy while he went over his lines. An auditory learner, his way of memorizing a part was to read it aloud over and over.

He wasted some time surfing channels. He stopped for a moment on a TV movie entitled,

My Life, My Choice. It seemed to concern a bright, attractive teenage girl who wanted to be sterilized so that she would never contribute to global overpopulation. Her uncooperative parents, played by one actor who looked a little like Larry Linville and another who looked like Dodie Goodman, were presented as moronic, Bible-thumping hypocrites.

"Creative," Will said. "Nobody's ever portrayed parents that way before. *'Get thee to a nunnery. Why wouldst thou be a breeder of sinners?'*" He switched the set off and tuned in a light rock station on the stereo.

Abelard had his exits and his entrances again. Finally, Will stopped letting him out and just left him howling by the door.

The knocking had been going on for some time before he noticed it. It wasn't coming from the door. It came from upstairs.

He stepped into the upstairs stair well, flipping the light switch. At the top of the steps he stood and listened. *Rap. Rap. Rap. Rap.* It was too regular. If he hadn't known he was alone in the house, he'd have thought a human being was doing it.

The sound was coming from further up, in the attic. Did the attic have a light? He couldn't remember. As a boy Will had been terrified of the dark, and under oath he'd have had to admit that he'd still rather not go into a room with the lights off. He stepped toward the hatch in the ceiling, then turned and went back downstairs for a flashlight. He got one out of the refrigerator, where he kept it to preserve the batteries. He also got a step stool and carried the things upstairs. He set the stool underneath the hatch, unfolded it and climbed up the three steps, then lifted the square wooden cover that sat, unhinged and latchless, on top of the opening. He shone the light inside.

The attic in this small house was not intended for more than minor storage. It was a triangular space between the ceiling and the roof peak, too low to stand up in. Anyone who wanted to walk around there would have to step on the joists, over the pink insulation, in a crouch.

Everything looked quiet to Will. He had an uneasy sense of being in a place where he didn't belong, as if his lease didn't cover this part of the house (which was ridiculous). The only sign of disturbance was that one of the three or four cartons someone, not he, had shoved up there at one time or another seemed to have fallen over. Maybe squirrels had done it. Could squirrels have done it?

He shone his beam on the clutter and saw that the spilled carton contained books, some of which lay open on the fiberglass padding.

If it hadn't been books, he probably wouldn't have examined further, but Will was not normal about books. He kept his own as pristine as humanly possible, never breaking the spines or removing dust jackets. It simply was not in him to look at books lying open, spines up, and not put them right.

He hoisted himself up through the hatch (it was cold up there—he wished he'd put on a jacket) and crawled cautiously over to the carton on two knees and one hand (the other held his flashlight), keeping his weight on the joists. It hurt his knees, and his hands were going numb. From downstairs he could hear Abelard, still singing his song of protest.

He picked up the books one by one and closed them, setting them gently on their sides. They were old books, some of them apparently Norwegian, in that old Germanic printer's font that would have been impossible to read even if he'd understood the language. Then he turned the carton upright and looked over its contents.

In spite of the cold and the dark he had to check the titles. He'd come this far, he wasn't going to lie awake now wondering what books were up here. More of the same—books on history; books of poetry; about two thirds of them foreign language. He lifted each out in turn and handled it with care. Will had never gotten over the romance of bound literature—the wonder he had felt as a boy, coming from a house of many magazines but few books to the school library, and more volumes than he'd ever seen in his life. Later he would learn that this had been in fact a pretty meager library even for an elementary school, but at the time it had been an epiphany. A book, to Will Sverdrup, was a treasure, even with crumbling pages and water-stained covers. He wondered about the people who had spent money for them, perhaps money they could ill afford, generations ago.

At the very bottom was a book different from the rest. "This is *seriously* old," said Will. It was leather-bound, with a raised spine and triangular corners, and the cover was recessed and tooled. It was larger than the others, taking up the entire length and width of the carton bottom so that he was hard pressed to get his fingers around it. It wasn't terribly thick, so it couldn't be a Gutenberg Bible—*Dream on, Sverdrup,* he told himself—but it was heavy and the paper was thick.

He crooked his icy flashlight in the angle between his neck and his shoulder, under his ear, and set the heavy volume on his lap. Carefully he opened the cover. He uttered an oxymoronic imprecation to an excremental divinity, the flashlight making his white breath numinous.

The title page said:

𝕿𝖍𝖊 𝕿𝖗𝖆𝖌𝖎𝖈𝖐𝖆𝖑 𝕳𝖞𝖘𝖙𝖔𝖗𝖎𝖊
𝖔𝖋 𝕳𝖆𝖒𝖑𝖊𝖙𝖍, 𝕻𝖗𝖞𝖓𝖘𝖊 𝖔𝖋 𝕯𝖊𝖓𝖊𝖒𝖆𝖗𝖐𝖊
𝖇𝖞 𝕿𝖍𝖔𝖒𝖆𝖘𝖘 𝕶𝖞𝖉

Eric Smedhammer sat before his computer screen, joystick in hand, intent on *Yggxvthwul's Gambit.* Just 40 more kills and he'd have access to the fourth level. The screen depicted a blasted, post-Apocalyptic landscape of ruined buildings and twisted, ravaged trees, through which the hulking, tentacled form of Yggxvthwul trudged. Long experience with the game helped him to avoid deadfalls and obvious ambushes, and he had learned to identify radioactive dumps and send his monster there (extra power points).

A human figure appeared from behind a building. *Yes!* It was an old lady! You got extra points for old ladies. He guided Yggxvthwul to her, ran her down and devoured her. Her caricatured figure waved its arms and legs and made screaming noises as it disappeared into the monster's mouth. *Cool*.

A vehicle appeared. A school bus! This was his night! School buses were a hundred points, but they took finesse.

Eric made Yggxvthwul lie down in the middle of the road, moving slightly, as if injured. This part was tricky. The artificial intelligence chip would alert the bus driver if he failed to do a convincing "bait wiggle." Then the driver would speed up and run him right over, and he'd lose 500 points.

But he nailed it. The school bus rolled to a stop, and he made Yggxvthwul leap up suddenly, jumping onto the hood and tearing the roof off, picking the children out one by one and chomping them down in a spray of blood and a chorus of screams. *This definitely did not suck*.

A knock on his door broke his concentration. From somewhere a Slime Dragon appeared and covered Yggxvthwul with ooze, which it then set afire.

End of game.

"Yahgummin," Eric said, bitterly.

His father opened the door a few inches and sort of sidled in. He never just walked in. Eric thought it was funny, but he wasn't amused tonight.

"Kind of late," said his dad.

Eric made a snorting noise.

"I'm just turning in. Wanted to say goodnight. Everything okay with you?"

"Mm." *It would be if you'd get your ass outta my space.*

"How's things at school?"

"Mm."

"Mr. Sverdrup said he'd seen you in a fight."

"Mm."

"I told him I was sure it was nothing serious."

"Mm."

"I mean, sometimes you get upset. That's understandable. But you're sorry about it, right?"

"Mm."

"Yeah, that's what I thought. So everything's cool. It won't happen again."

"Mm."

"You bet. Okay, sport. Don't stay up too late, huh? 'Night. Love you."

"Mm."

His father sidled out.

What a lamer.

Time to kill the room light. The game was

more fun in the dark, and no shining under the door would alert his father. Eric killed it without getting up by stretching his long tongue across the room and flicking the switch with it.

It wasn't exactly a tongue. It was more a tentacle, like one of Yggxvthwul's, with little suckers along its length. Eric had been frightened by it when it had first appeared, but now it was way cool.

Will barely remembered clambering out of the attic and downstairs to his den. He barely took his eyes from the book, afraid it would dissolve like the dream it must be.

Kyd's Hamlet! It was incredible! It was not to be believed! One of the great lost treasures in English literary scholarship, lying right over his head every night as he slept during the months he'd lived here.

Kyd's *Hamlet* was not much coveted for its own sake. Kyd had been a store-brand dramatist at best. But it may have been the missing link between Belleforest's transcription of Saxo Grammaticus and Shakespeare. So many questions about the play would be answered if we knew how much was Shakespeare's, how much (if anything) Kyd's. How in blazes had it ended up in a box in a farmhouse outside Epsom, Minnesota?

He set the book down on his desk and turned on the banker's lamp. Gently, reverently, he opened it and began to turn the pages.

Five minutes later he stopped reading straight through and began to turn pages at random, checking familiar sections. He paged faster and faster, forgetting for a moment his reverence for the yellow paper.

This was a nightmare.

It was almost word for word the play he knew.

Will had to step away from the desk and pace. It didn't make sense. Kyd was not this good a writer. Shakespeare was too great a writer, and too creative, to have simply plagiarized from a hack like Kyd.

But that was sure how it looked.

❊ CHAPTER III ❊

"Remember me," said the ghost in armor.

Will could have sworn the ghost appeared after he woke. But of course it had been a dream, before the alarm on his bedtable went off. A good sign, really—the play was working its way into his unconscious.

He did not want to talk about Thomas Kyd that day in class, but there was no getting around him.

"The revenge tragedy was the blockbuster entertainment form of Shakespeare's day," he told the class. "Kind of like special effects films nowadays. The form was introduced in England by a playwright named Thomas Kyd, who worked a little before Shakespeare got off the ground. His play *The Spanish Tragedy* isn't that hot as a work of art, but it sold wagonloads of tickets, and pretty soon everybody wanted to do one. Elements in

37

it even worked their way into *Hamlet*. Kyd may have also written the first version . . . the first stage dramatization of *Hamlet*.

"Why do you think revenge plays were so big for the Elizabethans? Any ideas?"

No response, as he'd expected.

"What was going on in Shakespeare's England? What was happening in his society?"

After a pause, Kimberly Olson said, "The Renaissance?"

"Yes, but that's not what I'm thinking of. What did Queen Elizabeth's father, Henry the Eighth, do?"

"He chopped off all his wives' heads," said Jason Nordquist.

"Two out of six wives," said Will. "Actually you're in the neighborhood. What was the big consequence of Henry VIII's first divorce?"

"The church thing?" said Kimberly Olson.

"The English Reformation, yes. Whatever your religious beliefs, it's impossible to underestimate the cultural impact of the Reformation. What were some differences between Medieval Catholic thinking and Protestant thinking?"

The students looked around at each other. They weren't used to discussion of religion in school, and it made them uncomfortable. It was much the same reaction a teacher would have gotten for mentioning sex a hundred years earlier.

"The Pope?" asked Kimberly Johnson.

"In a way. What did the Pope represent?"

No one said anything.

"I'm not trying to push my beliefs on you," said Will. "I'm not even going to tell you what my beliefs are, assuming I have some. But religion was a very important part of life in Shakespeare's day. It still is for a lot of people. If we're going to talk about ideas and the history of ideas, we have to consider religion."

"Did the Pope represent tradition?" asked Kimberly Engel.

"Yes. Or that's close, anyway. The English were new Protestants. They were enjoying a freedom of thought they'd never known before, and they were high on it. Instead of ideas coming down from headquarters, under the weight of tradition and authority, they had a new ideal—the plowboy with his Bible. The Protestants said that a plowboy with a Bible had as much authority as all the popes and councils that ever met. This was very heady stuff in that time and place. Did you know that the early Puritans were accused of being sex maniacs? It's true. They read the Bible and concluded from their reading that, contrary to what they'd been told, sex was a good gift of God, and ought to be enjoyed when it was used properly—which for them meant within marriage. Bishops had heart attacks when they heard that."

"What does this have to do with *Hamlet*?" asked Jason Weber.

"I was getting to that. What did I say yesterday about attitudes toward revenge in Shakespeare's time?"

Blank looks.

"All right, what I said was that Elizabethans made a moral exception for revenge. They were nominal Christians, but they set aside Christian teaching when it came to avenging the murder of a family member.

"That was an oversimplification. As I've been saying, England was a country in cultural revolution. The revenge rules were part of the tradition they'd inherited—not necessarily Catholic tradition, just cultural tradition. But the new ideas that the Protestants and Puritans were spreading led them to question these traditions. The Protestant teachers pointed to their Bibles and said, 'Show me where it says this in Scripture.' It was very confusing. Take revenge and the Protestants will call you a sinner. Don't take it and your friends will call you a coward.

"Look at the ghost of Hamlet's father. What does Hamlet think of the ghost? Why does he arrange his 'Mousetrap' play? Why not just take the ghost's word?

"Look at the end of Act 2, Scene 2:

> *The spirit that I have seen*
> *May be a devil, and the devil hath power*
> *T'assume a pleasing shape, yea, and per-*
> > *haps*
> *Out of my weakness and my melancholy,*
> *As he is very potent with such spirits,*
> *Abuses me to damn me. I'll have grounds*
> *More relative than this. . . .'"*

"That's ridiculous," said Kimberly Johnson. "Everybody knows Christians are the most violent people the world has ever seen. What about all those wars?"

"I asked a guy I know about that once—a Christian guy I act with in the theater. He said, 'Hey, think about it. What do people kill for? They kill for love. They kill for security. They kill for patriotism, or loyalty. Are those bad things because people kill for them?' The fact is, people kill for anything that's really important to them. The fact that they kill for a thing doesn't mean it's a bad thing, just that it's an *important* thing, at least to them. And I don't think you can make the case that the world has become less violent since large parts of it have stopped taking religion seriously.

"So, anyway, Hamlet may be superstitious by our standards, but by the standards of his own time he's a very rational, skeptical man. He doesn't accept anything on authority, not even the authority of his father's ghost. He's rethinking the whole world—he's a representative of an age that re-created the world—that invented modern science and universal education. Whether your family came from England or Norway or the Ivory Coast or Vietnam, if you're living here and now, Hamlet is your ancestor."

When class was done he couldn't stand it anymore. He'd planned to make the call after work, but he stopped Sharon the guidance counselor in the hall and asked if he could use her office for a private call. "It's long distance, but I'll use my credit card," he promised.

Sharon said that was fine, and he went into her office and closed the door. He dug a card and a slip of paper out of his wallet and dialed a number in Minneapolis—the office of Arundel Perry, his faculty advisor from his student days at the U.

He didn't really expect to reach Del on the first try—he had no idea what his schedule was these days. But it was Del himself who answered, not even a student assistant.

"Perry," said a smoke-scarred voice.

"Del? It's Will Sverdrup."

"Will. How the hell are you? You in town?"

"No. I'm calling from Epsom."

"Epsom?"

"Where I teach now."

"Oh, yeah. I heard you were someplace out in the sticks. How's it going?"

"Good. I'm playing Hamlet in our local theater."

Del congratulated him and made some vague promises to see if he could come down for the show (fat chance).

"Look. Somebody's asked me about a situation, and I said I'd talk to you." Will couldn't bring himself to connect himself directly to the Kyd volume. He was afraid it would commit him before he'd worked out a strategy.

"This person—who doesn't want his name

brought into it yet—he thinks he's found a copy of Kyd's *Hamlet*."

Silence at the other end. Will could imagine Del taking a long pull on a cigarette, though smoking was surely forbidden in faculty offices.

At last Del asked, "Have you seen it?"

"Yes."

"Bound?"

"Yes. *The Spanish Tragedy* is also in there, along with some sonnets."

Del said something Will didn't catch. Then he said, "What's it look like?"

"You mean, how does it read?"

"Yeah."

"That's the shocker. It's almost word for word the same as the Good Quarto text. It can't be right. It must be some mistake—some misattribution by a publisher."

"Hmm. Maybe, maybe not. I want to see that book."

"What do you mean, maybe, maybe not?"

"You can't be that far out of the loop, even in Morton, Will."

"Epsom."

"Whatever. We're reevaluating Shakespeare. He's not the shibboleth he used to be. T.S. Eliot had the nerve to say it, a long time ago— Hamlet's a mess. We've built this mythology around a play that's too long, too unwieldy, too self-contradictory. We keep looking for a central theme—a solution to a mystery. The fact is, there is no theme, no mystery. It's just a bad play. It's time somebody came out and said the emperor has no clothes."

Will couldn't speak for a moment.

"If we can prove *Hamlet* is just a bad play by Kyd," Del went on, "misattributed to Shakespeare, or even stolen by him to meet a deadline, maybe it'll help dethrone this whole Shakespeare religion."

Will almost croaked, "I can't believe I'm hearing this from you. You used to hate the revisionists."

"Things have changed around here since you graduated. We're dismantling the pedestals. The world has all kinds of great literature, and it wasn't all written by dead white males. We've got to knock some chairs away from the table so there'll be room for new voices."

"So you're knocking Shakespeare's chair away?"

"Forget that metaphor. Say we're taking away his tenure, making him fight for his job like everybody else."

"I don't think—I don't think the person who found the book will be eager to produce it if he thinks it'll be used to take away Shakespeare's tenure."

"He has an obligation to scholarship."

"I think—I think he—or she—will interpret what you're saying as more politics than scholarship."

"Then don't tell him—her—whatever—that. Tell them anything, but I've got to see it. If it's money they're worried about, there are foundations who'll pay big bucks— I mean six, seven figures—to acquire it."

"I'll . . . I'll see what I can do."

"You stay in touch. If I don't hear from you, you'll hear from me."

"Yeah. Thanks." Will said goodbye.

Blast. Del had blindsided him. He hadn't expected this conversion to political correctness. Del was a good scholar, but he wasn't discreet. Will had counted on his devotion to Shakespeare to keep him quiet. So much for that.

A woman was leaning against the driver's door of his Jeep in the parking lot when he left the building that afternoon.

Will cursed under his breath. It was Ginnie. He'd have liked to turn and walk back the other way, but that would have looked cowardly.

"Hello, stranger," she said. She was taller than she looked, her roundish face belying her long legs. Curly golden red hair, dimples, wonderful blue eyes. The kind of girl you'd be happy to fly off to Club Med with or take home to mother, if you had a mother. She wore jeans and a hooded jacket, the hood thrown back.

Will stood facing her, his briefcase in his hand, breathing white steam.

"You haven't returned my calls," she said, giving him a sad smile without the dimples engaged.

"There's nothing to say," he answered.

"I have things to say."

"I don't. I could sit someplace and listen to you, but it wouldn't change anything."

"You're saying you don't care at all? Our time together hasn't meant anything to you?"

"It meant something. But it didn't mean what you wanted it to. I can't be what you want me to be, Ginnie. I don't have what you want."

"Maybe you don't know yourself as well as you think you do."

"You're wrong about me. You think you can change me, make me into somebody you've imagined. Look, the right guy's out there for you, and you deserve him. Go find him. Don't waste time on me."

She looked at her feet a moment, bending a little at the waist. Standing straight she said, "You're a damn fool, Will Sverdrup. I'm a helluva fine girl, and I could have made you very, very happy. But you'll never know. Someday you'll be old and alone, and you'll think back on this day and you'll want to swallow Drano."

"Ginnie, you're probably right. I'm sorry."

She walked off, tall and graceful, oscillating her elegant bottom.

I must be terrified of commitment, thought Will. *Otherwise I've got to be crazy*. He imagined a world where he was a different kind of man; where he could give and receive the way this woman needed him to give and receive.

Will was one of the actors to arrive early for blocking that night. He usually was. He'd always loved just being in a theater, watching all the sundry activities that synergized to bring a production to term. On top of that, he hadn't the responsibilities of family and overtime that many others had. Bess was there already, as usual. She was onstage talking to Pat and to the middle-aged lady who painted the flats.

Peter Nilsson was also there, and Will went and sat by him in the audience seats.

"Got your part memorized already?" asked Peter with a smile.

"Not quite. Fortunately I've been teaching *Hamlet* for years, so a lot of it's already in my head. But it's still a challenge."

"I envy you your memory, kid. You make me wonder what I'm doing here."

"You underestimate yourself. You're on my short list of people I'm always glad to work with.

> " *Thou hast been*
> *As one in suff'ring all that suffers*
> *nothing,*
> *A man that Fortune's buffets and*
> *rewards*
> *Hast ta'en with equal thanks; and blest*
> *are those*
> *Whose blood and judgment are so well*
> *commeddled*
> *That they are not a pipe for Fortune's*
> *finger*
> *To sound what stop she pleases.'"*

"Thanks, but you just made another generous contribution to my inferiority fund."

"You'll be fine."

Peter shook his head. "I don't know why I keep doing this. Well, I do know. I love being on stage. I'm a ham. But the lines! I get them all down word-perfect, backwards and forwards, and then I start to put on my makeup and I get the jitters, and they fly out of my head."

"It's just nerves."

"My nerves are enough. I shouldn't put you other actors through it. You never know what'll come out of my mouth."

"It's not that bad. You're not really worse than anybody else. We all drop a line from time to time."

"No, it's worse with me."

"Really, it isn't. Relax, Peter."

"As you say, O Prince. Did I ever tell you I planned to teach English myself when I was in college?"

"No, really? What happened?"

"My sister got seduced by Lord Byron."

Will thought a moment. "You're older than you look," he said.

Peter smiled. "It was a sort of an intellectual seduction. Carrie was a nice kid—very straight-laced, very proper. Really pretty. But when I was in college and she was in high school, she discovered the Romantic poets. I'm afraid it was partly my fault. I was heavily into Byron and

Shelley. Anyway, she ran away from home. She left a note with a quotation from Byron:

'Tis vain to struggle—let me perish
    young—
Live as I lived, and love as I have loved;
To dust if I return, from dust I sprung,
And then, at least, my heart can ne'er
    be moved.

"This was the '70s. Everybody was doing it. There was never a sexual open season on young girls like they had then. 'If it feels good do it—it ain't hurtin' nobody.'

"Carrie got hurt though. She came home on a bus one day in 1976. We hadn't heard from her for years. She'd had syphilis and gonorrhea, and an abortion—a legal one—had left her sterile. She weighed ninety-six pounds and she was hooked on heroin.

"I always felt responsible for her running away. I'd heard from her now and then the first few months after she ran off. I knew what she was doing. It didn't seem so romantic when it was my little sister. She died of kidney failure in '78.

"The more I thought about those bastards—guys like Byron and Shelley and Robert Burns—the angrier I got. Here were jerks who treated women like Kleenex, and everybody talks about them like they were heroes. Even the Feminists don't criticize them. They were political radicals, so they have to be saints—who cares who got hurt? You know what happened to girls who got pregnant out of wedlock in those days? You can gas all day long about how society's hypocrisy was at fault, but that doesn't help the girls those predators ruined.

"So I changed my major from English to Business. Nobody studied Business in the '70s. I had my choice of jobs when I graduated. How I crashed and burned in that arena is another story."

They heard someone coming in and turned around to see Howie Smedhammer entering, followed by his hulking, black-garbed son.

"Ever wonder if the real Hamlet was like Eric? Just a big punk in a black T-shirt?" asked Peter.

"I wonder what he's doing here," said Will. "I know he's not much interested in the play."

Father and son stopped to greet them. "Eric's going to be helping with the tech crew," said Howie.

"Really?" asked Will. "You're gonna be a techie? I didn't think this sort of thing interested you, Eric."

"Techiesurcool," Eric mumbled back.

"You think so?"

"Sure. They wear black."

"I guess that makes me cool, too. Hamlet wears black."

Eric responded with the kind of smile he'd have given a stupid sibling, when he wasn't at liberty to hit him.

"Come up on stage," said Howie to his son. "I want to show you the trapdoor."

"Arrogant and sullen," said Peter as they watched them climb the stage steps. "But on the plus side he's condescending and offensive."

"He's been through a lot," said Will.

"Yes, that's what everybody says about Eric. 'He's been through a lot.' The whole town's become his enabler. We're not doing him a favor."

Various cast members entered as they talked. Will noticed with interest that Rosemary and Randy came in separately. He wondered if Randy had dumped her already.

Bess called them up onstage and they began working through Act I, playbooks in hand, making penciled notations in the margins about where they should walk so they wouldn't bump into one another or the scenery.

This production would open with Act I, Scene ii, beginning with King Claudius' speech. Sean showed up precisely in time for it. As they walked through the scene, Sean constantly edged toward the rear of the stage, forcing the other actors (Randy as Laertes, Peter as Polonius, Diane as the Queen, and Will, along with the two bit players who played Cornelius and Voltemand) to turn away from the audience to address him.

"Stop upstaging everybody, Sean," said Bess. "Move it down, move it down."

"Was I upstaging? I do beg your pardons. I only thought the secrecy and cunning of the

character called for me to seek out hidden, shadowed places—"

"You're a king," said Bess. "You stand in the
center of everything and enjoy the attention. You
know how to do that, Sean, I'm sure. Three
steps forward, please."

Then followed the scene with Hamlet,
Horatio (Howie) and Marcellus (Alan Johnson),
and the *"To thine own self be true"* scene with
Rosemary as Ophelia, along with Polonius and
Laertes. That ended Act I, enough for the first
night's blocking.

They ran through everything once more and
broke up at about 9:30. Bess said, "Will, Randy'll
be choreographing your duel. Have you got time
to run a few passes with him?"

Will said, "Sure," and he and Randy went
down to the basement together. Randy carried
a long, leather-covered box under his arm. He
opened it on a table, revealing a pair of beautiful cup-guard rapiers with grips that looked like
ivory.

"Wow," said Will. "These aren't genuine, are
they?"

"They're genuine swords," said Randy.
"They're not genuine antiques. Don't worry. It's
synthetic ivory and the points are tipped." He
took one out of its formed nest and gave it a
couple of the swishes no man, it seems, can
resist.

Will took the other and assumed the *en garde*
position.

"You've fenced before," said Randy.

"Just stage fencing, and not much of that. A couple classes in college."

Randy took his stance and they traded a few thrusts and parries. Randy got past Will's guard with one of his thrusts, landing a jab in his left pectoral muscle. Without padding, it hurt.

Will felt a sudden rush of adrenaline. His mind knew it was crazy, but his body went into defense mode. It believed it was being attacked, and it rather liked the feeling.

They traded a few more parries. Will's ego blossomed, convincing him he was defending himself with great skill.

Randy burst his bubble by scoring two touches in a row. They both stepped back. Will was panting. "*'A touch, a touch, I do confess't,'*" he said.

Randy smiled. "Ever see Erroll Flynn's *Robin Hood*? That duel between Flynn and Basil Rathbone? Rathbone carried him all the way. He was a world-class fencer. Flynn was too busy getting starlets drunk to put in time with a foil or a saber." He took his stance and attacked again. Steadily, relentlessly, he pushed Will back and back, toward the kitchen end. Will's confidence drained out through his armpits. He was on the defensive, and worse, he was certain Randy was holding back.

"I could kill you with a sword," said Randy. His dark eyes glowed, his face was flushed. Will thanked God for the buttons on the tips, but wondered what he would do when his back hit the wall.

For just a moment the lighted basement seemed very dark, a place of stone walls lit by flickering torches. Will thought he saw Randy coming at him with an untipped sword. They both wore doublets and hose.

"Swords! Ah, how I love the sword!" said a voice from the stairway. Randy turned to face it and once again he was dressed in his customary oxford shirt and jeans, in the old church basement. The duel ended. The voice was Sean O'Reardon's. He stood on the first step, leaning on the handrail. "Did I ever tell you about the time I almost fenced with Sir Laurence? Larry, we used to call him . . ."

Randy swung back and, with a swift lunge, disarmed Will and sent his rapier spinning toward the ceiling. He reached with his left hand and snatched the weapon, and in a few moments had both swords cased and was gone up the stairs.

"Arrogant son-of-a-bitch," said Sean. "I never could abide a prima donna."

Will didn't say anything, but sat in a folding chair, trembling. Sean looked at him a moment and decided, apparently, that there was nothing more to interest him here. He headed for the men's room, his original goal.

Will climbed the stairs and made for the seating area, where he'd left his jacket.

Bess and Rosemary were working through

some blocking on the stage. He stopped and watched them a moment. Rosemary moved ver ' well. She had grace. He enjoyed watching her. He wondered if she'd broken up with Randy, and how he could find out. But the thought of Randy made him nervous, and he knew he wouldn't do anything about it tonight.

He went out to his car for the duffel bag he'd brought. Back inside he caught Bess as she was packing her notes into a portfolio.

"Can I show you something?" he asked her. "I've got this thing I need to talk about, and you're the best one I can think of."

Bess said, "Thanks, I think," and they went to her office in the basement. Will took the Kyd volume out of his bag and undid the newspaper he'd wrapped it in. He laid it on her desk, open to the title pag .

"Hell's garters, ' said Bess. "Is this what I think it is?"

"You tell me."

They examined the book carefully. Finally Will wrapped it up and packed it again, and suggested they get a cup of coffee. Bess agreed and they left their cars at the theater and walked two blocks to the Home Maid Café. Will carried the bag.

"Jesus," said Bess as they walked. "Have you talked to anybody in the scholastic community? You went to the U, didn't you? Isn't there some-body up there you know?"

"Yeah, I did. I called my old advisor. He's

a Shakespearean scholar. But he's changed his politics. Turns out he's anti-Shakespeare now, and he wants the book for career purposes. He wants to prove he has no reverence for dead white males."

"God damn all political correctness. Except for gay rights, of course."

"Of course." They reached the café and went inside to sit in a corner booth, away from the few other customers.

"So what do you think?" she asked. "You think Kyd wrote *Hamlet?*"

"Absolutely not. A, Kyd wasn't that good. B, I can't imagine Shakespeare trying to pass off a known work of somebody else's—especially a hack like Kyd's—as his own. Artists have too much ego for that. Real geniuses may do all kinds of godawful things, but they have too much contempt for other artists to steal their work.

"No, the way I figure it, somebody printed up a volume of Kyd and threw *Hamlet* in out of ignorance or stupidity or sheer bloody-mindedness. It's got to be something like that."

"Makes sense to me," said Bess. The waitress came and she ordered tea. Will ordered coffee.

"I know a few people at the U myself," said Bess when the waitress was gone. "I'll make some calls, see if I can find you somebody without an axe to grind."

"Thanks." It felt good to share the burden. Will asked, "How are things with Minn?"

Bess shook her head. "It's over, Will. She's gone. I came home from work yesterday and she'd moved all her stuff out."

"I'm sorry."

"Thanks. Damn it, Will, I thought this was it. I thought she was the one. We'd even talked about having a baby. We discussed who we'd get for a donor. Your name came up, by the way. Would you have been willing to do it?"

Will had to smile. "I'm flattered, I think. It isn't something I'd ever considered. But I guess—no, I'd have had to say no."

"Why?" They'd moved into dangerous territory, and Will could read the defensiveness behind the question.

"Not for moral reasons. Not the kind you're thinking of, anyway. I guess—I know there are guys all over the place who've fathered children they never give a thought to. I know they do it. But I don't know how. If I had a kid, I'd need to be part of his life."

"You're a good guy, Will Sverdrup. A little square, but good. Don't mind me. How's your own love life? Who you seeing now—that redhead? What's her name—Ginnie?"

"It's over. No future."

"For a square, you don't stick very long. That was one cute girl. You don't suppose she swings both ways, do you?"

"Not to my knowledge, no."

The hot drinks came and they went back to the original subject.

"How do you think the book ended up in your attic?" Bess asked.

"Aye, there's the rub."

"Hmm?"

"It looks suspicious, doesn't it? Here I am, a teacher of English Literature and a Shakespeare fan—I'm teaching *Hamlet* in one of my classes and I'm playing Hamlet. And just now I happen to discover the lost Ur-*Hamlet*. How many mystery movies have you seen where the cop says, 'I don't like coincidences'? Well I don't like them either. That's one of the things that makes me cautious. I keep wondering, who do I know who'd want to go to all the trouble to forge the manuscript, break into my house and plant it? It's not impossible, but it's a lot of inconvenience when you could just scratch my car hood with a key."

"Probably one of your old girlfriends."

"There's only one person I can think of who'd have a motive for mounting a hoax like this."

"Who?"

"Me. I didn't do it, but it's me I'd suspect if I heard about it. If this is a fraud, somebody has gone to a lot of trouble and expense to wreck an already lackluster academic career."

Bess stirred her tea. "Probably the Masons," she said with a smile.

"More like the Illuminati."

"Or the Elders of Zion."

"The Liberal Media."

They played the name game for a while, and Will felt better.

He drove home, garaged the Jeep and went to the house.

The door was open, "heating the whole county," as his mother used to say. Inside, Abelard sat crouched in a corner, his teeth bared, shivering.

Every cupboard was open. Every drawer had been pulled out and dumped on the floor. The TV, the stereo and the computer had been knocked off their stands. His filing drawers hung open and all his books had been swept from their shelves.

Eric Smedhammer sat at his computer. He was composing an e-mail, to be sent to a long list of addresses he'd collected from web boards.

Dear Friend (it went):

My name is Megan, and I am 12 years old. I am writing to you because I got your address as someone who has a compassionate Christian heart.

I am writing for my mother, who has a rare form of cancer that attacks the hands and feet. The doctors say that unless she gets a very expensive kind of surgery, her hands and feet will have to be amputated.

I don't want my mommy to lose her

hands and feet. I want to be able to hold her hand and take walks. I want her to be able to comb my hair and cook me breakfast and teach me how to sew and work in the garden.

Mr. Van Houghton at Butterfield Industries says that if I get 10,000 people to read this e-mail and pass it on to their friends, he'll pay for my mommy's surgery. Please, please, please, forward this message to everybody you know. Mr. Van Houghton's company has tracking software that tells them how many people read this e-mail.

I don't want my mommy to lose her hands and feet. Please, if you consider yourself a Christian and have any love in your heart, forward this message to as many people as you can. I promise I will pray for you. Father McCarthy says God will never forgive anyone who turns his back on us.

Thank you.
Megan Underhill

Pretty good, Eric thought.

He could hear his father coming up the stairs. He'd gone into the den to exercise his grief after rehearsal, while Eric had gone up to his room.

His father had missed one of the stages in the grief process, and his counselor had assigned him to work on his Bargaining.

His father knocked at the door. Eric sighed, turned off his monitor and said, "Yeahcummin."

"Hey, tough guy," his dad said.

"Hey."

"You know what happened to the Flatten-bagger?"

"Flattenbagger?"

"Yeah, you know that machine I ordered from the TV. The one where you put stuff in the plastic bags and the vacuum cleaner sucks all the air out. So you can fit more in storage."

"Yeahaymember. I thinkismaybe in the spare room closet."

"I was sure I left it in the garage."

"No, I thinkis i'thuhspareroom."

"Okay, I'll check. Don't stay up too late."

"Mm."

"Well, goodnight."

"Mm." The door closed.

"Dork," said Eric.

JUTLAND, DENMARK, 501 A.D.

Feng shouted, "Everyone out!" The warriors and the thralls beat dust up from the rushes on the floor as they hurried out, leaving the prisoner and his uncle alone in the shadowed, raftered hall. The hall had a raised benche along each wall and a long-fire in a hearthway that ran down the middle. Along the walls hung tapestries, with shields and armor—trophies of war.

Feng took no great risk being alone with Amlodd. The young man was naked under a wadmal cloak, his hands bound with a belt, his wrists and bloody fingers swollen. He stood with his mouth open, drooling, making no attempt to cover himself where the cloak hung open in front.

Feng planted himself in front of his nephew. He drew his belt knife, just in case. As they stood, clothed and near naked, anyone could tell they were of one blood. Amlodd could have been Feng himself, twenty years since. Both had red-gold hair and beards, and gray eyes. Both were only middling tall, but wide in the shoulders, with chests so massive as to look unhealthful, like goiters.

They stared one another in the face for many heartbeats. Feng sought to force a way into Amlodd's mind with his gaze, as a man might lever a woman's legs open with a knee. But Amlodd kept his mind's maidenhead.

The look in Feng's eyes changed then. His brows lifted as if in sorrow. "Do not make me slay you," he whispered.

Amlodd thought, *You come late with that bidding,* but let no muscle of his face betray him. It was hard work, this lassitude.

"I ever loved you," said Feng. "Do you know why I loved you? 'Twas because you were so like your father."

Amlodd felt himself lose control then. He rolled his eyes and fell to the floor, rocking himself in the rushes and dirt and cast-off bones. He made animal noises to keep his grip on the secret he clutched in his mind.

"Odin's eye! It drives me mad myself to see you thus, so like your father you are!" cried Feng. "You'll not credit it—you're too young to understand. But I loved your father. He was a god to me."

Amlodd threw himself into a fit then, roaring gibberish and arching his back so that he stood on his heels and the back of his head. It took almost no art—it seemed the fitting thing to do.

Feng leaned against a pillar, like a man wearied in a fight. "You are young. You cannot understand how anyone could kill one they loved—kill them *because* they love them."

"I love you," said Amlodd from the floor, his eyes wide and sweet.

"I warrant you do," said Feng. "And I'll wager you'd like to prove it as I did with your father.

"Are you truly mad? Have the gods given me this gift, that you are mad, so that I need not put you out of the world? That would be a blessing— a mercy I'd not hoped for. To kill a madman would be shameful, and a sacrilege to Odin.

"Yet how can I know? Even if you are mad in truth, suppose you should regain your wits? Would I sense it soon enough to ward myself?"

He walked down the hearthway between the earthen benches into the entry room. On his left was the door. He opened it and shouted for Guttorm, his marshal.

When the tall warrior appeared, Feng told him, "Take Amlodd now, and keep him under guard in one of the old storehouses. When night comes, take him to the river and drown him there. We'll say he got loose and made away with himself."

Amlodd, on the floor in the hall, heard the words. "*Raven,*" he whispered, "*Bird of Odin—give me counsel. Help me to save my life, that I may get my vengeance and make you the feast I promised.*"

Odin answered him with a vision. He saw in his mind's eye the raven he'd met in the fen.

"*This will not serve,*" said the bird. "*You lack the art to feign madness. But you are lucky. I know where to get a feigning mind. If you would live and avenge your father, go now where I send you!*"

He saw a door before him in his mind—a rare door of wonderful workmanship—elegant wood gleaming bright as steel, of a strangely spare pattern, with an odd latch like a ball of brass. In his mind he put his hand on that latch and pulled the door open.

The words came out from his mouth without lighting in his mind—words in a tongue no man could understand—and those who came to carry him away stood gaping in wonder.

"Oh what a rogue and peasant slave
*   am I!*
Is it not monstrous that this player here,
But in a fiction, in a dream of passion,
Could force his soul so to his own
*   conceit*
That from her working all his visage
*   wanned,*
Tears in his eyes, distraction in his
*   aspect,*
A broken voice, and his own function
*   suiting*
With forms to his conceit? And all for
*   nothing,*
For Hecuba!
What's Hecuba to him, or he to Hecuba,
That he should weep for her? What
*   would he do*
Had he the motive and the cue for
*   passion*
That I have? He would drown the
*   stage with tears*
And cleave the general ear with
*   horrid speech,*
Make mad the guilty and appall the free,
Confound the ignorant, and amaze
*   indeed*
The very faculties of eyes and ears. . . . ?"

This was madness indeed—there could be no doubt of it. Amlodd was touched by the gods, like a devoted beast. None dared molest him.

* CHAPTER IV *

Will was up with the police until 2:00 in the morning. He worried the deputies would ask whether he thought the intruder had been looking for anything in particular, but they didn't approach law enforcement imaginatively. "Yeah, we see a lot of these break-ins," the one in charge said. He had a Smokey the Bear hat and a county-issue gut. "Lots of times they don't even steal anything valuable. You missing anything valuable?"

Will couldn't think of anything that was missing offhand. Thank God he'd taken the book with him.

"When I was a kid we left our house unlocked all the time," said the deputy. "Somebody got robbed maybe once every two or three years around here. Don't tell me society ain't on the skids."

He wrote up a report and left with his people. Will said the hell with it and went to bed without even trying to clean up, except for piling the toppled books neatly so they wouldn't lay open and crooked.

In the morning he went to work half asleep. The weatherman on the radio said to expect scattered snow flurries. *"They'll be getting heavy snow in parts of Iowa, but it won't come this far north."*

His first afternoon class got preempted by a school assembly.

Principal Hellstrom opened the proceedings with an announcement.

"I'm sure you'll all be happy to know that the School Board has authorized a new program to improve security in our school," the principal said. He was wearing a purple sweatshirt today that asked the question, DO I LOOK LIKE SOMEBODY WHO GIVES A RAT'S ASS?

"Beginning next week, we will have a Student Security Team," he went on. "The faculty and student council have met and agreed on the following list of outstanding students who will be your Security Team members. These students are:

"Jason Sunde

"Kimberly Lurvey

"Jason Chesley

"Kimberly Clow

"Jason Pedersen

"Kimberly Kaste

"Jason Cook

"Kimberly Anderson

"And Eric Smedhammer."

Wonderful, thought Will. *They've given Eric a badge.*

The assembly speaker was a woman from the Sociology Department of one of the state universities. She spoke on the subject, "Thinking Outside the Box."

Original, thought Will.

The gist of her talk was that the structures and traditions of our society confine us in prisonlike conceptual boxes. She exhorted the students to think of at least one traditional value they could set aside, in order to liberate their souls.

Then Principal Hellstrom dismissed them, suggesting they all go to their next classes and write a short essay about some tradition they would like to set aside.

And, behold, it was done.

Will collected his students' essays at the end of the hour. He looked through the essays once they had filed out.

Some traditions the students felt might be jettisoned:

  Marriage
  Religion
  Racial equality
  Gender equality
  Parental authority
  Police authority
  The incest taboo

Sobriety
Art
Literature
Law
The Golden Rule

Will sighed and dumped them all in his trash basket before leaving.

The students had cleared out quickly. The hall was empty as Will locked the room. From somewhere two men appeared and moved in, one on either side of him. They grabbed his arms with strong hands.

Will looked from side to side in panic. The men appeared young, but too old for high school. College age. They wore sweatshirts and sweat pants. He tried to see their faces, but a hand pressed his head forward against the door panel and held it there, flattening his nose.

"Where's the book?" they asked.

Terrified, Will said nothing.

They twisted his arm behind him. The pain radiated both ways from his shoulder.

"The book! Where is it?"

Will was no hero. He wasn't about to give his life for a book, even the Ur-*Hamlet*. He opened his mouth to speak.

Suddenly the hands let him go and he fell. Voices shouted; there were sounds of blows and bodies falling.

He turned to see Eric Smedhammer fighting the two attackers.

He saw a suckered tentacle dart from Eric's mouth and smack one of them. The college boy screamed and ran away, followed quickly by his friend.

Eric didn't chase them. He stood and looked down at Will, a superior smirk on his face.

"Goothingiwuzhere," he mumbled.

"Eric. What was that—your tongue? Some kind of tentacle—"

"T-shirt," said Eric, pointing at the silk screen of Yggxvthwul on the garment.

Of course that must have been it. In the confusion of the moment, he'd seen the picture and somehow superimposed it on what actually happened.

"Well, thank you, Eric. Thank you very much."

Eric shrugged and walked away. He didn't show any interest in why outsiders had attacked a teacher in school.

Will went out to his Jeep and found the lift gate jimmied open. Thank goodness he'd left the Kyd book with Bess. He drove home and straightened things in his house, then worked on his lines. He didn't eat supper.

When he drove back into town for rehearsal, snow had begun falling in light, fat flakes that became an array of fireflies that streaked toward him in his headlights like stars in hyperspace in a Star Wars movie.

"We're getting a little more snow than we expected tonight, but nothing to slow you down in the morning," said the man on the radio.

Will was early as usual. There were lights on in the theater, so somebody was there. He started to climb the concrete steps.

Footsteps pounded up from behind. Will turned in panic, still edgy after the attack that afternoon. The man who climbed up beside him, panting, was fat and short. Will didn't recognize Del Perry at first.

Perry said, "Will, hold up."

Will faced him. "Nice to see you," he said. "Run out of thugs?"

"Look, I'm sorry about that," said Del, taking a deep drag on a cigarette and flicking it away. He wore a wool overcoat with the collar up, no hat. His yellow hair was blowing away from where he'd combed it across the top of his head. "They were a couple jocks who were flunking my class. I said I'd pass 'em if they did me a favor."

"You're not even embarrassed, are you?"

"I'm embarrassed as hell, Will. But I've been so embarrassed for so long, I just don't give a rip anymore. I'm desensitized. Let's go inside. I'm freezing my butt off out here."

"There's somebody in there. If you threaten me, there'll be a witness."

"No more pushy stuff, I promise. I just want to talk. I suppose there's no smoking in there?"

"Fire marshal's rules."

"Like everyplace else. And me out of nicotine gum. Come on."

They climbed the steps and went in. Through the auditorium door they could see Bess on stage, kneeling over the trap door. They went down the basement steps. Will flipped on a light and they sat in folding chairs by a long table. Del sighed and shrugged his overcoat off.

"I may not get tenure," he said. "My wife left me; she took me for everything I've got and there's alimony and child support on top of it. I'm living in a one-bedroom apartment and I drive an '88 Escort, and I'm barely making it. If I lose my job there's no way I can pay my obligations. I'm a dead meat deadbeat."

"That's you, Del. Always quoting Shelley."

"Give me a break. I had to learn to talk like a thug to survive in the department. I told you, it's a different world. It's not an ivory tower anymore. Ivory's environmentally insensitive."

"Instead you take your gun and go slaughter Shakespeare."

Del's hand wandered toward his shirt pocket, where the cigarettes were. He touched it lovingly, then dropped the hand. "Don't get high and mighty with me, Will. If you're trying to withhold evidence that Shakespeare plagiarized Kyd, what does that make you?"

"I'm not withholding anything. I'll turn it over to somebody. But I won't give it to you."

"I need it. I thought we were friends."

"So did I. Until you sent people to trash my house and beat me up."

Del slumped in his chair. "I'm in a bad place, Will. I'm appealing to you."

"No. You disqualified yourself."

"Yeah, yeah." Del pushed himself heavily up out of his chair. "You remember I talked about money, don't you?"

"It's all you've talked about."

Del got up. "Yeah right, rub it in, you goddam prig. Young and good-looking and on the upswing. I was there once too, you know. You don't swing up forever. Someday you'll be in a bind too, and looking for somebody to do one little thing just to give you a hand up, and I hope they have more consideration. . . ."

He moved up the stairs talking as he went.

Will wished he could do something for the man. Del had been a good friend once, and the breaking of their trust was like losing a minor organ—a spleen, maybe.

He climbed the stairs, leaning heavily on the banister.

He found the other principal actors gathered with Bess at the front of the auditorium. She and Randy and Diane sat on the stage apron. Rosemary, Howie and Peter sat in the first and second rows. Eric sat a little further back, to one side. They were doing an imaginative exercise, talking about how life must have been in Shakespeare's time. As Will went down the aisle Sean came in, covered in snow and complaining about driving conditions.

"It was a very different world back then," Bess said as Will and Sean sat with the others. "Religion was as important as career.

Careers were generally decided for you by your family. Marriages were decided that way, too."

"God, that must have been a time," said Diane. "Can you imagine getting married that way?"

"Think of the wife abuse there must have been," said Rosemary.

"Not necessarily," said Peter. "I personally believe wife abuse was probably rarer then than it is now."

Diane sat bolt upright. "How can you say a thing like that?" she asked.

"Because I've thought about it in light of my actual experience, instead of romantic movies. If there's one thing I've learned about in life, it's dysfunctional families.

"What's the first thing you learn from dysfunctional families? That they reproduce themselves. Abused daughters go out and find abusive men to marry, men just like dear old dad. It happens almost every time. They swear they'll never marry anyone the least bit like their fathers, and then they infallibly pick out his clone. It's like salmon swimming upstream.

"But if you've got a system where dad picks his daughter's husband, what happens?"

"What happens is, he picks out a fat bastard just like himself for her," said Diane, unwrapping a breath mint.

"No, that's exactly what he doesn't do. That's a picture you get from sentimental novels. What happens in real life when one bully meets another? Do they slap each other on the back and become bosom buddies? No. Bullies flatter strong people and push weak ones around, but they don't like their own kind.

"This is what I see happening: Daughter says, 'I think Johnny over there is really cute.' What she really means is, 'I can sense that Johnny is the kind of s.o.b. who'll use me for a punching bag and make my life a living hell,' only she doesn't know that's what she means. Daddy says, 'No, I don't like him.' Daughter says, 'But why, Daddy?' Daddy says, 'I don't know—he's got shifty eyes.' What he means is, 'I can smell it that he's just as big a bastard as I am, and I wouldn't trust him with my garbage, let alone my daughter.'

"So he picks out a nice, dull, dependable husband for the girl, and she spends her whole life dreaming about the wonderful bad boy who got away, not realizing that her father, all without knowing it or even wanting to, has stepped in to short-circuit the natural cycle of abuse."

Bess said, "Very creative, Peter. I don't buy it for a second, but at least you've been thinking about it. That's the kind of thinking I'd like all of you to do, even if you only come up with this kind of crap. We're going to get our costumes about a week before dress rehearsal, so you can wear them awhile and be comfortable in them. I want you to think about the period too, like this, so you're comfortable in it."

Howie craned his head around. "It's getting late. Where is everybody?"

From the shadows in the back of the theater a slumped figure appeared, trudging down the center aisle. It was Del Perry. He had snow in his hair.

"The storm's getting really bad," he said, in an apologetic voice. "I couldn't get out of the parking lot. I'm afraid we're all stuck here for the time being."

Will introduced Del without mentioning the reason for his visit.

"Well," said Bess, "we might as well get to work on our blocking. If we get snowed in, we'll make a working party of it."

"If this is a party," said Sean, "where's the bar?"

"Put out that cigarette!" said Bess. She snapped her head to the side to face Del, who'd collapsed in one of the seats and lit up.

"Have a heart, lady," he said. "Do I really gotta go out in that storm to get a little relief?"

"The fire marshal says you do. You're a guest here, Mr. Perry. Please observe the rules of the house."

"Yeah, yeah." He headed out, pulling his overcoat on again.

Bess went to center stage. "Okay, kids, Act III, Scene iii. We've had the play within the play, Claudius has stomped out; Hamlet is certain of his guilt now. We've cut the first section;

Claudius, you pick it up with line 36; we'll have a little chapel thing set up back here—way upstage, where you'll feel at home. A small curtain'll cover it—it'll open to show you kneeling at the altar. By the way, everybody, try to stay off the trapdoor. I was checking it and I think the braces are loose."

Claudius made his prayer, stopping to make penciled notes in his script as Bess gave them, and Hamlet hovered over him with his own script rolled up for a sword, then let him live so as to kill him later in *some act that hath no relish of salvation in't.*

The theoretical main curtain closed and opened again to reveal Peter and Diane in the queen's bedchamber.

"Polonius, you'll hide behind a curtain upstage left," said Bess. "Gertrude, you stand here. Hamlet, you enter stage right."

They worked through the murder of Polonius, and Peter settled himself comfortably on his side with his head propped on one hand to watch them trace out the rest. They made use of all the space, Diane constantly retreating from Will's intensity, Will forever stalking her and blocking her escapes. Even doing it this way, forever rerunning sections and making small changes, the innate tension of the scene made Will's shoulders ache.

"Ha! have you eyes?
You cannot call it love, for at your age

*The heyday in the blood is tame, it's
    humble,
And waits upon the judgment, and what
    judgment
Would step from this to this? . . ."*

Bess told Will to grab Diane's wrist as he spoke the line, "*Nay, but to live in the rank sweat of an enseamèd bed, stewed in corruption, honeying and making love over the nasty sty—*" and Diane used her free hand to slap him across the face.

Will stopped, stunned, and put his hand on his cheek. It had been no stage slap. It stung.

"That's good," said Bess. "We'll use it."

Diane's eyes went wide. "I don't know why I did that," she whispered.

Will smiled ruefully. "Just pull your punch next time, okay?"

"Hold it like that for a moment," said Bess. "Gertrude, you're afraid of Hamlet. You're afraid that slap will push him over the edge and he'll murder you too. So you go from anger to pleading. Let's hear your next line."

Eric slouched on in the ghost's place, and they finished the scene. Bess excused Will from dragging Peter offstage for the time being.

Sean, Diane and Will went through the next scenes without Rosencrantz and Guildenstern, since Alan and Johnny weren't present.

"Okay, we skip Act IV, Scene iv—" said Bess.

"Skip it?" asked Will. "I thought we were doing Scene iv!"

"Did I say that? Sorry. I decided to cut it."

"You're cutting the '*My thoughts be bloody, or be nothing worth!*' speech?"

"We can manage without it."

"It develops Hamlet's character and sets up Fortinbras' arrival in the last scene!"

"I'm sorry. You'll have to live without it."

Will said something under his breath about *Reader's Digest* and Bess said, "You want to direct this play, Will?"

"I don't like it. Am I allowed to say I don't like it?"

"Why don't you just bottle it up inside you for now?"

"Fine."

"Fine. Shall we move on? Scene v, folks. Gertrude and Ophelia on stage, Horatio and Claudius, you wait in the wings."

Will went out into the audience and sat fuming as Diane, Rosemary and Howie blocked their scene. When it came time for Sean to enter he was nowhere to be found.

"Are all you people in league against me tonight?" Bess demanded.

"I'll find him," said Randy. "Heaven knows I have little enough to do in this play."

Bess put a hand over her eyes as he went for Sean. She stood motionless center stage until Randy returned with the truant. Sean seemed even unsteadier than usual. Turning to see them come in, Will noticed Del in a seat toward the back. Incredibly he had another cigarette lit, and was hiding the glow behind cupped hands.

Sean stumbled as he climbed the steps to the stage. Bess, Diane, Rosemary and Howie rushed down to him while Randy rushed up from below.

"'Mall right," said Sean. "I once had a walk-on in *The Skin of Our Teeth* and saw Richard Burton do Mr. Androbus brilliantly on twice the alcohol I've had." He pulled himself up the steps in a couple of tries. Bess and Rosemary helped him. Will, watching from his seat, noticed that Sean managed to rest his hand on Rosemary's bottom fully three times before he made it to the top.

"Watch your hand there, buddy," said Randy.

"What do you care?" Rosemary asked. "My ass isn't your property."

"You're right," said Randy, stepping back. "The line forms on the right, gentlemen; take your turns at Rosey's ass."

Rosemary took three angry steps toward him, but Bess caught her by the arm and turned her around.

"Back to work," said Bess. "Can you people try to play nicely?"

Sean groped her one more time and Rosemary slapped him. He fell down again.

"Stop it! Just stop it!" Bess shouted.

Eric, who was still on stage, said quietly, "Fire'n thentryway."

They all ran down the aisle to see, but the

fire was spreading quickly in the old woodwork, and the smoke and flames drove them back.

"The side door, through the sacristy," said Bess.

The group ran back toward the stage. They clattered up the steps and headed for backstage right.

They stopped, piling up into one another, at the sight of a tall man in a black suit and clerical collar, who stood barring their way with hot, angry eyes.

They ran back toward center stage. One by one, each of them found themselves poised on the edge of the trapdoor, which had somehow opened itself, and one by one they fell through.

❋ CHAPTER V ❋

Will opened his eyes. The first thing he saw was a woman's face. It was the most beautiful face he had ever seen his life.

It was a young blue-eyed face, the eyes so blue they hurt him, like a laser to the cornea. They were large and widely spaced. The forehead above them was wide, and a few strands of golden hair fell over it. The nose was short, freckled and a little snubbed. The mouth was very small, and he could somehow tell that it concealed a smile to melt the heart. She reminded him a little of an actress named Inger Stevens, dead many years, though this face was rounder.

The woman was speaking, in a language he could not understand. Her voice was high, sweet and musical.

"Her voice was ever soft, gentle and low—an excellent thing in a woman." Not perfectly apt, but he'd always liked the quotation from Lear.

He could lie here (on a blanket on straw) and listen to this woman speak all day, despite the fact that he couldn't understand a word.

Something in his mind wanted attention, like an itch. He tried to scratch it with a mental finger, but couldn't seem to reach the spot.

And then he found it. The itching eased, and as it did he knew what the girl was saying.

"You're not listening to me, are you?" the girl asked.

"No, go on," said Will.

"What?"

Will realized that he wasn't speaking the same language she spoke. He sought the place in his mind where he understood her, and spoke from out of it, choosing the words carefully, gaining confidence as they came.

"I'm listening," he said in the new tongue. "Speak on. Speak on forever."

"We have to be rid of love," the girl said. "That's the secret, don't you think?"

He wanted very much to agree with her, but had to say, "Well, it seems hard. . . ."

"No, not hard at all. 'Tis love that's hard. 'Tis love makes life unbearable. Without love we'd live forever, for there'd be no need to die. It should be the king, instead of love."

"The king instead of love?"

"Aye. The king must take the families away. If

the king owns all the land, and all the beasts and all the grain, he can give to each as they deserve. Let no one own a house, or a farm, or a ship. Let all be the king's. Let all the men live singly, or in companies. Let all the women be whores, and the men pay them to lie with them.

"When a child is born, let it be the king's. The king will let it live or die, as he pleases. Let the child be raised by strangers. Let there be no love for children, no love for parents, no love for a man or a woman."

"But why?" asked Will.

"So no one need die." She looked deeply at him with those lancing eyes. "'Tis love makes us die."

Will smiled. "You mean I've no hope that you'll love me?"

The girl's eyes went dark like the lights of a house at bedtime, her face went slack, and she whirled and fell into the corner, covering her head with her arms and weeping. Will felt as if he'd stepped onto a stair tread that wasn't there as he realized that the girl was out of her mind.

The corner where she crouched joined two walls made of some kind of rough plaster framed with wood, and the floor seemed to be dirt strewn with straw or something like straw. Will paid attention for the first time to his surroundings. The room was dark, lit only by sunlight from a triangular opening at the gable end of the roof peak.

It all reminded him of something he'd seen before. What?

His right hand hurt. He held it up and saw the fingers and the ball of the thumb had been slashed. The hand was brown with dried blood, and the wounds were crusted, but he saw no sign of infection.

He didn't recognize the hand. Looking farther down, he didn't recognize his feet.

They were someone else's feet. They were larger than they ought to be. The tops were hairy, and the hair was gold-red, not brown.

And why was he naked?

And how had he gotten so strong? He looked at his legs and his stomach, and his chest as well as he could. He looked at his arms and hands.

They were massive. They were like body builders' arms, except that these were not body builders' muscles. No one had trained for definition here. This was working muscle—the kind that looks almost fat; like a powerlifter's muscles, only not exactly.

He had a beard too. He could feel it. He couldn't see what color it was, but he bet it was gold-red.

This is some other guy's body, he thought. *Whoever traded this one for mine must be really pissed.*

"Fortunately for you he's far from here and out of reach," said a voice. A strobelike shadow flurry made the room blink, and a large black bird flapped down to light on the straw, facing him. It pecked in the straw, came up with a maggot, swallowed it, and fixed him with one bright black eye; it seemed to have only one.

"*Nevermore*," said the raven.

Will goggled.

"Couldn't resist that," said the bird.

"You speak," said Will.

"Fluently. In several languages."

Will felt an urge to cower in a corner himself. He drew his knees up to his chest in a defensive reflex. "Where am I? What am I doing here? Who am I?"

"That's easily answered. You are where you've no business to be; you do what you've no business to do; you are in fact whom you've only feigned to be heretofore."

"You make game of me."

"All is a game to me, and a losing one at that."

"Then there's no profit talking to you."

"Nor in anything else in this world, or others."

"Others?" Will thought a moment. "Other worlds? Is that where I am, in some other world? My name is Will Sverdrup, I come from Earth in the twenty-first century."

"You futurelings! You always drop your century like a king's name, thinking to cow the savages."

"*Futureling*! Then I'm in the past? That makes sense! This could be anywhere in Europe, anywhere in the Dark Ages, or even early Medieval. Raven! Think me no fool who vaunts himself because of the year of his birth! I am one who respects the past. I try to take all men on their own terms, rather than judging by the customs to which I was born."

"Know you Yggdrasil?"

"The World Tree of the Norse? Is that where I am? Among the Norse?"

"Know you Yggdrasil?"

"Yes. The tree that upheld the Nine Worlds. The dragon Nidhogg gnawed at its roots; the Norns poured spring water on them to heal them and give growth. Beasts of all kinds dwelt in the branches."

"Upheld! Gnawed! Poured! Dwelt! You lie when you say you're not bound to the future— you think these times past even when you're in them!"

"I beg your pardon. I spoke out of usage."

"Then listen. You must not think of Yggdrasil as a tree growing up from the ground. Yggdrasil has its root at the middle, and grows out in all directions. It grows ever; it grows at all times. Even I cannot see beyond the end of its growth."

"All right."

"All right? You've naught to say past 'All right'?"

"What would you have me say?"

"Fool's question! What you say is what you are! If you know not what to say, then you're not what I require. You're useless to me. Farewell."

And with a flapping of wings that seemed large as an eagle's in the small house, the raven

flew up through the smoke hole (for that was
what it was—Will recognized it now) and
departed.

Before Will could digest what had happened,
the door of the house opened and a huge man
entered. Will could not see him clearly, for the
sunlight that came with him hurt his eyes.

"And is it here you are, Katla?" the newcomer
roared. "Be gone with you! Is not one witling
plenty to a house?" He strode to the girl, lifted
her by the arm, clapped her bottom and sent her
out. She ran with speed and grace, laughing.

"And you'd not the sense to drive her out?" he
said to Will, standing above him with his hands
on his hips. Will could see him better now. Hulk
Hogan, but not bald. He had fair hair—almost
white—nearly shoulder length, and a short beard
of the same color. His eyes were bright blue, his
complexion ruddy. His yellow woolen tunic, or
shirt, had long sleeves. Those sleeves would have
been roomy on an ordinary man, but fitted snug
on this one. He wore rings of silver above
his biceps. His trousers were of reddish wool,
wrapped with woven bands below the knees
rather like World War I soldiers' puttees, and he
wore leather shoes. At his side hung a sword
which Will recognized immediately for a Norse
pattern and an early one—a straight, short guard
and flat mushroom-shaped pommel. It was decorated with silverwork and brass in the shape of
intertwined gripping beasts.

There could be no question. He was looking

at something like a genuine Viking. Somehow he had traveled back in time. He still did not know where he was—it could be anywhere in Scandinavia, or anywhere in Europe in fact, as far as the Vikings ranged. And the exact date could be anytime within centuries (the sword could be an heirloom). But he knew more than he had. It was something.

"Why should I drive her out? She offered no harm," said Will, pulling himself to a sitting position and drawing his blanket around him.

The big man squatted. It seemed a small thing, but Will marveled at his squat. He'd never seen a man do it so easily, as if it were no trouble, as comfortably as a modern man would sink into a chair.

"You really do not know? You've forgotten yourself so much?" he asked.

"I know not what I know or what I've forgotten."

"Do you know your name?"

"My name is Vill Sverdrup." To his irritation, Will found he could not say the later "w." It came out as a "v."

"*Sverdrup?* 'Sword-place'? A good enough name, I suppose, but 'tis not yours."

"Then tell me what my name is, you who know so much."

"You are Amlodd, son of Orvendil, nephew to my lord, Jarl Feng."

Will fell back against the wall, unable to speak.

"Lost your tongue with your wits?" the tall man asked.

"I am Amlodd?"

"Unless he has a twin, and I've heard of none such."

"Amlodd, prince of Denmark."

"Well 'prince' would be stretching matters a bit. Hrorek is king of Denmark, and of course he's your grandfather, so I suppose you could call yourself a prince. But you're heir to the jarl, which is a high station."

"Amlodd the Dane. 'Tis I, Amlodd the Dane."

"None other."

"What of Katla? Why should I have sent her out as you say?"

"You do not know? You mock me not?"

"I swear by—let's say by Yggdrasil."

"Then I shall tell you. There are two reasons why you should never be alone with Katla. How did she behave with you?"

"She spoke of love. She was against it. When I used the word she broke down in tears."

The big man nodded. "Poor Katla. 'Twas because you spoke of love she did not touch you."

"Touch me?"

"Touch your manhood. She can't keep her hands off any man, old or young, rich or poor, hero or coward. And it drives her madder than before that none of them will lie with her."

"None will lie with her? Why not? Is such a woman as she thought ugly in this time?"

"No, of course she's fair. But she's mad."

"Yes?"

"Yes."

"And so?"

"So what?"

"So why can't a man lie with a madwoman, if she's fair? I'd think it might be good sport."

"It might, I suppose, were it not dangerous."

"Dangerous? How?"

The tall man looked him hard in the eyes. "You truly do not know?"

"You keep asking me. I swear I do not know."

"You're mad yourself. I suppose it follows you'd not understand about madness."

"I'm not mad. I just don't know."

"Of course."

Will realized, with irritation, that the man was humoring him. He said, "Tell me."

"Then listen," the man said. "Madness is a thing of Odin's. He speaks out of it. He uses it to give victory, or to destroy great men. A woman mad is a holy thing, like a beast marked for sacrifice. Her holiness and death might pass to the man, like fleas."

"But if I'm mad as you say, what harm could come to me? I've the fleas already."

" 'Tis different in your case."

"How different?"

"You're sure you don't know this?"

"For the last time—"

"All right. Katla is your sister."

"My sister."

"Your half-sister to state it clear. Her mother was a thrall but Orvendil was her father. He set her on his knee and owned her."

"My sister."

"Aye."

"My sister. My sister."

Guttorm decided, apparently, that the madman would continue to say "my sister" for some time, so he rose with another oiled movement and went out, closing the door behind him and barring it.

❧ CHAPTER VI ❧

"Is this Hell? Are we dead?" The voice was Diane's. They could make out one another's forms in the darkness, but one could only be told from another by voice.

"I'd say it's not bad if it's Hell; a bit of a disappointment if it's Heaven," said Sean.

It was neither very hot nor very cold. An occasional air current stirred, but nothing violent.

"It seems to be an open space, but sheltered," said Howie. "Some sort of hall or amphitheater?"

"I've got a lighter," said Del Perry, "but you probably don't want me to use it again."

"You mean since you burned down our theater?" asked Bess.

"Let's draw and quarter the man later," said Peter. "Right now I'd like to see where we are."

Bess said, "Yeah, okay."

They heard the fizzing sound of a butane lighter catching, and they squinted at Del's round face in its glow.

"Well, walk around, man," said Howie. "Give us some idea where we are."

Del began to walk, holding the lighter out in front of him. The exercise was not very helpful. "Black stone floor, black walls. No natural features; no furniture."

"If that's everything, you'd probably better put the light out," said Bess. "No point wasting the fuel."

"So what have we learned?" asked Peter when it was dark again.

"Not much," said Rosemary. "It doesn't make any sense. We were in a burning theater. Now we're here. Where is here, and how did we get here?"

"I think it's plain enough," said Diane. "We're dead."

There was a moment of silence, as if in memorium.

"I don't buy it. Where's the near-death experience?" said Howie. "The only light at the end of the tunnel we've seen is this guy—what's your name?"

"Del."

"Del. And he isn't exactly my idea of God."

"All near-death experiences aren't the same."

"There's a very simple way to figure out if we're dead," said Sean. Diane gave a sudden cry and the sound of a slap was heard.

"Proof we're not dead," said Sean. "If this was a near-death experience, we'd be out of body. If we were out of body Diane wouldn't have cared that I grabbed her. Ergo, we still have bodies, and we're still alive."

"Maybe we only think we have bodies," said Rosemary.

"Then Diane would have had no way of knowing I'd grabbed her in the dark. Am I wrong?"

Silence for a moment.

"I guess that's a relief," said Rosemary. "But how did we get here? Is this some sort of secret crypt beneath the stage?"

"Unlikely," said Bess.

"We haven't got enough information," said Howie. "It is a capital mistake to theorize in advance of the evidence, as Sherlock Holmes used to say."

"Did I ever tell you I almost got a part in a play with Basil Rathbone once?" asked Sean, and everyone told him he had.

"There's at least one of our company who hasn't said anything yet," said Peter. "And that's odd because he's normally pretty talkative. What about you, Randy? What do you think about all this?"

Randy's voice, a clear tenor, came out of the darkness. "What do you know about quantum physics?"

"Quantum physics?" said Sean. "I try to know as little about quantum physics as possible."

"Gluons and quarks and Heisenberg's

Uncertainty Principle," said Howie. "I can use the words, but I don't really know what I'm talking about."

"Have you ever heard of alternate universes?" asked Randy.

"Anybody who's read science fiction knows about them."

"What about infinite universes?"

There was silence.

"Some physicists theorize that at every instance in the history of the cosmos, wherever there is a choice between one thing happening and another, both things happen, and each option goes on in its own universe."

"Seems like a hell of a way to run a cosmos," said Sean.

"You think we're in some kind of alternate universe?" asked Rosemary.

And then there was light. Their eyes turned toward it hungrily. The light was a column, which resolved itself into the shape of a man. They recognized him. It was the red-eyed man in the clerical collar they'd seen in the fire.

"More than alternatives in matter make new universes," the dead man said.

"If you're who I think you are, this isn't Heaven," said Peter.

"This is not Heaven, nor is it Hell," said the ghost. "This is the place of Hamlet."

"Funny, it doesn't look like a hamlet," said Sean.

"The stories told among men have a reality

of their own. Surely you've all felt that there is a sense in which Don Quixote and Sherlock Holmes exist in their own rights, more than other fictional characters but less than real people—than most people at least."

He paused for effect.

"Some characters and stories," he went on, "—only the greatest ones, and only the ones which hold and compel human belief—can become the bases of universes in their own rights."

"How?" asked Peter.

"There are beings in the universe, greater than men and lower than angels. They are known to you, in story and legend, under many names. These beings know the doors between the universes, and they have the power to take quiet empty ones, where little or nothing is going on, and re-furnish them, so to speak."

"Let me get this straight," said Diane. "This universe has been sublet to Hamlet?"

"It remains to be seen. The operation is a delicate one. Real humans must be found to take the major roles, and to play them out. If the story goes awry, the experiment fails, the graft does not take, and the universe reverts to its former state."

"What about the human actors?" asked Bess. "What happens to them if the graft doesn't take?"

"For that matter," said Rosemary, "what happens if it does take? As I recall, we all die in this play, except for Howie."

"And what about the rest of us?" asked Bess. "There's me, and Eric who's a techie, and this pyromaniac from the U, whatever his name is."

"Del," said Del. "Hey, you know what I just figured out? I figured out there's no No Smoking rule in this universe." He lit a cigarette and everyone moved away from him.

"You will find your places in the drama, fear not for that," said the ghost. "As for dying, you do not wish to, as I did not in my time. I would say that your only hope is to break the play—to refuse to follow the script, and so frustrate whatever Old One has set you here. Perhaps if you can do that, you will undo his work and be drawn back where you came from."

"Perhaps?" said Peter. "*Perhaps* is the best you can do?"

"I am only a fellow actor in this drama, drawn like you from our home universe. I am not a Watcher or a Holy One. My knowledge is limited."

"What about the play? What about *Hamlet* the play?" asked Bess. "What happens to it in our world if we break it here?"

The ghost did not answer, but dissolved, leaving them in the dark except for Del's cigarette ember. But it wasn't as dark as before. They could recognize one another now. Perhaps the night was lighter; perhaps their eyes were adjusting.

"I don't like this," said Bess.

"Really? And I was having such a good time," said Sean.

"Will Sverdrup," said Howie. "There's one more of us who hasn't said anything since we got here. What's the matter with you, Will?"

They had drawn together in a cluster as the ghost spoke, all but Del and Will. Will sat alone, arms on knees, his back against the stone wall.

"If you speak to me, call me by my name," he said.

"I'm doing that, Will," said Howie.

"I know nothing of your Will."

"Hey, this is confusing enough without playing games."

"Speak not to me of games, churl. I know you not, nor any of you. I know not how I came here, or aught of the matters whereof you speak. But offer me violence, any of you, and in spite of this puny body I wear, I'll wring your necks, one of you or many."

"What the hell are you talking about?" asked Howie, stepping toward him.

"Don't do that," said Peter, drawing him back. "Who are you, stranger?" he said to the one who looked like Will. "You seemed to be our friend; forgive our familiarity. If we're to call you by your right name, we must know it."

"Then call me Amlodd, son of Orvendil."

"Dear God," said Bess and Del, in the unison of a Greek chorus.

❦ CHAPTER VII ❦

"All right, let's say I'm Amlodd," Will told himself. "What happens to me? What do I need to prepare for?"

He got to his feet, wrapped his blanket around him, and began to pace. Pacing in the straw in bare feet was an adventure—under the straw was dirt, and stones, and small bones and things that wriggled.

But he found he was less fastidious than he'd been in his own body. He was vaguely aware that he itched most everywhere—no doubt he had lice and fleas like everybody else in the Dark Ages. But he felt no distress about it. The soles of his feet were tough, insensitive to what they trod on short of knife blades or red-hot coals.

His strength sang under his skin. He'd never

felt anything like it. He looked around him for something to lift or bend or break. Nothing in the house recommended itself.

He tried the door and found it barred. He gave it a shove and it burst open, the wooden bar outside snapping and flying off in two pieces. He stood in the doorway with no plans to go anywhere, just enjoying his ability to smash barriers. Strangers stared at him, but no one challenged him. He felt an ease of tension as he stood in the open air, and he realized that he hated being cooped up.

He didn't, however, care to be outdoors wearing just a blanket, so reluctantly he went back in.

He needed to concentrate. Amlodd had a story, and it lay over him like a death sentence. He needed to prepare himself for it.

The trouble was, to know what Saxo wrote was not the same as knowing the story. Saxo's account was a garbled collection of legends and folk tales. Half of them probably hadn't even happened to Amlodd, and the other half were remembered wrong. Still, it was all he had.

He remembered with a shudder that some scholars judged Amlodd a myth—a culture hero who existed only in legend. Scholarly habit gave him a frightened moment of fear that he might disappear; then he laughed at himself.

What had happened to Amlodd?

They had tested him, to see if he were really insane. How did it go?

Feng's men had taken him out riding, with

some plan about putting him in contact with a woman and seeing what he would do. Why this would be a test of madness, no one could say. Will remembered a Monty Python routine about a village idiot, which ended with the idiot in bed with several attractive young women, saying, "I may be an idiot, but I'm no fool."

Amlodd's response made no better sense. He had gotten away from the witnesses and enjoyed the girl, then gone home and admitted he'd done it. Why hide it in the first place then? Another example of Saxo's sloppy storytelling and garbled sources. There was some wordplay involved too, Hamlet's famous riddles.

Then Amlodd had talked privately with his mother, discovered a spy in a pile of straw and killed him—the inspiration for the death of Polonius in the play. He had disposed of the body by chopping it up, dumping the pieces into a drain and giving them to the pigs. He had been sent to England (he actually got there, had adventures and married the king's daughter), and returned to burn the jarl and his household in their hall. And he'd lived to fight another day— Shakespeare had taken a dramatic liberty in killing him off at the climax. The real Amlodd had been a Viking, not a Greek, and knew nothing of Aristotle's *Poetics*.

He heard footsteps approaching and turned to see two big men coming toward the house. They were dressed like Guttorm. One carried an axe, the other an unsheathed sword.

"Trying to break out, madman?" asked the one with the sword as he stepped through the door.

Will tensed with fear, and a feeling he'd never known surged through his body. All the reflexes that would have sent him running away in his own time and place hurled him in the opposite direction now. Before he knew it, he had attacked the swordsman, bare hands against steel, ducking under the man's slash, grasping his arm and breaking it over his knee like a stick. As the weapon flew free he caught it by the grip, wheeled and faced the axeman, stepping back so he wouldn't trip over the injured one.

"Want some of the same?" he asked, dancing the weapon from hand to hand, rejoicing in its balance and keenness. The axeman's eyes went wide, and he backed away and fled.

Will found himself laughing. It had all been done without thought—his nerves and his muscles had reacted as they'd clearly been trained to. It was wonderful to be strong and skillful and dangerous. He danced the sword in a figure eight. It felt like a drug, but better than any he'd ever tried in his brief flirtation with chemicals in college.

Guttorm reappeared at the door. "Give me the sword, Amlodd," he said, holding a hand out.

"You've only to ask," said Will, and he returned it, presenting it over his forearm in a gesture that would not be seen again for hundreds of years.

❖   ❖   ❖

Bess and Del approached the man they knew as Will carefully, as they would have a Ming vase or a manticore.

"You're Amlodd?" asked Bess.

"I am, and I demand to know what witchcraft has made me a weakling."

"You heard the ghost. You know as much as we do."

"He spoke words without meaning. What is 'physics'? Who is Hamlet?"

"We have a friend named Will. The body you're wearing is his. Somehow his . . . his soul and yours must have got switched."

"Ah," said Amlodd. "That I can grasp." He rubbed his chin a moment, then said, "What are you people? You wear fine clothes, though the pattern is strange. You men wear paltry rings and no weapons, and your hair is short like thralls' and you have no beards. You women dress without modesty, in trousers like men. And you're all weaklings, except for the troll over there." He gestured toward Eric.

"You might say we're *skalds*, poets," said Del. "But we don't tell our stories in verse. We take the words and deeds of the people in the saga, and relive them."

Amlodd's eyes widened. "You must serve a great king, if he can keep so many skalds to tell tales in this manner."

Howie, from behind them, said "We don't have—" but Peter put a hand on his arm to stop him. "Culture shock," he whispered, and Howie shrugged.

"We've been working on a . . . a saga of a hero called 'Hamlet,' " said Del.

"I have not heard of this hero."

"Hamlet is Amlodd."

Amlodd was silent a moment. "I've ever purposed to have a saga of my own," he said. "But I've done naught as yet to make my name known in so distant a place as this must be."

Bess and Del exchanged a look.

"We're not just distant in miles," said Bess. "We are distant in time as well."

Amlodd shook his head like a horse agitated.

"Hundreds of fathers and sons and grandsons have lived and died since your time. We are from your future."

Amlodd drew himself up in a ball for a moment, like a hedgehog. Then he stretched himself and got to his feet.

"I am dead then? This is Hel? I see no great feasting, no mighty warriors, as in Valhalla. I must have died in bed, and have come down with the women and thralls to Niflheim."

"We don't know what place this is," said Howie. "But we think we're alive. And, at least in that body, so are you."

Amlodd crouched, pushing his fingers back through his hair. "There are so many things I cannot grasp," he said. "This place. You people. That troll—"

"What do you mean 'troll'?" asked Peter.

"That thrall-faced boy over there." He pointed at Eric, who sat apart, sulking. "Can you not see the magic in him?"

"None of us can see magic," said Peter.

"Has the race grown so weak?" asked Amlodd. "Puny bodies and no vision? Well might you relive the sagas of heroes. It's clear you've none of your own. My counsel is to kill the lad now, if we can, before he makes trouble."

Howie got up and took a step forward. "The boy is my son," he said.

Amlodd, still crouched, said, "Then your son is a troll."

Howie took another step and raised a fist. "I don't know who you think you are—"

Amlodd rose from his crouch like a cat and rushed at his attacker. At the same moment Eric moved swiftly between them. No one could tell clearly what happened in the darkness, but there were shouts and the sounds of blows on bodies. When all was done, Amlodd lay on his back, Eric was running off into the darkness, and Howie stood where he had been, looking confused.

Amlodd shook his head and sat up. "Curse this wretched body!" he said. "If I'd had my own arms and legs, I'd have snapped his spine for him."

"Eric!" Howie cried, walking in the direction where the boy had run. "Eric! Come back."

"Can you expect him to stay in the state he's in?" asked Amlodd.

"In what state?" asked Bess.

"He became a monster. Surely you saw it. Arms like a squid he had."

Howie turned on him again. "Will you stop telling lies about my boy? I don't care who you think you are, my boy is—"

"A troll and a warlock."

"Will you shut your—"

He rushed on Amlodd with a fist raised, and quickly found himself on his back on the floor. Amlodd stood above him, hands on hips.

"I may not be the man I was," Amlodd said, "and my nerves may be slow, but I've skill enough to handle such as you. I've no wish to kill you, for that would be shameful as killing a child. But goad me not."

Howie got to his feet again and said, "I've got to find Eric." He headed after his son.

Bess stopped him with a hand on his shoulder. "Maybe it's best we all stay together," she said. "Eric's a tough kid. He'll be able to take care of himself. And he'll find his own way back."

"He's all I've got left, Bess."

"Getting lost yourself won't help him."

Howie slumped his shoulders, hesitated a moment, then went and sat with the others.

There was silence for a time.

"I don't like ghosts," said Peter at last in the half-darkness.

"Few people do," said Sean.

"No, I mean I don't like getting directions from ghosts. I don't believe in them as such."

"As such?" asked Bess.

"What we saw was clearly a supernatural presence. Lots of people have seen presences like that over the years. But just because they're supernatural doesn't make them ghosts."

"What else could they be?" asked Rosemary.

"For want of a better word—demons."

Randy said, "Oh yes, we have a Bible-thumper among us, don't we? Everything's either black or white for you."

"I don't believe that human souls stay around after death—not for very long, anyway. If something looks like a ghost, I think it's probably an evil spirit."

"You forget," said Sean. "Even if it were true in our world, this is Hamlet's world, and Hamlet's ghost was real."

"I think you're mistaken, Sean. In two ways. First of all, this isn't Hamlet's ghost, it's our friend from the theater, the child molester, tab collar and all. He got sucked out of our world just like us. Secondly, I've always thought that Hamlet's ghost was a demon, too."

"That's ridiculous," said Diane. "Hamlet's ghost told the truth."

"And led Hamlet on to disaster. Hamlet wonders about it himself. That's why he sets up the Mousetrap play."

"But the ghost passed the test," said Rosemary. "He told the truth."

"The error wasn't in the information he gave. The error was in demanding revenge."

"Oh jeez," said Bess. "You don't understand about the Elizabethan view of vengeance—"

"And you don't understand about the Protestant teaching on vengeance, which was a hot new idea in Shakespeare's time."

"What you're saying," said Rosemary, "is that we shouldn't trust this ghost."

"That's my suggestion."

"Have you got a better explanation than his for where we are?" asked Howie.

"Not at the moment. His information may be correct, like the ghost's in the play. But his guidance might be disastrous."

"Well, I agree with you on one thing," said Howie. "I don't like ghosts. But for different reasons."

"Scientific?"

"Of course. I can believe in alternate universes. But I don't think ghosts or spirits of any kind exist in any universe."

"You seem to know a lot about the unknown."

"I can't claim to know it. I just don't believe it."

"Because you'd have to rethink your whole world if there were spirits."

"And you'd have to rethink yours if there weren't."

"*Touché.*"

"I understand how you people come to believe in eternal life," said Howie. "It's understandable when you think about it. We all once lived in a world of eternal things. When you're a baby, and a small child, unless you live in a really screwed-up situation, everything seems eternal. Your parents and grandparents have always existed; you probably live in the same place you've always been; nothing much has changed as far back as you can remember. As you grow older, things start to change. Naturally you hanker for the time when everything seemed secure and immatable. That's where religion comes from."

"What do you say to that, Peter?" asked Randy.

"I . . . I can't prove it wrong. I just don't believe it's true. It's not the only possible explanation."

"Just the best one," said Howie.

"All real scientific and cold-blooded," said Diane. "It explains love, too. When you're little, everybody takes care of you, so you think love exists. You grow up and find out that everybody doesn't love you, but you still hold on to the childish belief that love exists, and that it can give meaning to your life."

"I believe in love," said Howie.

"The illusion is understandable, once you analyze it scientifically," said Diane.

"I'm hungry," said Amlodd. Everyone jumped at the opportunity to change the direction of the discussion.

"Yes, what are we going to do for food here?" asked Sean.

Amlodd clapped his hands twice and shouted

"Thralls!" as if that was how he always dealt with hunger, as indeed it was.

Straightway there came a rushing of feet and a dozen shadowy, dark-clothed figures appeared, bowing.

"Set a table," said Amlodd.

The figures bowed again and rushed off. A few moments later they returned with a large tabletop and trestles, which they proceeded to set up. They covered the table with some dark cloth, then set out metal plates and goblets made of what looked like pewter, along with spoons and knives. They brought in long benches then stopped and looked toward Amlodd.

"Feed us," said the main character, and they rushed off to return shortly with platters and bowls heaped with . . . something.

The company sat down to dine and poked their knives tentatively into what they found before them.

"This seems to be meat," said Peter. He cut a small piece and put it in his mouth.

"Don't tell me it tastes like chicken," said Sean.

"It doesn't taste like anything. It's just a bland, generic sort of meat product. If you told me it was beef, I'd believe you, but I'd call it pretty poor beef. If you told me it was horse, I'd believe that too."

"But it's edible?" asked Diane.

"It doesn't taste rancid or anything."

"This seems like some kind of vegetable

mush," said Rosemary, taking a chance with a bowl. "The same thing—nothing unpleasant, but nothing to enjoy either."

"Well, I'm starving," said Diane. "Better to be poisoned than starve." She dug in and soon they all joined her, hungrier than they had realized.

After a few minutes Sean said, "Hey, I'm the king. If Will the Barbarian there can get service, why can't I?" He tapped his metal goblet with his knife and called, "Servants!"

The dark shapes gathered.

"I want some light. Bring torches or something."

The servants bowed and turned, but Peter stalled them with a question. "May I ask for something else to drink?"

"What's the matter with what we've got?" asked Howie.

"I'm not sure, but it smells a little like wine. I suppose that's what they'd serve in this world. But I'm a recovering alcoholic. If I can get water, I'd rather not mess up my sobriety."

"God, not only a Jesus freak but a Friend of Bill," said Randy.

"It seems to me I read that the water in Shakespeare's time was so polluted you'd get dysentery and typhoid from it," said Rosemary.

"Well, let's see what we get," said Sean. "*Garçon,* bring this man water. Clean water. Water from a spring."

The servants trotted off. A couple minutes

later they returned with a flagon of what Peter pronounced perfectly good water. "Bland of course, but in water that's a virtue."

They also came with torches which they set into sconces in the walls. The company took the opportunity to get a better look at the servants, but they all wore hoods, and somehow the light did not seem to reach under them.

They feasted for some time, and even Howie grew cheerier. At last they put their knives and spoons down. "I wonder where we sleep?" said Diane.

Amlodd put a hand on Rosemary's arm. "Are you a wife?" he asked.

Rosemary said no.

"Betrothed?"

"No."

"You're a virgin?"

Rosemary laughed. "Not for a few years now—"

"Good, then you're a whore." Amlodd picked her up off her bench and began to carry her away. Rosemary struggled and screamed.

"Do something, Randy, she's your girl," said Sean.

"Not for a couple days now," said Randy, grinning.

Peter got up and walked into Amlodd's path.

"I probably can't fight you any better than Howie could," he said, "but this is not how we treat our women."

"She's yours?"

"No. But I can't let you take her against her will."

"I can hurt you."

"You'll have to then."

"It's okay, Peter." Rosemary said it.

"You want to go with him?" Peter asked.

"Better this than a fight. And, hey, he's Hamlet."

"And you're Ophelia. You know how she ended."

"I'm tougher than her. I'll see you in the morning."

Peter stood and watched as Amlodd and his conquest disappeared down a sort of corridor that hadn't been there before.

"Well, if we're going to be in character, would you care to retire, wife?" Sean asked Diane. Diane smiled and gave him her hand.

"I don't like this," said Peter. "Once we start living our roles we may not be able to stop."

"The old lament of the born-again Christian who isn't getting any," said Diane.

"Servants! Conduct us to our bedchamber!" cried Sean, and the servants appeared with lamps to lead them down the same corridor Amlodd had taken.

Howie sat watching, still at the table, and was startled by the voices of two shadowy men who approached him.

"Master Horatio," they said,
"Bearing on thine affect for Lord Hamlet,

Much remarked and praised by all and
    general,
Who holding high conceit of his
    discourse and parts
Would see him eased from the dark
    address
Of his late melancholy; for his good weal
We'd tell thee of a wonder.
Strange visitation, wondrous to the sight
Hath us o'ertaken in our nightly watch
Portending woe and horror in the land;
The form of him we knew as liege,
By name King Hamlet, walking in the
    night
Upon the bastion; as may be t'hold
An eye upon the lands which once he
    swayed.
Straightway we saw him, stiffened all our
    limbs;
Burst sweat upon our chill and smoking
    flesh
Be-rimed to kiss the cold envenomed air.
We thought he made to speak, but in
    our fear
We fled that place. And thought we then
Of thee, a man of parts and subtle
To discern.
We pray thee, as a friend and
    Christian man,
To honor us our company to bear,
Upon our watch, to view this prodigy;
Grant us, men plain and dull of wit,

Benison of thy rarer schoolman's sense,
To ravel truth from lie—"

"Get out!" Howie shouted. "Get the hell away from me! I'm Howard Smedhammer, not Horatio! There is no Horatio! If I have my way, there never will be!"

The servants fled.

❦ CHAPTER VIII ❦

A woman walked up behind Guttorm and he moved aside for her. She stood in the doorway and gazed at Will.

Will returned her gaze, pulling the cloak tighter around him. She was a handsome middle-aged woman dressed in a long pleated dress with a sort of wraparound apron over it, held up at the shoulders by brooches shaped like tortoise shells. She covered her hair with an intricately folded white linen headdress, and she wore a lot of gold and silver jewelry. She had a rather long face, but it was a lovely one, and she carried herself with a grace Will had seldom seen. He mentally cast Greta Garbo—but softer. She looked in his eyes, as if searching for something there.

"Do you not know me, my son?" she asked.

Will went with the script. "Mother?"

She took a step forward, then hesitated. "You wouldn't hurt your mother would you, Amlodd?"

"I may speak knives, but will use none," he said. There was no word for "dagger" in the Danish tongue.

She took another step, uncertainty on her face. Her gaze dropped to Will's hands.

"You've hurt yourself, my son," she said, forgetting her fear and rushing forward. She took his hand and pulled it out to examine it, not caring that the blanket came open. Will pulled the hand from her and turned away.

"Why do you turn your back on me, Amlodd?"

"'Tis nothing. A scratch."

"You always let me see to your wounds. Don't you remember the time you took the Saxon arrow in your chest? Or that axe blow that broke your wrist?"

Will could actually feel the shadow of an ache in his left wrist.

"There's no need," he said. "The hand is well."

He felt her hand on his shoulder and moved further off.

"Will you not bear to let me touch you? Do you hate me so?"

"I do not hate you. But I . . . I do not care to be touched just now."

"Will you put on clothing and come to the feast tonight, my son?

"Of course. I meant to ask for clothing."

"And will you—will you try to stay inside

your skin? Act as you did while your father yet lived?"

Will was still looking away from her. "I shall try."

A short-haired girl in a light-colored, undyed dress appeared with folded garments, a belt and shoes. "Take these and put them on, then," said Amlodd's mother.

Will took the clothing from the girl. "This is a wonderful shirt," he said, examining the garment. It was rust-colored wool, edged with braiding at the neck and cuffs. There was ornate embroidery on the sleeves and across the chest—writhing and intertwined forms of what (he remembered) historians called "gripping beasts."

"'Tis just a shirt," said the woman. "I've made you dozens such."

"You made th s?" He faced her, holding the shirt before him for modesty.

"Of course. I'd not let thralls sew shirts for my son."

"You made this *for me*?"

"Why do you wonder at that?"

Will's eyes went wet and he had to blink. "No one ever did such a thing for me."

"Oh, my son, you only forget because your mind's unwell."

Will shook his head to clear it. "Yes, my mind's unwell. That must be the reason. Please go and I'll dress myself."

"Do you want help?"

"Perhaps at the end, if there's something

I've . . . forgotten. But I can don trousers and shirt on my own."

"I'll be without then."

As she turned, he said, "Mother?"

She turned back, smiling. "Yes?"

"You're a—" He groped for a word. There was no word for "artist" in this language. "You're like a poet with a needle." The word for poet was Danish—*skald*.

Her eyes widened and a blush brightened her cheeks. "What a sweet thing to say, Amlodd. Your mother thanks you."

The door was closed and, before dressing, Will sat on the bench and wept into his hands.

He remembered an evening after school one October, coming home to find his mother had gone to bed with one of her headaches. He had been afraid to ask, but had felt he had to.

He had pushed the bedroom door open a crack and, seeing that she responded to the noise, had asked, "Did you make my Halloween costume?"

His mother had moaned and said, "What costume?"

"You said you'd sew me a pirate costume for trick or treating tonight."

"Can't you wear what you wore last year?"

"The ghost mask?"

"Yeah, right, the ghost mask."

"It's just a mask. It's not really a costume."

Suddenly his mother lurched out of bed and

rushed to the door. She grabbed him by the shirt collar.

"Do you know how hard I work?" she shouted. He could smell the alcohol on her breath.

Will opened his mouth, but thought better of answering, knowing it would only make her angrier.

"I work my fingers to the bone to make a home for you! I come home with a stinking headache, and want just a little rest before I have to make your damn supper, and do I get to rest? Do I get to rest?"

Will stood with his mouth open.

"Answer me! Do I get to rest?"

"No?"

"No! No, because my selfish little boy can't think about anything but a stupid Halloween costume! A stupid Halloween costume! Do you know what 'selfish' means?"

Will didn't want to answer.

"Answer me!"

"Someone who only thinks about himself?"

"Who do you think is selfish? Who's the most selfish little boy in the whole damn world?"

He had to answer. "Me?"

Then she had started hitting him.

The linen undertrews and wool trousers tied with drawstrings. There was a linen undershirt and he pulled on the embroidered rust one over it. He had a single-edged knife in a peculiar tooled sheath with two loops so that it hung horizontally on the belt, along with a purse which also had two loops. He checked inside the purse and found a carved horn spoon and several bits of silver rings, hacked up.

He pulled on wool socks and leather shoes. There was no right or left shoe—they were interchangeable, except that they fastened with a triangular flap that crossed the instep and buttoned on the side with a bone fastener. He assumed it would be best to wear the buttons on the outside.

There were no furry leggings as seen in movies. There were woven puttees such as Guttorm wore. He remembered with amusement that it had been traditional for stage Hamlets to wear cross-garters up through the nineteeth century. Well, why not? He cross-gartered the puttees.

It felt good to have clothes on. He wished there was such a thing as a mirror in this time and place. He felt a confidence in his appearance he'd never known before. He wanted to take his new body out for a spin.

He pushed the door open and stepped out. Everyone in the yard looked at him. He rather enjoyed it, but hoped he'd put everything on right.

"Mother," said "How fine you look, Amlodd," and adjusted the shirt here and there. Then she called the girl to re-wrap the puttees in the same fashion as Guttorm's. She fastened them with little silver hooks.

Guttorm came striding up. "My lord Amlodd," he said. "Word just came. A whale has washed up on the strand. Will you come see this thing with us?"

Will said, "Aye."

More short-haired people in undyed clothing brought horses. Will reckoned they were slaves—"thralls" would be the word. The horses were smallish, more like ponies, dun-colored with their manes trimmed to stand up straight. He looked at the saddle of the one brought to him. He seemed to recall that the Vikings had possessed the technology of stirrups, but this was before the Vikings. After hesitating a moment, he tried to mount by jumping, and slid over the other side, landing awkwardly on one foot. There was laughter, and he felt his face burn.

The horse thrall quickly knelt down on the horse's left side, making a stirrup with his two hands, fingers interlaced. Confused, Will came around again, put his right foot in the hands and swung up. It was the wrong foot. He found himself seated backwards in the saddle, facing the horse's rump. The laughter erupted again.

Mortified, Will remembered a passage from Saxo's *Gesta Danorum*: "*When he was told to mount his horse he sat on purpose with his back to the creature's mane, facing the tail. . . .*"

"I suppose you're all wondering why I've asked you here," said Sean the next morning

when he and Diane appeared in what seemed
by general consensus to be the dining hall.

"You haven't asked us here; we've all been
here for hours," said Bess. "There's still some
breakfast if you don't mind cold generic."

"'Twas a manner of speaking. I'm not hungry myself, but I could profit from the hair of
the dog, as Jason Robards used to say." He
clapped his hands. "Servants! Wine for the king!"

"And something hot for the queen to eat,"
said Diane.

"And how did you all sleep?" asked Sean.

"The sleeping wasn't too bad," said Rosey.
"The bathroom arrangements could have been
better."

"The antic charm of the chamber pot," said
Sean with a smile. "At least we can tell the servants to empty them for us. And thank God
this isn't the Middle Ages. We'd have to use
oubliettes."

"The best I can figure the rules out," said
Peter, "is that we can have anything we ask for—
as long as it existed in Shakespeare's England."
Peter's face was red and his speech a little
slurred. The others noticed that he was drinking what they drank, but no one said anything.

"Which means, I suppose," said Sean, "that
there's no such thing as a morning cup of coffee—not even for the king." Peter looked at
him sadly.

"When was coffee introduced in England?"
asked Bess.

"Hold on. Hold on. I think we need to talk about this right now," said Howie, who had been sitting with his head on his hands at the far end of the table.

"Talk about what? Coffee?" asked Sean.

"Not coffee, you imbecile. This king and queen thing. A, we're Americans and we're not supposed to believe in monarchy. B, I thought we'd agreed we'd do our best not to live out our parts. I thought we weren't going to allow the Hamlet thing to happen, because that would mean that all of you except me would be dead by the end of the play."

"Most succinctly put," said Sean. "Your concern for us does you credit. However, you have to look at things from my point of view. This is the only chance I'll ever have to king it, and frankly I think I have a gift for autocracy. I've never made a great success of my life—you probably all know that—but I've come to believe that perhaps it's only because I've had no outlet for my true gifts. Perhaps I'm a man born to be king."

"Don't get too excited, Sean," said Peter. "Everybody feels the same way. It's human nature."

"I don't want to be a king," said Howie. "The whole idea offends me."

"I think you're jumping the gun, Sean," said Bess. "So far the only orders you've given have been for meals."

"Has there been any sign of your son, Howie?" asked Diane.

Howie dropped his chin on his arms. "No. I don't care whether it's dangerous or not—I'm going out to look for him if he doesn't show up soon. I don't know what's outside the castle in this universe, but as far as I can tell, it's daylight now."

The dark servants came and set wine and warm mush before Sean and Diane. Peter suddenly leaped from his bench and tried to catch one of them, a male, by the arm, but the servant slipped from his grasp and sped away down the corridor. Peter fell onto his hands and knees. "Did you notice what he was wearing?" he asked the group as he got back to his feet.

"Pretty much the same as last night," said Diane. "Vaguely Elizabethan in basic black."

"There's more detail today," said Peter. "He was wearing hops and slows—slops and hose. I'm sure the men only had hose last night. And up close there was embroidery. And look at this wall—"

He went to the wall. He put his hand on it. "There's squared stones and mortar here. I'll swear that last night it was just flat stone. It's as if this place is . . . defining itself."

"Like a living thing?" asked Rosemary.

"Yeah. Like an embryo. Or a work of art. The artist starts with a general outline, then refines it and adds detail as he goes along."

"And who would the artist of this be?" asked Randy.

"God maybe. Or maybe us. Maybe it's drawing

images from our minds—our imaginations of what Elsinore was like."

"*Mr. Data, please report to the holodeck,*" said Del, who was sitting apart from the others as usual. "You know what? I'm sick of this charade."

He got up and turned to face Bess. "Ms. Borglum—that's your name, right? Ms. Borglum, when are you going to tell these people what's really at stake here?"

Bess scowled. "You think I know something the rest of you don't?"

"Yeah. You know it and I know it, and maybe one other. I'm talkin' about the book."

Bess looked down at her folded hands. "I don't think the book has anything to do with all this."

"Oh, you don't, huh? Then why don't you tell everybody and let them decide for themselves?"

"What's he talking about?" asked Howie. Everyone leaned in at the table.

Bess shrugged. "I guess there's no harm talking about it, though I still don't think it has anything to do with our situation." She told them the story of Will and the Kyd *Hamlet*.

"I'm with Bess," said Sean when she was done. "I don't see how it relates to our predicament."

"Look at it from the alternate universe point of view—everything the ghost told us," said Del. "Suppose fully realized works of art create their own separate universes. What if the great work of art stops being great? Does its universe go on, or is it destroyed? Suppose it's destroyed, or emptied. Wouldn't that create a kind of vacuum? Kyd's book is gonna destroy *Hamlet*. Maybe the vacuum of a universe collapsing was what pulled us here. Maybe this universe needs us to fill the roles to keep its existence going."

"That doesn't sound like very good news," said Randy. "If we don't become the roles, we'll only create a greater vacuum that will keep us here forever. If we do become the roles, we die."

"Unless the ghost was right," said Del. "He said that if we broke the play, we'd just go home."

"Maybe the play is worth our lives," said Sean, stroking his chin.

"You're missing my point, people. The point is, the play isn't great. It never was great. It's not worth dying for, and it's not worth staying here for. Let's all do our best to unwrite it. It's our only chance of getting out alive."

Amlodd rose from his seat. "I do not understand all you people say. But it seems you hold that my saga is not a great saga."

"Not your fault, son," said Del. "You fell into the hands of rotten writers."

"A man's saga is his only wealth in the end. Would you take that from me?"

"Oh, can it, Sverdrup. Do you think I really think you're Amlodd?"

Amlodd's face went white. "What mean you?"

"Can the corny diction too, kid. You're a good actor—probably the best actor in this bush league troupe. You made us swallow your little game for a while. But if you expect me to believe that Amlodd Orvendilsson was a real historical person, and not a character from an old myth, well, find somebody else to sell your swamp land to."

Amlodd started to move toward Del, and Peter and Howie restrained him with hands on his shoulders.

"The whole thing's a myth," said Del. "Historians have proved it. All these stories about war and revenge in ancient times—they're all frauds."

"What are you talking about?" asked Bess.

"It was all invented by the Christian conspiracy. Scholars know now that there was never any violence of any kind in the world before the appearance of Christianity. All the atrocity stories were invented by Christian historians, so they could justify their aggression against their peaceful neighbors."

"Wait," said Sean. "Let me get this straight. You're saying there was never an Assyrian empire; never a Roman empire; never an Aztec empire—"

"They existed, but they were purely voluntary, peaceful arrangements. War, murder, revenge, slavery—they were all invented by the Christians, who then projected them back on history by forging the records."

"That's B.S.," said Bess.

"There's nothing I can do about your closed

minds. The very fact that you disagree with me proves you're bigots. But take my word for it— there was never a Hamlet; never an Orvendil; never a murder and never a revenge—"

Amlodd pulled free and leaped the table like a flying hawk. Del ran out just ahead of him. Amlodd stopped and let him go, spitting at his back. "'Tis a waste of breath to chase cowards," he said.

He turned back. "You—" he said to Howie. "Did you say you meant to search for your troll son?"

"My son, yes," said Howie.

"Then I'll bear you company. I'd see what world we're in."

"Will you attack my son again?"

"Your son attacked me. In any case, you saw how it turned out. I'm unarmed, and he is stronger than I."

"I suppose two is better than one, not knowing what's out there," said Howie, getting up. "Anybody want to come along?"

"I'll go," said Randy.

"Yeah, why not?" said Peter.

"Might as well take the whole scout troop," said Sean. They all got up and followed Amlodd down the corridor.

The three women were left alone at the table. Diane immediately got out of her seat at the head and moved down beside Rosey. "Tell me all about it," she said.

"About what?" asked Rosey, with a smile.

"Will—Amlodd—whatever the hell you call him. What was it like with a *real* barbarian?"

Rosey half-lowered her eyelids. "He was all right."

"All right? Just all right?"

Rosey laughed. "He was wonderful. He was so . . . enthusiastic. Didn't you hear him? And he kept telling me what he could have done if he'd had his own equipment—frankly I'm glad he didn't. He might have killed me."

They laughed and Bess laughed with them.

They stopped laughing when the men came back and they got a look at their faces.

"What's wrong?" asked Bess.

"We found this in the corridor," said Peter. He held out a pack of cigarettes.

"Cigarettes—the only cigarettes here belong to—"

"To Del. He wouldn't have left behind the only cigarettes in the world."

"And there was blood there," said Sean. "Quite a lot of blood."

Rosey sought the chamber where she and Amlodd had slept. She had hardly known Del, and hadn't liked what she'd seen of him. But she'd never come so close to death before.

The room was large and high-ceilinged. There was a huge four-poster bed there, draped with curtains, and the walls were hung with dark tapestries on which embroidery could be dimly made out.

She lay on the bed with her knees under her chin. The strangeness of the whole situation sifted down on her like a century of dust. She thought about the family she might not see again, the friends and familiar places that might be lost to her.

She wept until a hand on her shoulder startled her.

"The nearness of death always rouses a need for life in me," Amlodd said, letting his hand wander.

She pulled away and fled to a corner of the room. "I'm not in the mood," she said, hugging herself.

"Then I must give you a gift, I suppose." He dug awkwardly in Will's trousers pockets and came out with a few coins. "I don't know what these are worth, but some of them seem to be part silver—"

She stalked forward, fists at her sides. "Let's get one thing straight, Melancholy Baby. I'm not a whore. I slept with you because I wanted to, and I'm beginning to think I made a big mistake."

"Then why did you come here to bed?"

"To be alone and cry."

"You weep over that . . . nobody?"

"He was a human being."

"And so?"

"Every human being is important."

"Who told you a thing like that?"

"It's something we believe."

"Then you're fools."

" '*No man is an island, apart of himself...,*' " she quoted. " '*Every man's death diminishes me, for I am involved with all mankind.*'"

"A death like that? He was a little man, without strength or courage. He had no honor and died like a slug. He might as well have never lived."

Rosey sat on the bed cross-legged. "Have I told you yet what a horse's ass you are?"

"You take offense because I can tell the difference between a man of honor and a thrall? If you think all men of equal worth, what do you honor? How do you choose between right and wrong? How do you choose who will lead and who will serve?"

"It's complicated. Look—a man died and I'm upset. Do I have your permission to be upset? Didn't you ever weep for a pet—an animal that died? Even though it wasn't human?"

Amlodd fell silent for a moment.

"You've touched his heart," said Randy, who had walked in without either of them noticing.

"Doesn't anybody knock in this universe?" asked Rosey.

"A fascinating conversation," said Randy. "You're right, Rosey. Every death does matter."

"Thanks for your support."

Randy came in and sat on the bed with them. Rosey thought it was like the Mad Hatter's slumber party. "Imagine if you will a world—this one, perhaps—where no one died. How does that sound to you?"

"Wonderful," said Rosey.

"Dull," said Amlodd.

"One for Amlodd. It would be dreadfully dull. Do you know why?"

"No shoot-em-up Westerns?" asked Rosey.

"No courage. Did you ever play poker for no money? It's as boring as radio static. People's lives are the stakes they play for in the great game. Without something at stake, nothing matters much."

❧ CHAPTER IX ❧

Will finally got himself arranged on the horse and rode out with of a party of about fifty men. The steading they left, a cluster of buildings around an open yard, was one of several such steadings grouped within an area of cultivated fields surrounded by forest. He'd never thought of Denmark as a heavily forested place, but all he knew of the country were conditions in the twenty-first century. The day continued cool, the sky mostly clear.

Guttorm rode up beside him as they passed a large bog. "Do you remember anything?" Guttorm asked.

"Nothing. Tell me, is it late fall or early spring? The trees are bare; I can't tell from them."

" 'Tis spring. There are a hundred ways to know this."

"I've forgotten them."

Denmark was a wooded and watery land, tree-covered except where there were lakes and bogs, with farms and meadows scattered here and there. All the farms had steadings similar to the one they'd come from, though none so large.

He smelled the ocean before he heard it, and heard it before he saw it. It was incredible how noisy-quiet the pre-industrial world was. He thought the volume of ocean, wind, bird songs, frog songs, insect songs, etc., was not much less than the ambient noise he'd known in his own world, but each sound seemed more distinct, more easily identified, unlike the mechanical drone he was used to. He couldn't name all the noises, but he could tell them apart.

Their road took them up over a grassy dune onto the wide shining beach. The green sea pounded itself into white surf and scattered in thunder. They turned their horses and rode south along the beach until Will made out a great black shape in the surf. Coming nearer he saw that the whale was still alive and moving, and men were rushing in to kill it with spears. The surf surged red all around.

His stomach sank at the sight. In his mind beached whales were for saving. For these people, beached whales meant protein for the community.

The others gathered to watch the killing. Will went down the beach, his back to the slaughter, marveling at the whiteness of the sand, the clarity of the water. He saw a bright orange thing half-buried, and stooped to dig it out. It was a piece of amber, about the size of an egg. He held it in his hand and it warmed.

A child came up to him, bare of leg and dressed in a white shirt, with hair cropped short. Will reckoned he must be a slave. He handed the amber over to the child. "Take it," he said.

The boy's eyes widened. "For me?"

"Yes."

"It's very costly."

"Good. Give it to your parents. It will help them buy their freedom."

Will heard laughter and looked up to see that Guttorm and three of the warriors were watching and listening. "He makes gifts to thralls," said one of them. "A piece that might win the love of a girl or the friendship of a warrior he throws away on one who can return him nothing."

"He's mad," said the other. "Such is the way of madness. Madmen cannot tell the worth of things. They think silver just another metal. They think Danes no better than Saxons. They look at, say, the sand on this beach, and imagine it to be . . . oh . . ."

"Meal," said Will. "A great granary full of barley meal." The words were almost straight out of Saxo. Since they'd fed him his cue, he'd picked it up.

"Meal?" the man asked. "Where do you think they could grind so much meal?"

Will knew the answer to that, too. "In that great mill," he said, pointing to the ocean.

The watching men laughed and the three he didn't know ran to tell the others what he had said. Will didn't think it was that funny himself, but he happened to know that he'd made a joke that would be retold for more than a thousand years. There'd be another joke along soon, if he remembered correctly. Something about a knife . . .

Guttorm stepped close to him and spoke in low tones. "*Be wary,*" he whispered. "*They're planning something. I know not what, but you're in danger.*"

Will almost answered him seriously, but it might be a trap.

"*Conscience does make cowards of us all, and thus the native hue of resolution is sicklied o'er with the pale cast of thought,*" he said. Or words to that effect, in translation. He fought to cover the actual fear he felt. Why had he come with these people? He'd thought his madness would protect him. He shouldn't underestimate their intelligence because they were primitive by his standards. There was more than one kind of primitive.

Someone started shouting, and Will turned to see one of the warriors gathering the thralls into a group and herding them southward along the beach. He asked Guttorm what was going on.

"Someone's found a bit of salvage," said

Guttorm. "He's getting the thralls to take it to the jarl."

Will looked at him, expecting more.

"All salvage belongs to the king," Guttorm went on. "You've forgotten this too?"

"So it would seem."

In a few minutes the thralls came back. Three of the men were carrying a large wooden object, shaped rather like a knife.

"What's that? A giant's knife?" Will asked.

Guttorm scowled. "Now you're making game of me. Are you saying you don't even recognize a ship's rudder?"

Will said, "Oh God." He had walked into Saxo's story again. This was another of Hamlet's riddles.

How was it possible that he was living the story out without intending to? Was he being compelled by some force? He felt no compulsion— he was only reacting naturally.

He remembered a writer—he forgot whom— who had said something about how our freest actions seemed to be the ones in which we were aware of the least choice. He'd thought it hogwash when he read it. Now he wasn't so sure.

Another man had come up to them and heard the exchange. "What use would there be for a knife as large as that?" the man asked.

Will thought he might as well finish the scene. "To slice that huge ham," he said, pointing again to the sea.

The man found this hugely funny. Laughing, he said, "What a grand *kenning*—the sea is the ham of the rudder-knife! Someone should put it in a poem!" Then he went to tell the others. Once again, Will knew, history had been made.

One of the men came down to Guttorm and said, "Somebody's got to herd the thralls back to the village with that rudder. Left to themselves they'll pilfer the thing and it'll end up in pieces in a dozen houses."

Guttorm said, "Then see to it."

"I'm in charge of the whale. All the men were sent on that errand, save you. So it's you must go with the salvage."

Guttorm shrugged. "Very well. I'll take Amlodd with me."

"No, best to leave him with us. It takes many men to hold a madman if he throws a fit."

"We'll be all right.'

"The jarl told me to keep my eye on him. We'll look after him."

Guttorm looked at Will, then at the others, and saw no way out. He went to Will and said, "Watch yourself," quietly, then mounted his pony and rode off with the thralls.

Will looked about him and felt suddenly cold, as the only man who'd shown him friendship disappeared into the forest shade.

One by one and then in groups, the jarl's men came and gathered around Will. They clustered in a semicircle, just a little overclose for friendliness. Will stepped back and wet his shoes in seawater.

"Hot day," said one of the warriors.

"Hot?" asked Will. It was chill so that he wished he'd worn a second shirt.

"I've never known it so warm so early in the year," said another warrior.

"No, believe me, 'tis very cold; the wind is northerly."

"You mistake, sir," said the same man, " 'tis warm. A wonderful day for a swim." He took another step forward, and the others moved in with him. Will stepped back and now stood in water to his ankles, with the waves wetting him to the knees. The men on the ends of the crescent that hemmed him in stood as deep in the water. It occurred to him that no one could see what was happening from the shore. If any of the whale butchers chanced to glance this way, he'd only see a group of men standing in the surf. He took the only defense he could think of.

"Suppose I were Odin," he said.

The men grew still.

"Suppose Odin spoke from my mouth. Suppose I had the power of Odin to curse my enemies."

A few of the men actually backed up a step.

"Suppose I could call a monster from the sea to slay you all."

Will was amazed at the power of his words. The men's eyes grew wide and their mouths fell open, as if they actually saw such a monster rise from the waves. Not only did they goggle, they turned on their heels and ran, so that Will couldn't help turning to see what had frightened them.

It was a woman on a horse, rising from the water. She had hair white as silver, but she was not old. She wore nothing at all and rode bareback, and she had a face Will knew well—his mother's face. With all his memories, he often forgot his mother had been beautiful.

"Will Sverdrup! Come with me if you'd save your life!" she cried.

Will sloshed backwards. "No!" he cried. "Not you! Not with that face!"

The woman widened her eyes, and the face around them changed. Now it was Katla's face. That he could endure. He splashed to her and she hoisted him up on the horse behind her with amazing strength.

The warriors scattered as she spurred her mount through them and straight into the forest—not up the roadway but over the dune and into the depths of the wood. The sunlight turned to dappled shade, the trunks of the trees a blur around them, and Will held tight around the woman's small waist, feeling no sexual desire whatever for the moment. Her silver hair chastised his face.

The ride ended as suddenly as it had begun, in a green glade where there was a stream. The horse halted and the woman flung a leg over its neck and slid to the ground. "Come down. Sit beside me on these stones and we'll speak," she said.

Will dismounted rather more clumsily. The horse galloped into the woods, and the woman showed no concern about it.

Will did not wait for small talk. "Who are you and why did you wear my mother's face?" he demanded. He stood and she sat, but he felt no advantage in the position.

"I beg pardon if the face troubled you," said the woman, reclining on one arm. "I merely plucked the chief woman's face from your mind."

"You can't put a man at ease by appearing naked with his mother's face."

"Yes, I should have remembered that. But you humans have so many rules and kinships, 'tis sometimes hard to keep the straight of them."

"Even now I'd rather you put something on. Unless you want to make love."

The woman sighed and a scarlet gown covered her.

Will felt more at ease, and sat on a mossy stone. "Who are you then? What do you mean by 'you humans'?"

The woman laughed, and a crowd of butterflies came from all directions to cluster around her head like a halo. Only it was too early in the year for butterflies. "My name is Hlin," she said. "You may call me one of the Old Ones—I'm not prideful about youth like mortal women."

"You're not mortal?"

"Why should that surprise you? You've seen my deeds; did you think I was someone's wife and daughter?"

"I didn't know what to think."

"But you know of the Old Ones, surely?"

"I do not."

"Then how came you here?"

"I fell down a hole."

"You did not summon one of my kinsmen? Make a pact? Win or lose a riddle game?"

"No."

Hlin sat up and set her chin on her fist. The butterflies scattered and vanished. "Yet you must know one of us," she said, frowning. "Only the Old Ones know the ways between the worlds."

"I've never seen anyone like you before."

"Hm." She thought a moment. "*When* did you come from?" she asked.

"Where?"

"Not *where*, *when*. Do you know when in time we are now?"

"Sometime in the sixth or seventh century, I'd guess. Pre-Viking."

"That's right, by Christian reckoning. When did you fall down your hole?"

"It was the twenty-first century."

"That's it then. That far in the future I've never fared. We have little power in your time—the christening still has some effect, and you've grown far from the earth. Still there must have been one of us. Wasn't there someone there when you fell—someone fair to look at and strange in temper? Someone who brought excitement wherever they came, with whom time and place sometimes seemed loosely bound?"

Will said, "Randy."

Hlin smiled with Katla's small, sweet, beautiful mouth. "I'm sure you're correct. So now I've done you a favor. You know how you came."

"What did you mean by the ways between the worlds?"

"There are many worlds. You must know this."

"So I've heard."

"We Old Ones travel between them. These Danes think we live under hills or in the mountains, but we've a world of our own, which we enter by doors men cannot find. The doors lead to other doors between all the worlds, and we know the ways."

"But you can take people through."

"Yes."

"Can you send me back whence I came?"

She lounged on the rock again. "I could, but it wouldn't solve your problem. You're not only in another's world, you're in another's body. You must change souls with him to go back properly. You don't want to be a stranger to your family and friends, do you?"

"I suppose not." Will's shoulders slumped. "Have you any idea how I'd manage that trick?"

"I might have ideas, but why should I answer your questions without something in return?"

"What have I to offer you?"

She smiled and the scarlet gown disappeared. "Sit beside me," she said.

Will sat on the dry grass at her side. He was growing excited.

Instead of reaching for him, the woman put her hand in the grass and plucked some plants. "Do you know herbs?" she asked.

"No. I can tell a rose from a dandelion, not much more."

"This plant with the big silver, hairy leaves is the horseshoe. It's good for curing cough. This one with the spotted purple stem and the notched leaves in pairs is the cock's comb. It also helps with the cough, and it can sharpen the eyesight. But not now. The winter killed these."

"I know what this is," said Will, pulling a reed from the stream bank.

"Tell me then."

"It's what they thatch houses with. I noticed that." Will put his hand on her ankle. Her skin was extremely smooth, and warmer than he expected.

She shook him loose. "What I mean to say," she said, "is that you are like an herb in winter. It may keep green for a time, but it's lost its life-channel. It looks alive; it may think it's alive; but it is dead. You and all your people are dead in the same way. Why would I want you? Except as food?"

He put his hand on her knee. "Would you eat me?"

"Don't laugh at me, time-tramp. I've eaten better men than you, and I know nothing of guilt. Don't judge me by the tales told to children in your time."

"All right then, what can I give you in return for what I want?"

"You have one thing I can get nowhere else than from a mortal man."

"And that is?"

"Your pain."

"What?"

"Your love."

"My pain or my love?"

"They are the same. It's what makes you do what you do—build what you build, say what you say, dare what you dare. That worm in your gut that eats you from inside, pushing you to go to a new place; make a new thing. We never do these things, for we have no pain."

He nearly made a joke about S/M.

"The first of our race was called Cain," she went on. "He slew his own brother, but the High One did not exact blood from him, because there had never been murder before, and he could not have understood. Cain feared that others of his kin would take vengeance, so the High One freed him from death and pain. That was his punishment."

"How can I give you my pain?"

"Open your thoughts to me. Relive the great wound of your life, the one that shapes your every choice. Give me that pain, and I shall give you my body."

The lust drained from Will like water out of a colander. He stood and turned his back to her.

"Your fear is a great one, mortal man," the woman said. "It makes you pale as death."

"There's nothing you can offer that would make me live that again."

"Your fear makes me hungry! I drool over pain such as yours!"

"I don't think—I don't think I've ever known the meaning of what we call 'perversion' before today."

"And is it not perversion that excites you mortals most?"

"Some of us."

"The word means to go in a wrong way. You find something upon the main path that frightens you; so you take a side path, or make your own. You think you are bold to go on side paths, but the truth is that it's what you met on the straight one that frightens you. I want to know what you found on that path, man of the future. What monster did you meet there?"

"Which way is it to the village? It'll be a long walk, I expect."

"Don't your folk believe that there is health in uncovering your scars?"

"Let me see—we went west toward the sea. If it's afternoon now, and the sun is there, then west must be that way . . . I think. We entered the forest south of the road, and didn't cross it again . . . I think. So if I head north, I should cut the road—"

Suddenly she was beside him, her hand on his arm. "I need what you feel," she said. "Have pity on me. Give me a taste."

"My pain is mine."

She pressed her rich body against him. "Just a little," she said. "You needn't do anything. Just let me snatch what crumbs I can while we couple."

He loved knowing he'd reduced this proud creature to beggary. He took her roughly in his arms and pushed her to the ground. They fornicated in the grass and wild beasts sent up howls in the woods.

❊ CHAPTER X ❊

"A sword!" said Amlodd. "Thralls, bring me a sword!"

Within a minute the servants appeared with a sheathed rapier and a sword belt.

"You call this a sword?" Amlodd cried. "'Tis an awl for stitching leather! Get me a proper sword, a slasher with a blade three fingers wide!"

"A broadsword," said Sean from the bench. "The man wants a broadsword."

The servants returned with a Pappenheimer war sword. Amlodd frowned at the complicated steel basket that guarded the grip, but smiled after he'd swung the thing a few times.

"A man is naked without a weapon," said Amlodd, belting it around his waist. He fumbled with the buckles for a moment, but figured it out. Then he began a routine of exercises with the blade. "North-under with this weak body,"

150

he said as he posed and swung, his muscles quivering and sweat standing out on his forehead.

"What do you need a sword for?" asked Bess. They had finished breakfast but remained in their chairs around the table. "I'd like to remind you we're not planning on any duels in this version."

"I need a sword because I'm not a woman," said Amlodd. "Besides, someone must hunt the troll. I see no other man here fit for the work, except perhaps Randy, and him I do not trust."

"Don't mind me," said Randy, who was lounging with a foot on the table. "Just pretend I'm not here."

Amlodd asked, "What manner of man are you?"

Randy sat up straight. "What's that supposed to mean?"

"I can sense the Old Ones. There's something of them in you, but it's weak. I'd think you were half-blood with them, only they do not whelp."

"What you sense," said Randy, "is called deodorant. We don't glory in stinking as you do. Unfortunately we didn't bring a supply, so we'll probably sink to your level."

"We Danes bathe every Saturday night!"

"Then I suppose we should do the same, if this is Denmark," said Sean. "Only I wonder when Saturday is."

"Ask the servants," said Diane. "We really ought to do something for them, you know. Everything that gets done around here, gets done by them."

"But are they even human?" asked Rosey. "Has anybody tried to talk with one of them? We know they can speak, but are they just repeating words? Can you have a conversation with them?"

"I've tried," said Peter. "They don't seem to like talking much." He took a drink of wine. He was drinking openly now.

"They are thralls. What does it matter whether they're human or not?" said Amlodd. "What we need to think on is the troll. He has killed already. We must hunt him down. If I can get no help from you men, I must do it myself."

Howie got up and walked around the table to face Amlodd. "I'm telling you again you're talking about my son. You'll hurt my son over my dead body."

"If I must," said Amlodd. "This son of yours has killed one of us already. Shall we all die at his hand to spare your feelings?"

"How do we know it was him? It could have been anybody here!"

"We were all together when Del was killed, Howie," said Bess. "Eric was the only one missing."

"Well, how do we know it wasn't a stranger? So all the natives we've met have been these mimes who wait on the tables. We don't know who or what else might live here. We don't even know that the mimes aren't murderous."

"Fair enough," said Amlodd. "Let's track the killer and see what we find. But I say it again—

your son is a troll, and will have to be put down. No doubt you'll want revenge then, so I'll have to put you down too."

Howie shook his head. "You don't understand. I lost my wife just a few months ago. You can't take my son away too. Surely you have a little pity!"

"What a strange word is this 'pity' of yours," said Amlodd. "You'd leave a deadly monster at large, putting all of us, even the women, in peril of our lives every minute, simply to keep you from a sad feeling. Is there no honor in your heart? If I'd become what your son is, my father would have hunted me down the first day, and he'd have been right. Thank the gods I had such a father."

"Listen. You lost your father. Don't you see that you'd be doing the same thing to me that your uncle did to you?"

"Yes. What of it?"

"So can't you see that if it was wrong for him, it's wrong for you too?"

"Why?"

Howie looked stuck for an answer.

"Because right and wrong are the same, everywhere and for everyone," said Peter, leaning his chin on his crossed arms.

"I didn't mean that," said Howie. "I don't believe that."

"Then what did you mean?" asked Peter, and again Howie had no answer.

"It's simple, he loves his son," said Randy.

"He'll let any number of people die to protect him. I love love. It brings people together, if only in cemeteries."

"I kill my enemies," said Amlodd. "My enemies try to kill me. The one the gods favor wins. That is how the world is. It has nothing to do with right or wrong."

"That's right," said Diane. "If it feels good, do it. See, Peter? You Christians always talk as if you're defending traditional values—but there are traditions older than yours."

"If I thought right and wrong were the same for me and my enemies, how could I kill them?" asked Amlodd. "Now, who will help me hunt?"

Everyone stood silent, embarrassed to hurt Howie.

"If you're going after my son, I'm going to be there," said Howie. "There's got to be somebody to talk to him."

"Then I'm coming too," said Peter.

"I wouldn't miss it," said Randy.

"I'll come," said Bess.

"A woman?" asked Amlodd.

"A damn strong one," said Bess. "I felt silly yesterday, staying back here while you guys went out. Anyway, who'd you rather have? Me, or the majesty of Denmark over there?"

"Don't mind me," said Sean, still at the table. "I felt rather silly myself yesterday. I wouldn't go now to save my life. In fact that's my very purpose. I once said to Maurice Evans—"

"I'll come too," said Rosey.

"No," said Amlodd.

"Why not?"

"I need you for bed. If you were killed I'd have to sleep with Bess."

"In your dreams, sweet prince," said Bess.

"We'd better all get swords, I suppose," said Peter.

"No. Spears are better," said Amlodd.

"Spears?"

"Much better for hunting. Especially for men without skill. You can throw them or use them close. I'll get a spear myself. My sword is for other things."

He called for spears and soon they were outfitted.

"Let us go then," said Amlodd.

As they set out Bess turned back. "You're really not coming, Rosey?"

Rosey looked at the floor and shook her head.

Bess went with the others.

"Does anyone actually know the way out of this castle?" asked Randy.

"First we hunt an exit, then we hunt the monster," said Peter.

"Eric," said Howie. "His name is Eric."

They followed the main corridor until it took a right turn.

"Perhaps we should scatter bread crumbs," said Randy.

"This is folly," said Amlodd. "Thralls!"

A servant appeared, coming from the direction in which they were headed.

"Lead us outside," said Amlodd to him, and the servant turned and led them. As it happened, the corridor led straight out to the main door of the hall. They emerged into the grass-grown bailey. The gate was not far to walk. Past that there was an even shorter walk through the outer bailey to the main gate.

" 'Tis Denmark," said Amlodd, breathing deeply. " 'Tis home. But not Jutland, I think."

They stood on a solitary cliff, surrounded by low hills covered with trees, dotted with lakes and marshes and seamed with rivers on three sides. To the west writhed the sea, troubled by a stiff wind. Seagulls hung motionless in the wind's face before diving for their meals. Two weathers contended—a blue storm over the sea and golden sunlight over the land. A winding track led down the cliff face to a harbor.

"Elsinore, I imagine," said Bess, shielding her eyes from the wind with a hand. "What you Danes call Helsingør."

"I know Helsingør. It has no mountain."

"No. This is Shakespeare's Elsinore. Shakespeare was a great storyteller, but not much of a geographer."

"The ghost said this was an 'unused' world," said Peter. "Does that mean a world without people, do you suppose? What would that kind of world be like?"

"I thought we decided this was Hamlet's world, with all the good stuff sucked out," said Bess.

"Could be both."

"More important, who's at the top of the food chain?" said Randy.

Amlodd knelt on the path. "He went this way," he said, touching the soil. "Three toes, like a bird, but large."

They set off down the track, Amlodd in the front and Randy bringing up the rear. It was a harrowing descent, the path sometimes little more than a yard wide, with a sheer drop on the seaward side.

"In our world they'd install handrails," said Diane.

"When all of you go home, remember to leave me here," said Amlodd. "From what I've learned of your world, I'd as soon live with the troll."

Amlodd was standing on a hairpin in the path as he spoke, somewhat ahead of the others. There came a whistling and a roaring as of some large object through the air, and it snatched Amlodd and carried him down to the beach sand below. The two bodies landed feetfirst; Amlodd's spear went flying out of reach. Eric (or Yggxvthwul, for it was his body with Eric's head) rebounded immediately, while Amlodd had more trouble freeing his feet from the sand. While he struggled, Eric reached a tentacle and casually disarmed him, drawing his sword and casting it into the sea.

Amlodd knelt with his arms spread, shock on his face. He closed his eyes and began to sing, a song that was not a tune by the modern folks' standards.

Ahead of the rest, Howie and Peter rushed breakneck down the switchback pathway, protected from falling only by their momentum. At the last hairpin but one, Howie leaped straight down to the sand, and Peter followed him, falling on his hands and knees. Eric could have finished Amlodd off by then, but had held back for some reason.

"Eric, for God's sake!" Howie cried.

"Hey Dad," said Eric's head atop the grotesque body. The torso and legs were like a lizard's, or a dinosaur's. Instead of arms there were suckered tentacles of various lengths, in constant motion so it was difficult to count them. They seemed to emerge from all around the upper trunk except for the scaly chest area. He towered over them, about eight feet high. He smelled more or less like a chicken carcass. "How's it hangin'?" It was the most clearly anyone had heard him speak in a long time.

"What's happened, son? Who did this to you?"

"Hey, nobody does nothin' to me. I worked for this. It took me a long time to master Yggxvthwul and then to get him inside me."

"He's possessed," said Peter, getting to his feet.

"Don't bring that supernatural crap into this," said Howie. "Look at you, Eric, this isn't what you want to be." By now the whole company was down on the sand, keeping well back. Peter stood midway between the father and son and the half circle of watchers. Amlodd knelt to one side, looking at the sky.

"Whadda you know about what I want to be?"

"I didn't raise you to be a killer."

Eric gaped his mouth and laughed. The laugh came up from Yggxvthwul's lungs, booming like a whale song, echoing off the cliff face.

"That's great, Dad. That's really bad. I remember everything you taught me. I've heard you say it a hundred times—'All human progress comes from breaking taboos, from killing hypocrisy.' You used to brag how your generation smashed all the sex rules."

"Well, that's not all I taught you—"

"And I thought, hey, you guys already broke all the taboos. What's left for us to break?

"And then I realized, there's still one taboo. There's one thing everybody does but they lie about it; something everybody keeps secret. It's hate.

"Everybody hates. Everybody hates somebody in their heart. But everybody says they love everybody.

"So that's the taboo my generation's gonna break down. We're bringing our hate out of the closet.

"So I thought about hate. I thought about it all the time—who I hate; what I'd do to them. You know what I discovered?

"Hate is a person. Hate is a god. I started to worship hate. Then I discovered Yggxvthwul. Yggxvthwul became my god. I prayed to him.

I asked him to give me his power. He answered my prayer."

"He's definitely possessed," said Peter.

"Shut up, Peter," said Howie. "Eric, I taught you about love, too. We believe in love in our family."

"Like your parents believed in virginity until marriage, Pop," Eric answered. "That was then, this is now. Get with the program.

"Now listen—I'm telling you how it's gonna be. I don't wanna kill any of you today. There's lots of animals on this world for me to hunt, and frankly, they're more fun than most of you would be.

"So leave me alone. Keep this caveman off my back. You let me be and I'll let you be— for now, anyway."

He crouched and sprang, and was up the cliff face and out of sight in a moment.

Amlodd's voice rose in a wail. "My enemy disarmed me, and he taunted me to my face! He thought me unworthy of killing! Give me one of your spears, that I may slay myself with it."

They gathered around him and led him up the path to Elsinore castle. He did not resist them.

They were a silent group at supper that night. Sean's attempts at jokes found no audience. Amlodd ate nothing at all, but crouched in a dark corner. Peter drank continually.

Three dark figures approached Howie in the dining hall as he went towards his chamber.

"Master Horatio," they said,
*Bearing on thine affect for Lord
        Hamlet,*
*Much remarked and praised by all
    and general,*
*Who holding high conceit of his
        discourse and parts*
*Would see him eased from the dark
        address*
Of his late melancholy; for his good weal
We'd tell thee of a wonder—"

"Lead on, MacDuff," said Howie. "Why the
hell not?"

❈ CHAPTER XI ❈

Will ducked in out of the night, through the low door into the entryway of the great hall. He came into the main hall through another low door.

The room went silent. It was like Wild Bill Hickok entering a saloon in a Western movie. Will would have enjoyed it under other circumstances.

He wasn't sure how he'd gotten here. He wasn't sure he wanted to come inside. But the shadowed forest frightened him. The last thing he remembered was his hot coupling with the Old One woman. He wasn't even certain he'd enjoyed it. And if he'd hoped to learn how to get home from here, he'd been badly disappointed.

The benches along the walls were crowded with the jarl's men, feasting at trestle tables.

Thrall women moved among them, keeping the ale horns filled.

Midway down the north wall, on Will's left, Jarl Feng rose from his high seat and cried, "Amlodd! Amlodd my nephew, we'd given you up for hill-taken!"

Will stood silent, scratching his head.

"Come up and drink with me, Amlodd!" Feng said. "Tell us what passed with the woman from the sea!"

Will trudged down the rush-strewn hearthway. He climbed up on the bench and sat at Feng's right. He took the horn offered him and drank deeply. His throat was dusty; he needed the drink. The drink, he discovered with a cough, was not ale but mead—a fermented honey drink too strong for a man confused.

"Who was the woman?" Feng asked. "Some say they did not recognize her; others say she looked like Katla."

"'Twas my mother," said Will. It didn't sound right, but he felt fuddled.

"Your mother? No one said aught about your mother!"

"'Twas Katla."

"Katla! Did Katla leave the village today?" Feng called out.

"No," said Amlodd's mother from the women's table at the end. "She was here all day. I was with her much of the time. Surely she never went as far as the sea."

"'Twas one of the Old Ones," said Will.

The room went silent again. Hands crept behind backs as men crossed their fingers against the Evil Eye.

"And what happened with this Old One?" Feng asked.

"We lay together." The words seemed loud in the breathless hall.

"Where did you lie?" Feng asked, hoarse. "Did she take you under the hill with her?"

"We lay on a horse's shoe, and a cock's comb and a bit of roof," said Will. The words sounded familiar. Oh yes, it was Saxo again. So be it.

Whispering, like a swarm of flies over a dead thing, filled the hall. Will sensed he was in danger. He was too weary to care.

"We have a gift for you," said Feng. He clapped his hands and thralls came in carrying a long bundle wrapped in woolen cloth. They offered it to Will, who took it.

He unwrapped the cloth. He found a sword in a sheath there.

"A sword," he said. "It's beautiful."

"Don't you know it?" asked Feng.

"No."

"'Tis your father's sword. You cut yourself with it, so we made a change to protect you."

Will tried to draw the sword. He couldn't get it free. He looked at it closely and saw that a rivet had been fixed through sword and sheath together.

The hall erupted in laughter. Will's face burned.

Amlodd's mother came and took the sword from Will's hands. "'Tis naught, son," she said. "We'll hang the sword on the wall in honor of your father."

Feng coughed and took a drink from his horn. To Amlodd he said, "Perhaps you are tired and would go to your house to sleep."

Will clutched his arm. "Not alone!" he cried. "And not in the dark!"

"Gerda, take your son to his house," said Feng to Amlodd's mother. "Guttorm, you go along. But bear this in mind—he's already injured a man, and I'll not have my people put at risk by madmen, even of my blood. If the boy kills anyone, I'll send him to England on a raid. There he may die honorably, or perhaps get his wits back."

Amlodd's mother and Guttorm led him out to the house where he'd woken. Guttorm lit a fish-oil lamp with a bit of flaming stick from the hearth. Will lay down on the bench.

"I dreamed," said Will. "I dreamed I lived in a distant land, where men can fly, and travel at great speeds in carts made of steel, and speak to others across the sea as if face to face. They have lamps without oil there, and no one is sure what the difference between a man and a woman is. And my mother tried to kill me."

"Your mother loves you, my Amlodd," said Gerda, sitting and taking his head in her lap. "She would never do you harm."

"Beware the pearl in the cup, Mother," said Will. He wrapped a blanket around him and curled up to sleep.

He dreamed it again, as he had so many times.

How his mother had wakened him on a Sunday morning, saying, "Get up and get dressed. We have somewhere to go."

He had brushed his teeth and combed his hair, wondering where they could be going. A visit to relatives? Certainly not to church. They never went to church.

When he went downstairs to the kitchen, his mother found fault with his shoes and slapped him. She told him to shine them, "And God help you if you get any polish on your nice white shirt!"

He toiled with the polish and brushes and soft cloth, checked himself desperately in the mirror and recombed his hair, and went down to her again in the kitchen. He was hungry and wondered if she had forgotten breakfast. He didn't dare ask.

When she saw him, she quickly put down the glass from which she'd been drinking. She came close to him and looked him over, running a finger over his wet hair like a Marine officer with white gloves. It was a touch without tenderness.

"I suppose it'll have to do," she said. "Come upstairs with me."

I thought we were going somewhere, he thought to himself, but he said nothing. He had learned never to question her orders. He didn't question them now, even though she told him to lie down on his bed. He started to take off his shoes, because shoes on the bed were grounds for a beating.

"Leave 'em be," his mother said. "Just lay down."

So he lay down, trembling with the strangeness of the thing. How was he supposed to know what to do when the rules kept changing?

Then his mother took a pillow and pressed it down on his face.

"DON'T FIGHT ME!" she cried. "YOU DAMNED DISOBEDIENT CHILD, CAN'T YOU JUST ONCE DO AS YOU'RE TOLD?"

But this time he fought her, terrified of the dark and choking. He thrashed his way out from under the pillow, tore his way out of the clutching hands, and ran downstairs and out to a neighbor's garage, where he crouched in fear for more than an hour, still trying to keep his clothes clean for her.

She hadn't come searching for him. When he had finally returned to the house, not to enter but to peek through a window, he had smelled gas. . . .

When he woke he felt clearer headed. He seemed alone in the house. The hearthlight cast low shadows on the walls, and he knew, though he could not remember, that he had heard someone speak.

"Who's there?" he whispered, crab-walking back to the wall, drawing his belt knife.

"No one's there, but I am here," said a woman's voice. Katla stepped out of the shadows into the half-light.

"*Nymph, in thy orisons be all my sins remember'd,*" said Will.

"I heard you speak of your mother as you slept," Katla said, sinking to the bench. "Tell me of your mother."

"Which mother? My true mother, or my . . . true mother?"

"You said your mother tried to kill you. I'd know more of this."

"I never speak of it."

"I understand—'tis like a worm under a rock. It grows in the darkness."

"If I turn my rock for you, will you turn yours for me?"

"I cannot share what I do not have. My memory is a ring that fell down the privy. 'Tis there, and I know where it is, but I'll not leap in to fetch it."

"Then why should I dredge for my ring?"

"Because you wish to."

"*You would play upon me; you would seem to know my stops; you would pluck out the heart of my mystery.*"

"I am mad and you are mad. We both are mad together. One of a kind knows the other."

Will ran his hands through his hair. She was right. He wanted to speak of it. Far from his home, far from his time, no person in the world could be hurt by his unburdening to this woman.

"I was born in a place called Minnesota, in a distant land," he said.

"Were you free or thrall?"

"Both. We were free in law; we were thrall in our hearts. My father was a thrall to his fears. My mother was a thrall to her past, and to drink.

"My father bore his fears as long as he could, but he could not carry the weight of them. I think my mother wed him because he was weak and could be ruled; yet she hated him for the same reason. She shamed him before outsiders, she shamed him before me. He stood it as long as he could, and one day he was gone.

"Without him to torment she turned to me. I was just like my father, she said. I was nothing and would never be anything. Nothing I did was good. That which was not flawless was a crime, and all crimes were treason.

"One day she dressed me in my best clothes and tried to slay me. I fled her, and she slew herself instead.

"I spent the rest of my childhood in foster-age in the homes of strangers. No one loved me, or if they tried, I would not let them. I've fled love ever since. My own mother could not love me; how can I hope for love from anyone else? It hurts less to push them away than to wait to be pushed."

"But your mother loved you."

"No. You think of Gerda, but that is not the mother I mean."

"No. I meant the mother who tried to kill you. No mother ever did such a thing but out of love."

Will almost snarled. "Love does not kill."

"You are wrong. Love is the murderous thing, and the more love, the more murder. When we love someone more than all, more than life, more than wealth, more than the gods, then we make them our god. We expect them to be as gods to us, to give us what only gods can give. This they cannot do. They always fail. And then we hate them. We may even hate them enough to kill.

"'Tis for this reason we must make love outlaw. Of all man-slayers, love is cruelest."

"I have been cruel for love," said Will. He laid a hand on her arm, lightly. "Perhaps we should love each other. We are wiser than the sound minds. We'd know not to trust so much to love."

Somehow Katla did not run from these words. Instead she put her face near his and giggled. "Would that not be a sight—a madman and a madwoman, together in incest, with all their mad children?"

They laughed then, long and hard, like a boy and a girl at some silly game. Will had not laughed this way in a very long time. And he had never in his life felt such closeness to a woman.

They lay down together—to sleep, no more—and Will spread his cloak over both of them. She smelled of barley meal and flowers. She was precious. He cherished her. Having her there warmed him, deep in his heart.

They were wakened when their cloak was snatched away. The light from the open door said morning. Guttorm stood over them, eyes wide.

"What have you done together?" he demanded.

"Nothing of shame," said Will. "I would not dishonor my sister."

"Well begone, Katla," said Guttorm, "before tongues begin to wag." The girl dashed out.

"Your mother would speak with you, Amlodd," said Guttorm.

"We shall obey, were she ten times our mother," said Will.

"Ten times?"

"Tell her I'm coming."

"I'll bear you company."

"As you wish."

They walked to the kitchen, a small building hard by the great hall. Guttorm waited outside while Will went in through the entry.

The kitchen had a floor of stone flags and a large hearth in the center. The house had been built over a small rivulet, which ran down the hearthway to one side of the fireplace. Hams and iron pots of various sizes hung from the rafters, along with cleavers and spits. Gerda sat on one of the benches, working at a sock with a single bone knitting needle. She stopped her work and looked up at Will.

"We must speak," she said.

"*Now, mother, what's the matter?*"

"I need to know. Are you mad or do you feign?"

"*I am but mad north-northwest: when the wind is southerly, I know a hawk from a handsaw.*"

She threw her knitting down and stood to face him. "I am your mother! Play not your games with me! If you've set aside our plan, then tell me plainly; if you carry on as you have, I can only believe you've truly lost your wits!"

"Our plan?"

"We are alone, Amlodd. You may speak plainly, so long as you shout not."

Will did not know how to answer.

"I truly know not what you mean, lady," he told her.

"Mad indeed?" asked Gerda. "I feared it— you've been so far unlike yourself; I never marked in you such a gift for snakishness."

He sat beside her on the bench. "Is it true?" he asked. "Did we have a plot, you and I?"

"Dare I tell you? Can I trust a blood secret to a madman?"

"Believe me, lady, I am a fool of silence— nonsense, like bubbles in a well, buoys in me and bursts to air; matters of weight, like gold, sink down and lie secret."

She sat again. "What avails it?" she said. "'Twas your own plan, whispered to me when first they brought you back from the hunt. We thought to get vengeance for your father by stealth— feigning your madness to lull Feng's fears, then burning him and his men in the hall when the time was right. But what can we do now, when you are mad in truth?"

"The man I am—the man who speaks to you—is not a killer," said Will. The theory of revenge in literature was one thing. To kill men, for an injury not even his own, was another entirely.

"So I feared. What shall we do?"

The noise brought Will to attention before his mind had recognized it. Amlodd's reflexes still functioned. He knew the noise meant danger and he knew where it came from—behind a chest in a corner. He hurried there and found a man crouching in the shadow.

The man pulled a knife and leaped to meet him. Will drew his own, with Amlodd's skill. The spy, whom he recognized as one of those who'd threatened him in the surf, aimed a cut at his ribs and Will did not parry, but leaped backward to avoid the cut, then moved in with a stab as the man's momentum left him with his flank exposed.

The man twisted away and came around in a full circle, aiming a slash at Will's knife arm. Will avoided it by dipping the arm, at the same time grabbing for the man's shirt with his free hand. The man sprang back and slipped on one of the wet stones that lined the rivulet. Will was upon him in a second, straddling him with one knee in the water. Each held the other's knife hand, corded muscles standing out on their necks.

Slowly, with bull-like strength, Will pushed his own knife down toward the man's chest. *I can't be doing this,* he thought. *This is not something I'd do.* For just a moment he hesitated, paralyzed by the fear in the man's blue eyes.

Then he drove the knife home. He felt it scrape along a rib—his gorge rising. The man's back arched and he shuddered. He did not die at once. It took a few minutes, as Will restrained him. The horror was compounded by the thoughts in his own head.

Don't fight me, he was thinking. *Can't you just once do what you're told?*

The rivulet ran red from the corpse to the outlet under the wall.

A violent shaking overtook him and he swung away from the dead man to sit on the bench with his back turned.

Gerda had been standing, watching. Her face showed no emotion. "If this killing comes out, you'll go to England. It would delay our vengeance long. Can you bear to cover a man-killing?"

"Manslaying is not a thing I take pride in."

"Indeed you are not yourself."

"Go. I'll handle it."

She looked searchingly at him, then went out the door.

Will followed her out and looked around the yard. People were everywhere—there were no idle hours in the steading. The thralls at least were always about at some duty or another. He walked toward the low stone wall that ringed the yard. The rivulet that ran through the kitchen drained into a pond on its other side. He saw that there were bones there, and many two-toed tracks in the mud. He knew those tracks from childhood visits to a farm.

He remembered how Amlodd had concealed the body in Saxo's book. He didn't want to do it that way. But for the life of him he couldn't think of a better one.

He went back into the kitchen house, steeling himself for nasty work.

His mother appeared at the door with a bundle. "You've blood all over your clothing," she said. "Change into these clothes."

"In a moment," said Will, taking them and closing the door on her. "What I'm about to do is best done naked.

"In what sense am I Will Sverdrup?" he wondered as he undressed and knelt by the corpse. "I'm doing things Will would never do." He wondered what it was that defined a man—what he thought or what he did.

The worst part (well, almost the worst) was knowing he'd have to go to England anyway.

So why was he doing this?

Because he had a mother here who loved him, and she wanted it. For her he'd have chopped up the whole village.

Except for Katla.

❧ CHAPTER XII ❧

In the morning they found the dining hall furniture rearranged. Gone was the long table where they had eaten and held their discussions. Now there was a dais at one end, and upon it two thrones, the one on their left larger than the other. Tapestries covered the walls—still predominately black and gold, but currents of red and blue had emerged there as well.

Bess was the first to arrive. One of the servants blocked her way as she tried to get a closer look at the thrones. He carried a halberd and looked like a dark Beefeater. Bess stayed near the door, waiting for reinforcements.

Randy came next, then Peter, then Rosey, who led a hangdog Amlodd by the arm.

"Have you tried asking the guard what's going on?" Randy asked Bess.

"Do you think he'd answer?"

"Only one way to find out."

Bess asked him, "What happened to the dining hall?"

"The dining hall is shifted," said the servant. He sounded something like Alexander Scourby. "Go down the corridor towards the gate, and left at the turning."

"What's happened here? Where's our people?"

"If you mean King Sean and Queen Diane, they are indisposed, but will see you later. Breakfast will be served in the new hall. One of the servants will conduct you, if you wish."

"We'll find it," said Bess, and the Beefeater bowed. They all turned and went the directed way. "What do you suppose this means?"

"The castle keeps revising itself," said Peter. "At first it was mostly undifferentiated space, like a stage in Shakespeare's day. But it's becoming a real, working castle."

"And what's this business about 'King Sean' and 'Queen Diane'?"

"Sounds like a palace coup to me," said Randy. "I'd say Sean found a power vacuum, and like a good bit of putty, rushed to stop it up."

"He can't do that,"said Bess" Doesn't he know he's putting us all in jeopardy? We've got to do everything we can to keep the story from happening. Your lives depend on it, for God's sake!"

"You're determined to prevent the re-creation, then?" asked Randy. "Even you, who love the play so?"

"My first obligation is to survive, and help us all to survive. The play'll have to take care of itself."

"It may be doing just that," said Peter.

They found the new dining hall, which looked quite a lot like the old one. The familiar table was in place and each of them now had a chair. As they sat, servants appeared as usual and began to set out food. The food had evolved into identifiable items—bread and porridge and smoked fish—and wasn't half bad. Peter emptied a flagon of wine immediately.

"Don't Sean and Diane realize how all of you end up in this play?" Bess demanded. "Let Sean be Oberon or Falstaff. Why does he have to be the king of Denmark?"

"What the hell does it matter?" asked Amlodd, who sat eating nothing, staring blankly ahead.

"Some of us still want to live," said Bess. "Though I'm beginning to think we're a minority."

"If we're voting on it, I vote to live," said Randy.

"Me too," said Howie, as he came through the door.

"Howie!" said Peter. "How are you?"

"I'm fine. I'm better than fine."

"Has there been news about Eric?"

"I was with him all night."

Everyone turned and stared at him, except for Amlodd.

"Those servants who took me away last night,

they led me to the battlements," said Howie, standing with one foot on a chair. "Eric met me there and we talked a lot of things out."

"Tell the whole story, from beginning to end, omitting no detail however insignificant," said Randy.

"The personal stuff is none of your business. But he told me about this universe, too. Because he's in this superior body, he understands things we don't."

"If you consider monsters superior," said Peter, more loudly than he probably intended.

"You're judging him by stereotypes," said Howie. "Just because he doesn't look like us, doesn't mean he's evil."

"There's a little matter of killing a man."

"Will you let me tell my story?"

"Yeah, go ahead."

"All right. Everything we thought about this being an alternate universe is correct. There are . . . beings in the cosmos—intelligences who don't grow old and don't die, and they navigate the universes. Eric has become one of them. He is the god of this universe."

"*Not an option!*" yelled Peter. He banged his flagon on the table and spilled wine.

"Will you let me talk? This world was remodeled for Hamlet. It is the will of its god that we live out the play."

"I don't believe it," said Peter. "Eric doesn't give a rip about Hamlet. Whoever set this up, it wasn't Eric."

"As I was saying," said Howie, "it is the will of the god of this world that we should live out the play."

"And die, all but you?" asked Bess.

"No. That's the best part. We can change the end. Look, the original Hamlet—our friend Amlodd over there—he survived, right? He can do the same thing here!"

"Interesting concept," said Randy.

"Wait a minute . . ." said Bess. "The whole point of the story is Hamlet's revenge. If he survives, Sean has to die."

"I trust there aren't any monarchists here," said Howie. "You've got to break some eggs, as the man said."

"Your son has killed one of us already," said Peter. "Now you want to kill another."

"Not us. I don't think any of *us* could hack it. But there's one person here who's killed before."

All of them turned to stare at Amlodd.

"Leave be," said Amlodd. "I'm no warrior now. I'm nothing."

Howie walked down to Amlodd's end of the table and sat on the chair on his free side.

"You want to be a warrior again, don't you?"

"With this body? With these spidery muscles and sappy nerves? I've become a thrall. I must learn to bow and grovel, and serve true men."

"What if there's another way?"

"What way?" For the first time, Amlodd turned to face Howie.

"Did you ever hear it said that when you kill a man, his strength goes into you?"

"Some men believe so. Mostly ones who've never killed anyone."

"That's true in our world. But this world is different. Listen—my son explained it. This universe is still being built. In this universe we can make the rules. If we believe it, we make it so."

Amlodd stared at him. "You mean, if I were to kill a man here, and truly believe I'd take his strength, I'd get it?"

"Exactly."

"This isn't you, Howie," said Peter. "You're a humanitarian. You don't believe in murder."

"You're still thinking in terms of the old world. This is the new world. The old rules don't apply here."

"I can't believe this. You're telling me *everything's* up for grabs? Incest? Matricide? Cannibalism?"

"We'll have to see. It all depends. It's about love, Nilsson. That's what you Christians believe, isn't it? I love my son. He's all I have in my life. I have to take him as he is, and love him on his own terms. In this place, where he calls the shots, I don't get to shove my beliefs down his throat. I have to be flexible; learn new ways."

"So you're the Virgin Howie of this dispensation? Will we have to revere you?"

Howie's face showed no reaction, neither humor nor anger nor embarrassment. "We'll have to see," he said.

"Give us a break, Howie," said Bess. "Peter hasn't won me to his religion; I'm not about to go for yours."

"Eric's no Jesus, and no Jehovah either," said Howie. "He doesn't stand to one side and let people do whatever they want, and judge them after they're dead. Eric's a hands-on god. There'll be no ignoring him."

"Great. Our god is a juvenile delinquent," said Randy, leaning back in his chair and folding his arms.

"He's not my God," said Peter.

"Your God's not in this universe," said Howie.

"I don't believe that. And even if it were true, it wouldn't make any difference. I'd stand by Him even if there were no way to Heaven from here."

"Spoken like a Norseman," said Amlodd, glumly.

"Then remember it. Eric—the troll—will want your worship. Your gods aren't my God, but they're better than Eric. Don't be taken in."

"Every land has its own gods," said Amlodd. "Where they rule, they must be honored."

"And Eric rules here," said Howie.

"That, I think, remains to be seen," said Randy, his feet up on the table now.

His feet came down when he heard the trumpets. They all got to their feet involuntarily as a troop of Beefeaters entered the hall, conducting Sean and Diane, who had dressed themselves like Arthur and Guinevere in *Camelot*.

The procession made its way toward the head of the table. Strong hands suddenly grasped each of them by the arms and moved them to new seats. The final arrangement went like this: Sean at the head, with Diane on his left. Next down from her was Peter, then Randy and Rosemary.

On his right sat Bess, then Amlodd, then Howie. Then the Beefeaters marched off, except for about four guards, who kept watch near Sean.

"All right, Sean, what's with the pomp and circumstance and the seating arrangement?" asked Bess.

"Informality might work in the twenty-first century," said Sean, "but it's inappropriate for our present situation."

"I don't recall anyone consulting us about it."

"That's one of the advantages of monarchy," said Sean. "Things get done without a lot of fuss and red tape."

"You can't just set yourself up as king," said Peter.

"Why not?"

"Because it's wrong . . . and because it's dangerous."

Sean leaned forward. "*How* dangerous?"

"There are people in this group who want to break the play," said Bess. "One way to do that is to kill the king at the beginning."

"Is someone plotting my death?" asked Sean. "Who is it? Tell me." The old geniality was gone from his face. It was a face none of them had ever seen before.

"Do we have treason already?" he asked. "Who is for me? Who is against me? Let's have it out, so we'll know where we stand!"

"If you're gonna play king, then I'm against you," said Rosey.

"If it's a question of killing, I'm against that," said Peter. He poured himself another drink.

"If anybody kills you, Sean, you've only got yourself to blame," said Randy.

"*Treason!* I'm surrounded by traitors!" cried Sean. His face had gone red.

"FOR GOD'S SAKE!" shouted Bess, standing. "Have we forgotten who we are? We're a bunch of amateur actors! Part-time players! We do shows in a converted church with a mildew problem! We don't have enough money to get the furnace replaced! We're not the nobles of Denmark and Sean is not the king!

"The only way we've got to keep alive is to remember who we are! If we lose touch with reality, this story will suck us in and we'll end in blood up to our ankles! Can't you people get that through your heads? It's only a story!"

"Bess, it's hopeless," said Randy. "Only a story? You think a story is a puff of breath; a piece of paper you can throw in the fire? Don't believe it. There's nothing more powerful than a story in any universe, except perhaps for the High One Himself.

"Your scholars think they've got stories tamed because they can trace them down centuries and cultures and retellings. They follow the Hamlet saga back to the story of Brutus in Rome, and they think they've pinned it to a card like a moth. Once they've tied a story to a legend, they think they've proved it couldn't actually happen in history. They don't see the simple truth—that anything that survives so much time and change must be eternal indeed—and that eternal forces can bend your precious real world to their own shape.

"You think you can fight being 'sucked in' by this story? You might as well throw yourself off a cliff and fight being sucked in by gravity. You might as well fight being sucked in by time itself."

"We still have freedom," said Bess.

"Your freedom will ensure the tragedy."

"It's your death too, you know."

"Would that it were so. Sadly, I cannot die."

He drew Bess to her feet, folded her in his arms and gave her a Rudolph Valentino kiss. "From one fairy to another," he said.

And Randy vanished before their eyes.

There was stunned silence except for repeated screams from Diane. Rosey ran to her and put her arms around her.

"What the hell was that about?" asked Howie.

"He is an Old One," said Amlodd. "I always thought so, though the feeling was faint. Probably that came of my senses being so dull in this body."

"What do you mean, old?"

"One of the Old Ones. The folk who live

under the hills. The ones who lead travelers astray and snatch children."

"Elves?" asked Bess.

"I'd not use that word if I thought one was listening," said Amlodd. "And they're always listening."

"This is too weird," said Diane, who had stopped screaming but was hyperventilating. She grabbed a cup of wine and drained it. Sweat stood out on her forehead.

"I don't think I want any breakfast," said Rosey.

Nobody wanted breakfast. They wandered off one by one.

Diane answered the knock at the bedchamber door. It was Peter.

"I thought you were Sean," she said.

"He isn't here?" Peter looked nervous. His face was red.

"No. I'm not sure where to tell you to look for him. He goes out like this. Maybe he does king business. Maybe he drinks or screws the servant girls. I don't know."

"Are you all right? You seemed pretty shaken up at breakfast."

"I don't know, Peter," she said, turning back into the room. Peter followed her, hesitant'y. "Everything's so confusing. Do people really want to kill us?"

"I don't know about anybody wanting to kill *you*. . . ."

"But Sean?"

"He's got this king thing in his head. Kings are natural targets. That's the way it is, I'm afraid."

"Even among friends?"

"I think . . . when a man says 'I'm the king,' he's saying, 'I don't want to be your friend anymore.'"

There was a small table with a flagon and a cup on it, and Diane went to it and poured herself a drink. "It's all so horrible. I miss my daughters, I miss my job—hell, I even miss my ex-husband. You want a drink?" Her face showed that she regretted saying it, but by then Peter was helping himself.

"I'll go now and try to catch Sean later," he said when he was finished. He turned to the door.

"Wait. Don't go. Please."

"I really don't think—"

"I'm not coming on to you, Peter. I know that's hard to believe from me—ha—but I'm not. Don't take it personally, of course."

"We can talk another time. I don't want people to get the . . . the wrong idea."

"No, wait. You—you know God, don't you? I mean, you don't just know *about* God, you really believe you know Him personally?"

"Well, yes."

"I never thought about God much. I went to church when I was a kid—my mom made me go—but I always thought, hey, how can you know for sure? So why bother about it, you know?

"But here we are. I mean, here we are—in this place, where there's a ghost, and a monster, and the castle keeps changing, and the servants will get you anything you want. What am I supposed to make out of it? There's no point asking if there's another world—we know there's at least one, and we're in it. So maybe the God thing's true too. What do you think? Wait, I know what you think already."

"What do you want, Diane? Do you want me to introduce you to Jesus?"

"I don't know. What do I have to do? I have to give up drinking and men, right?"

"No, not really. It's a gift; you just accept it. But if it's real, you do change. You never completely stop being a sinner though. Look at me, drinking again. I'm ashamed and sorry, but it doesn't mean I'm lost."

"Ha. Can you see me, sitting in a church, singing hymns? That would be a hoot. You think they'd accept me in church?"

"If it was a decent church, yes. With open arms. There's good churches and bad churches, of course. Some churches forget what they're there for."

"What *are* they there for?"

"To offer good news for free. I remember the church I grew up in. If you asked them what they were there for, they'd have told you it was to bring salvation to the world. But they were so busy driving their children away they didn't have much time for that. The offer stands though, and it's yours for the taking."

"And then everything's wonderful, right? All your burdens roll away, like in the songs?"

"Those songs are musical junk food. It's sins that get rolled away. The problems stick around. Most of the time they get worse. Believe me. The promise is that you'll get a special kind of help with the problems, not that they'll disappear."

"Sounds like bait-and-switch to me."

"You've got to check out the original promises, in the Bible. Not what people say about them."

"Where do I get a Bible? Have you got one?"

"Yes. I asked the servants for one the first night. It's a period Bible, of course—big as an overnight case and the print's hard to read, but I'll go get it."

"No. I want one of my own. I'll ring for a servant and order one."

"You've got a bell pull?"

"Why not?"

"No reason, I guess. It just seems kind of pointless, when they come whenever you call."

"I don't like to think about that. It's kind of creepy, you know? I like the bell pull better. Then I can pretend they aren't always nearby."

"Like God?"

"Yeah, I suppose." Diane sat on the bed and drained her cup. "I mean, what is it with God? Always watching. Keeping a record of all your sins, so He can find a good excuse to throw you in Hell. Who needs that?"

Peter sat in a chair by the wall that neither of them had noticed before. "Is that how you see God?" he asked.

"You know how I lost my virginity? I lost it to my mother's boyfriend, when I was fifteen. He was a married man, and a member of the church. He used to tell Mom he wanted to help me with my prayers, and then he'd come in my room and use me. He told me I was a temptation out of Hell to him; that I'd seduced him with my eyes. Sometimes he'd pray with me after he'd done it to me. He said I had to pray God to forgive me for being a seductive little succubus. Those were the words he used— 'seductive little succubus.' He died of cancer a few years ago. I hope it hurt him a lot. And I hope he's burning in Hell now."

"I'd say there's a good chance of it. From what you tell me, he was an evil man."

"But according to you, God forgave him if he said he was sorry."

"It's more than just saying the right words. It means a kind of dying."

"Well, he can't die enough to suit me." She sat quietly for a moment. "Why do you think my mom did it?"

"Did what?"

"Let him be alone with me? She must have known. Nobody prays that long."

"I don't know, Diane. We all have needs. We

try to get them met, and sometimes we lie to ourselves to hold on to whatever seems to be meeting them. For me it was the bottle. I didn't get free until I realized the bottle wasn't really satisfying, and that I couldn't meet my own needs no matter what I did. That was when I died. It killed my pride. It hurt. A lot. But it was the only way to peace."

"Peace. God, I don't even know what peace is," said Diane with a sob. "I've never known a moment of peace in my pardon-my-French life."

"Do you want me to pray with you?" Peter asked. "I know that must sound creepy to you, but I'll stay right here in this chair. I won't ask you to pray to become a Christian, if you don't want to. We can just pray that God will give you peace, and let Him answer it however He sees fit. If you'll open the door just a crack for Him, He'll start to come in."

"I want you to sit beside me. I want to pray with you and for it to be a clean thing. Is that okay?"

Peter breathed deeply. "Okay," he said. "If that's what you want."

He sat beside Diane and folded his hands. Immediately she began to sob, her shoulders convulsing, and despite himself he put his arm around her.

He began to pray. He prayed fervently, his head bowed, his eyes closed.

The opening door and the scream startled

him, but he only had a confused view of Amlodd
towering over him, sword raised, before the
blade fell and struck off the light for him.

"Dead for a ducat, dead!" cried Amlodd.

Diane stood screaming, hands on either side
of her face, like Munch's painting. She stood and
screamed for several minutes while Amlodd
stood staring. He said, "It's not Sean. It's not
Sean," over and over again.

Faces appeared at the door. Bess came in and
shouted at Amlodd. "You've killed Peter, you
goddam psychopath!"

Amlodd struck her backhanded across the
face. "Be silent, woman! I have to think!"

Bess picked herself up and threw herself on
him. "Give me that sword, you idiot!" she yelled.

"No man disarms me, and surely no woman,"
Amlodd answered. He pried her off and slammed
her against the wall, then set the point to her
throat. The people at the door rushed forward,
then hesitated.

They saw blood in Amlodd's face for a
moment. Then he went pale.

"Great honor I'd get of killing a woman," he
said. He lowered the sword, pushed through the
door and fled. He turned back in the corridor
and said, *"Thou wretched, rash, intruding fool,
farewell! I took thee for thy better."*

❧ CHAPTER XIII ❧

Will thought there were better ways to spend the night before embarkation than working up a hangover, but that was the Danes' way. *"It is a custom more honored in the breach than the observance,"* he thought. People took that line the wrong way, he remembered. How did they take it wrong? He couldn't recall.

There had been a general search for the dead man, whose name had been Halgeir, and Feng and his men had questioned Will particularly. "He swam away down the brook," Will had told them. Not exactly what Saxo recorded, but close enough. Will wondered idly if he was capable of withholding the lines Saxo fed him. As an academic, he felt something like a compulsion to give the right answer when he knew it, and as an actor he hated to miss a cue.

He got up from the bench and left the feast

to use the privy. Men looked away from him as he passed. No one smiled. Ever since Halgeir's death, suspicion had hung over him, aggravated by the taboo of his madness. All but Guttorm, Katla and his mother gave him wide berth.

He shivered as he left the hall. Accustomed as he was growing to living in the past, Will had trouble with the nights. It was truly dark in the Dark Ages—dark as he had never known it in the twentieth or twenty-first centuries. The stars were holes burned by cigarettes in a velvet curtain draped before an ammonia fire.

He had feared the dark in his old life. In this one it was worsening with each night. The darkness teemed with watching eyes and coiled power. He had a creeping sensation of being at the bottom of the food chain, like a rabbit or a mouse.

He remembered the elf woman speaking of "the christening" as an event that had restrained and restricted her kind. He'd studied enough history to consider Christianity a historical disaster—the beginning of an era of repression and violence that had destroyed everything beautiful and gentle in European culture.

But the people who wrote the history books had never stood in one of these unchristened nights and faced the things that lived in it.

He was used to a friendly universe, one where he could imagine that the only spirits around were angelic ones—perhaps motherly black women or lovely Irish girls. But that was a universe after the christening. Students of history wouldn't believe it, but anyone who passed, as he had, from one age to the other would understand.

He thought of pagan images he had seen—not the humanistic sculptures of later Greeks, but the works of real pagans—bulging eyes and gaping mouths and brazen Canaanite molochs with outstretched hands meant to be heated red so the babies could be laid on them.

He shuddered from head to foot. He was a murderer. He had blood on his hands. He felt it like Lady MacBeth. Anyone with eyes to see, he was sure, would know him for a manslayer—one who had killed coldly and with a certain pleasure. That made him different from the Will Sverdrup of the twenty-first century. If he ever returned to his own time and place, he wouldn't be the man he had been. And the spirits there, he was sure, would see his guilt as easily.

He slid a silver ring off his arm, one he had found in Amlodd's personal chest. He threw it deep into the trees, calling out, "Take this! Leave me alone!"

He did his business in the privy. On his way back he was stopped by two men named Hrolf and Gudbrand. They were the standard Abbot and Costello pair, only blond and not funny. Hrolf was Abbot and Gudbrand was Costello.

"We're for England in the morning," said Hrolf.

"So it would appear," said Will.

"A grand adventure."

"Let's hope so."

"A pity Halgeir couldn't be with us," said Gudbrand.

"Perhaps he'll show up."

"What do you think became of him?" asked Hrolf.

"Down the drain," said Will.

"How would a big man like Halgeir go down a drain?"

"Very carefully."

Hrolf stepped forward, hand on sword hilt. "Are you jesting about Halgeir?" he asked through clenched teeth. "Halgeir was our friend. What are you saying about him?"

"Nothing but to show you how a king may go a progress through the guts of a . . . porker."

"We do not like your jests," said Gudbrand. "And we do not like you."

"Then take your leave of me. *You cannot, sir, take from me anything that I will more willingly part withal.'"*

"Would that we could. But we are bound together, we three, for the voyage."

"How so?"

"The jarl has set us as your keepers, to see you come to no harm."

"'Such officers do the king best service in the end. He keeps them, like an ape, in the corner of his jaw, first mouthed, to be last swallowed. When he needs what you have gleaned, it is but squeezing you and, sponge, you shall be dry again.'"

"Say what you will, madman, we'll do our duty by you and the jarl. Get used to our faces." They sauntered off with the bravado of fear.

"Rosencrantz and Guildenstern," said a thin voice in English.

"Just what I was thinking," said Will, before he thought to wonder who spoke. He turned to see a silvery-blue light shining in a man's shape among the trees. The light coalesced rapidly into a recognizable form—a man in a clerical collar and black suit. He recognized the apparition he'd seen in the theater just before he fell through the trapdoor. It did not look as frightening now, but its eyes were still red.

"You're the ghost from the theater," said Will. As in the movies, the ghost was somewhat transparent, but Will had a feeling he was no less transparent to the ghost.

"Say the rest," said the ghost.

"What?"

"Say, 'the hypocrite, the child abuser, the suicide. The man who brought God's ministry into disrepute.'"

"It's no concern of mine."

"You're a careful man. If you'd accused me, I'd have thrown your murder in your face."

"Murder. I can't believe I've murdered a man."

"When in Rome. Killing doesn't shock these people."

"No, but hiding it does. Amlodd would have announced the manslaying from the housetops, paid a few pounds to the family, and come out with respect."

"As I said, when in Rome. You've killed your first. You must do it again to survive. You know that, don't you?"

Will sat on a tree stump. "I don't think I can."

"You're very young, aren't you? When you're older you'll realize that we do what we need to do in life. Things that would have appalled us at first become possible when we must do them, and easy when we've done them enough."

"This is what I have to look forward to? To becoming you? Will I kill myself as well?"

"Let's not compare sins, shall we? I never killed anyone. Except myself."

Will rose and turned away. "I do not like this conversation," he said.

"Stay," said the ghost. "I've come far to speak with you. I've traveled the way between the worlds."

"So have I. We both came down the same rabbit hole."

"Not quite. I was in Hamlet's world with the rest of your troupe."

"Hamlet's world?"

The ghost explained what had happened to the other actors.

"I can't believe it," said Will.

"I should have been Hamlet's father," said the ghost, "but the monster boy pushed me from my place. I didn't know what I'd do, but the raven showed me the way here."

The one-eyed raven Will had met before flew down from somewhere and lit on the ghost's shoulder. How does a bird sit on a spirit?

"And what do you mean to do here?" Will asked.

"I shall be the ghost here. I shall show you the way."

"I'm not sure Hamlet's father's ghost wasn't a demon. Come to think of it, I'm not sure you aren't either."

"Of course I'm a demon. We're all demons— me, this bird, and you. You're possessing someone else's body—what do you think that makes you?"

"My friend Peter Nilsson says all dead souls go to Heaven or Hell. He said ghosts are just demons, impersonating the dead."

"He's generally right. But people who die in despair, especially suicides, sometimes remain awhile in the place where they died. That was my case, until I was pulled down the trapdoor with the rest of you."

"Neither Heaven nor Hell?"

"No, it's Hell. Hell is a state of being more than a place. Wherever I am, there is Hell for me."

"All right. *What would your gracious figure?* What's your plan?"

"The raven will teach you how to carve runes, so that you can do what needs to be done with Rosencrantz and Guildenstern. Then, when you've gotten Amlodd's revenge, I'll show you the way to Hamlet's world. Once there, you can meet your old body in the flesh, and your souls will naturally return where they belong."

"Why not show me the way back now, and save a lot of trouble? You can bring the real Amlodd back here, and let him do the business."

"Because I'm nothing to him, and can teach him nothing he needs to know. I want to play my part.

"Like all men in Hell, I am a failure—more than most. I failed in my duty to God, I failed as a man. This is my last chance to matter in the world. In this place I can be Hamlet's father, a great figure in history."

"Will that make Hell easier for you?"

"Nothing makes Hell easier. But it's a matter of pride. If I'm damned, I'd rather be damned for pride than for my other sins."

"You swear you know the way between the worlds?"

"The oath of a damned soul means nothing. But I tell you it is so."

"I'm not sure I can do what I need to do next. To kill a man in self-defense is one thing. To kill with premeditation—that's something else."

"The death of those men is no less self-defense than that other. They're in league with the jarl to kill you by premeditation of their own."

"Hamlet wasn't sure whether his father's ghost was a damned spirit. I have no doubt of it, yet I'm going along with you."

"Good," said the ghost. "Raven!"

The bird took wing and flew onto Will's shoulder. "Learn the riddle of the runes . . ." it began.

An hour later Will headed back into the steading. He met Gerda walking in the yard.

"Amlodd!" she said. "I was looking for you."

"Now, mother, what's the matter?"

"I'd speak with you. You sail on the morning tide. You've always bid me farewell alone the night before embarkation, and I've always made you a gift. I have a new shirt and trousers for you, and a new shield." She motioned and a thrall girl came forward with the clothing, while a thrall boy came with the shield—flat and circular, painted red and decorated with bronze plates in the shapes of ravens. The thralls set the gifts on the ground, and Gerda sent them away.

Will embraced Gerda and kissed her. "I wish I could stay with you always," he whispered.

"Silly boy. If you stayed by your mother all the time you'd never do great deeds to make her proud."

"Would you really rather have me risking my life in England than staying by you?"

"Of course."

"Suppose I should die?"

"Do not die. We have our vengeance to finish."

"What if we forgot about vengeance? What if we forgot the past and simply tried to be happy?"

"Happy? Unavenged? Honorless? You frighten me, Amlodd. You talk like a madman indeed."

"Then why not do it tonight? Burn them in the hall as we planned?"

"Because they are watching you. They do not trust you yet. Time is the thing. In time they will grow easy with you, and then we shall eat our vengeance cold."

Will sighed. "All right, Mother, forget I said it. I shall make you proud in England and get your revenge for you when I return."

"Only do not feel too much at home in England."

"Why should I?"

"Have you forgotten all? Your father's mother was a British princess. She loved you much. Surely you remember her."

"I've forgotten much indeed. But I shall not forget you, though I sail to the house of the west where the sun sleeps."

They embraced again. Looking over her shoulder, Will saw Katla standing nearby.

"Katla," he said when he'd released Gerda. "Will you do me a favor?"

"Surely," said the girl.

"I think you're in no danger. Saxo said nothing about you dying."

"Who is Saxo?"

"A man not yet born. Will you promise me this? Stay away from rivers and streams."

"If you wish it."

"Good." He gave her a quick kiss and went to his house to sleep alone.

❧ CHAPTER XIV ❧

Diane found Rosey in the kitchen, a vast room with heavy wooden tables, chopping blocks and two great fireplaces large enough to walk upright in. She had swung a large copper kettle on its hinged crane over an inexpertly built fire.

"What are you doing?" Diane asked.

"I'm boiling water. I want a bath."

"The servants will draw you a bath."

"You know what's the worst thing about this place? Everything's done for you. I haven't got an occupation here." Rosey wiped her forehead. She was perspiring and her sweatshirt showed dark crescents under the armpits. It had been laundered several times since they'd arrived, and would need another washing soon. Diane and Sean were still the only ones who'd ordered period clothes from the servants, but the others were all thinking about it.

"It does get boring, between murders," said Diane.

"Damn!" said Rosey, turning to sit on a stool, her face in her hands. "How could he do that? Kill Peter? I was there in the hallway—I heard the noise and came running. Will—Amlodd— he ran by me. He had blood all over him."

"Peter was a nice man," said Diane. "Yeah, he was a religious fanatic, but he didn't really shove it down anybody's throat. He wanted to help me. You know how long it's been since any man has tried to just give me something, without wanting anything back?"

"He fell off the wagon."

"I think I liked him better for it. He wasn't standing up above me, talking down. But he felt bad about it. I was sorry about that."

"I can't believe Amlodd did it. I mean, I knew he was violent, over-the-top, but that was just sex. That was what made him exciting.

"You know, you fantasize about a barbarian— some kind of Fabio guy from the cover of a romance novel, a noble savage. But I never thought what a barbarian would really be like."

"You can't even say there's other fish in the sea. In this world, there aren't many."

"That's the worst thing. I don't want another fish. I still love Amlodd."

"Even after—"

"Didn't you ever find yourself drawn to a man *because* he was dangerous?"

"Oh yeah. Been there."

"Somebody once told me that there are only two kinds of men—Jimmy Stewarts and Errol Flynns. The Stewarts are kind and dependable, but they bore you. The Flynns cheat and lie and run around, but every minute with them is an adventure. They make the whole world more vivid, like a drug."

"First Randy and now Amlodd. You must have a thing for Flynns."

"I guess I do. They weren't the first. But there was never anybody like Amlodd." Diane saw tears running down Rosey's cheeks.

"You really care about him."

"Yeah. I know it can't come to any good. I know I'll get my heart broken. I could even end up dead. But I've got to follow my heart, right?"

"Peter once told me that was the biggest lie in the world—that you've always got to follow your heart. He said always doing what your feelings tell you is like saying 'always go north.' That'll get you to some places, but not to a lot of others."

"So what are we supposed to follow?"

"Well, you knew Peter. His idea was to follow the Bible. Hell, I used to laugh at him and now listen to me—I'm his mouthpiece. I suppose somebody's got to do it."

Rosey took Diane by the arms. "Don't go holy on me, Diane. You're the only friend I've got here."

"We're all your friends, honey."

"No, it's not true. All you people have worked together before—you're part of some kind of club. I'm an outsider. I didn't even audition with you guys. You know why Bess cast me, didn't you?"

"She thought you were the best person for the part."

"No. She's got the hots for me. I can tell."

Diane shook her head. "No, no. I'm not saying she isn't drawn to you. But Bess doesn't cast for that reason. She *cares* about these productions. She doesn't let personal stuff enter into it. Look at Peter. She knew what Peter believed. She knew he thought being a lesbian was a sin. But she cast him anyway, time after time, because he was a good actor."

Rosey said, "She wants me, and she's gonna make a pass. What do you think'll happen when I turn her down? We're all turning into killers here."

Diane gave her another hug. "Don't think that way, honey. What does it say in *King Lear*? *'That way madness lies'*?"

"Madness," said Rosey, sobbing. "That's what's going to happen to me, isn't it? I'll go crazy and then I'll drown. Randy was right. The play's sucking us in. It's like a black hole."

"No, no—" Diane was soothing the girl when Sean entered.

"There you are, my lady," he said, paying no attention to the women's embrace or the tears on Rosey's face. "I missed you at the trial."

"What trial?" asked Diane, letting Rosey go and sitting up straight.

"I had Howie arrested by the servants, and tried him for treason."

"For treason?" said Rosey.

"Of course. He was inciting the rest of you to assassinate me. What's that but treason?"

"You didn't—didn't—" said Diane.

"Have him executed? No. I'm still not comfortable with the idea of having an old friend killed—though that didn't seem to bother Howie. No, I've placed him in durance vile."

"Where?"

"The dungeon."

"We have a dungeon?"

"What's a castle without a dungeon?"

"Where is it?"

"God knows. Somewhere in the cellar, I assume. I just had the servants take him there. I hope it's cold, and full of rats. The bastard."

"This is getting out of control," said Diane.

"On the contrary. It's coming under control. I'm taking control," said Sean.

Diane took his hand. "Be careful, Sean. I say this because I care for you. We're like little kids playing with knives here. We don't understand the danger we're in."

"You're so sexy when you're motherly," said Sean, hugging her and tracing circles on her back with his index finger. "I missed you last night."

"I was upset."

"Then I'll see you tonight?"

Diane turned away. "I'm still upset."

Sean held her. "Don't be upset too long. I might lose interest."

Diane opened her mouth to speak, then just smiled and glided away.

Sean shrugged his shoulders. "We'll see you for lunch," he said, and went out.

When he was gone, both the women said, *"We've got to see him,"* simultaneously. They called for a servant with a torch to lead them to the dungeon.

It lay at the bottom of a series of stepped passages, and looked just like a dungeon in an old movie, complete with cobwebs and rusty hanging manacles. Howie's cell was equally cinematic— it had a heavy oak door with iron hardware and a small barred judas-hole. Bess was already there, looking through the hole. They joined her. They could see Howie's face.

"He can't do this!" said Rosey.

"Of course he can," said Howie. "He's playing his part. It's all in the plan."

"The plan?" asked Diane.

"The plan of my god. I had always wondered why Horatio stayed on in Denmark after Hamlet had gone, supposedly on a long voyage. Why didn't he go with Hamlet? Or if not that, why not just go back to school at Wittenberg?

"Now I know. He stayed to plot against the tyrant. He was a revolutionary."

"Revolution's a dangerous game to play," said Bess.

"Nothing can happen to me. I'm under the protection of my god."

"You mean Eric?"

"Of course. My god has the power to protect me, unlike some other people's—Peter's for instance."

"Don't make fun of Peter," said Diane. "He was a good man."

"Peter was an idiot."

"Howie!"

"He was a Fundamentalist. Q.E.D. He couldn't understand that right and wrong might not always be the same from one situation to another. He couldn't understand that it's okay— no, call it mandatory—to change the rules depending on time and place.

"In our old world, we thought revenge was wrong. That was then. This is now. In this world, revenge is the law. Revenge is the greatest virtue. I will get my revenge on Sean."

"Easy for you to say," said Rosey. "You're the one who doesn't die in this play."

"I've explained that to you before. We'll change the ending."

"If we believe Eric," said Bess.

"A monster who killed a man," said Rosey.

Howie moved back and paced in the cell. He was only visible to each of the women for a moment on each pass. "You're not getting it!" he cried. "Those words—*monster*, *kill*—they're just ideas from another world. They don't fit here. New places, new cases—that's the way it is. Eric explained it to me—if we want to survive this thing, to change the ending and go home—we've got to throw all that baggage out."

"What kind of baggage?" asked Diane. "Exactly what ideas are we supposed to drop?"

"Everything! Every preconception we brought here!

"I used to rag on the Peters of our home world, because they held on to old-fashioned ideas that didn't work in the modern world—religion, chastity, nationalism. But I didn't realize that I was as narrow-minded as Peter.

"I had all these assumptions—I thought love was always good. I thought forgiveness was always good. I thought lies and hypocrisy were always bad.

"But who said so? Where is it written? If we have the courage to open our hearts to new ideas—*really* new ideas—are we so certain things will go bad? What do we mean by 'bad,' anyway?

"We think Ghandhi was good. Who says? We think Hitler was bad. Who says? We've got to rethink everything!"

There was a moment of silence.

"Why?" asked Bess at last.

"For the only reason that's ever mattered. Survival. Survival by whatever means is necessary."

"People don't survive alone," said Bess. "We need to get along in communities, to help each other. That's why we've got to be good to each other. Not because a law came down written in stone, but just so we have somebody around us we can trust and depend on."

"In the old world, maybe. In some times and places. But how can you be sure that's true here and now?"

"How can we survive otherwise?"

"How do we know unless we try?"

"Because it makes no sense! And if it fails—*when* it fails—there aren't that many of us here. One dead is a lot . . . especially if it's me."

Howie came up close to the hole. "It doesn't matter," he said, smiling. "because I don't need your help. I can do this all on my own."

"You forget, you're in a cell," said Bess. "I was going to say we need to get you out, but now I think you'd better stay right where you are till you remember how to play nicely with the other kids."

"You can't keep me here," said Howie with a smile. "Sean can't keep me here, and these stone walls can't keep me here. My Savior is coming."

"What's that supposed to mean?" asked Diane.

"Watch," said Howie.

"What the hell—" said Bess.

A golden light turned the blackness of the dungeon to blazing, reflective white. They all shielded their eyes with their hands.

At the center of the light stood a white-robed figure with a golden beard and long golden hair, parted in the center.

"Jesus Christ!" said Diane, not entirely in vain.

But in a moment they saw that the face under the beard was a familiar one. "Eric!" Diane corrected herself.

"Peace to you, my children," said Eric, and the light faded to a more comfortable level.

"What's this crap?" asked Bess.

"I thought you people would be more comfortable with a kinder, gentler god," said Eric.

"When did you stop mumbling?" asked Bess.

"It was a way to get attention," said Eric. "I've got better ways to get attention now."

"I don't like this," said Diane. "I don't like you playing Jesus. It's offensive."

"Sorry, Diane. I know how sensitive you are." He reached an arm out and pinched her left breast. She jumped back, red-faced, and Eric grinned.

"You don't know diddly squat about me," said Diane, rubbing the place he'd touched.

"You're wrong. I know everything about everyone. I'm God."

"Some god."

"You think I don't have power? You think I'm all talk? Behold, unbelievers!"

The cell door opened before their eyes and Howie came forth. He held his hands out at his sides like a man transfixed by an epiphany.

He fell on his knees before his son and cried, "My Lord and my God!"

❧ CHAPTER XV ❧

I will tell you the tale of Amlodd the Dane, son of Orvendil. Not the great saga you've heard of how he avenged his father, but the tale of what he did while he raided in Britain, when he was parted from the army for a time. I have the tale from my father, who heard it from Amlodd himself after he rejoined the Danish host.

Amlodd had come to Britain with Stuf and Wihtgar and their Saxon fleet. He was a marked man, for his uncle Feng had sent messages carved on rune staves to King Cerdic, bidding him put Amlodd to death straightaway. But Amlodd, suspecting treachery, stole the staves in secret from the king's messengers while yet at sea, and read them. He pared the carving away with his knife and carved a new letter, bidding Cerdic slay the bearers, and this was done when they disembarked.

Then Amlodd pulled a wrathful face, demanding to know why the king had put his good friends out of the world. Cerdic, none the wiser, hastened to pay weregeld, giving Amlodd two bars of gold, which he packed away with a secret smile.

The Danes and Saxons met the Britons in battle and put them to flight. But as they stripped the fallen, they were set on by a party of Picts. You know how it is fighting Picts—they go to war stark naked except for war paint and armrings. If you can catch them on the approach, and meet them with arrows and spears, you can tear them to pieces. The trouble is they rarely give you a chance to do that. You don't know they're coming till they're already in your armpit.

So there they were, leaping and screaming and trilling and swinging bronze swords, all blue paint and spiky hair, and no time for our side to link up a shield wall—and it was slaughter. They were everywhere—behind every tree and rock, in front of you, behind you—you didn't know where to run because you didn't know where *away* was. Amlodd was a demon with sword and shield, and he fought on the move until he'd gotten to a place that seemed safe. He leaned against a tree for breath, and in a moment an arrow thrilled in the wood by his ear, and there were five Picts on him. He raised his shield and defended himself, but he was worn and outnumbered, and it was but a question of time.

Then in a moment the wheel of things turned over, and the Picts were screaming in fear, not bloodlust, as they were set upon by two battle-trolls, two wolves of Odin—to put it plainly a man and a woman. They were Britons, armed and fighting against the Picts. The man bore sword and shield, while the woman wielded a spear, and did it wonderfully. There's no arm like a spear for one who understands its use, and this woman fought like a Valkyrie. No weapon, whether swung or cast, came near her. The Picts were gone then as quickly as they'd appeared, and the two men and the woman stood facing each other.

The man had a bright red mustache and wore a kilt of plaid. He was tall and skinny, with the kind of ropy muscle that's more powerful than it looks, and is quick to boot. The woman had bright red hair and a face all cheekbones and angles, but fair for that. She wore a green kirtle.

Amlodd knew not what to expect, and kept his guard up. The man and the woman spoke in their gibbering tongue to one another. The woman sounded angry, and pointed often at Amlodd. The man shook his head; the woman stamped her foot.

The man spoke a final word and turned to Amlodd, speaking with a strange music in the Danish tongue.

"My sister Elen's for slaying you now," he said. "But I say 'twould be shameful to set on a man a-weary."

"I'd not make you look unmanly," said Amlodd, "you who've done me service. I'll fight you if you will."

"No, get your wind again. No man shall say that Llary son of Casnar Wledig slew a brave man on the cheap."

"I'm pleased to make your acquaintance. I am Amlodd, son of Orvendil, of Jutland."

The man's eyes went wide, and he spoke to the woman, who jabbered back, no friendlier than before. But she measured Amlodd from the corner of her eye, as if giving a second look to some dish she'd turned away at supper.

Llary spoke again. "You say your name is Amlawdd?"

"Amlodd, aye."

"But that's a British name."

"My father's mother was a Briton."

Llary paused and studied Amlodd's face, so that Amlodd felt himself going red. "What means this staring?" Amlodd said at last. "If you think me laughable I'll give you cause for sport—on the edge of my sword."

"No, you mistake me—I make no sport. 'Twas common of me to goggle so, but I'd not looked to see the prophecy fulfilled in a Saxon."

"Prophecy?"

"Aye. My sister and I are on a quest. We were sent thereon by Holy Mother Angharad. She prophesied that we'd be aided by a man who was of our kind yet not of our kind. 'Twas surely you she meant."

"You expect me to help you?"

"I hope it may be so."

"Why should I?"

Llary smiled. "Because 'tis a great adventure. Mother Angharad said we would face perils and fearful enemies, and fight through to our goal hardly if at all. Unless you're not the man I think you, you cannot turn your back on such."

Amlodd smiled in return. "I feared you'd offer me my life in exchange. Had you done so I'd have laid on with iron in an eye's blink. But this—this is, I must grant, a worthy offer. Yet 'tis a strange one, and I must think on it."

He leaned down, took the skirt of his tunic and used it to wipe the blood from his sword. Poor use for a good shirt, but it was spoiled with rips and his own blood, and these Pict savages they'd killed wore no clothing for him to use.

Amlodd was thinking that anything that helped the Britons must harm the Danes. A common enmity for the Picts was not reason enough to make an alliance. On the other hand, the Danes were servants of Feng, who'd tried to kill him. Yet still they were his comrades, and he'd stood with them in the shield wall. Yet again . . .

Fat drops of rain began to plop down through the leaves overhead.

"I know where we can shelter," said Llary.

That decided Amlodd.

When in doubt, get out of the rain.

Llary and Elen went together behind a tree and came out with each a leather pack. Between them they carried a bronze cauldron, about the size for cooking in a great house, all hammered out in twining patterns and men's faces.

"What's in that?" asked Amlodd.

"The treasure of Britain," said Llary. "Touch it and die."

They trudged up a steep forest path into a broad meadow. The path led across the meadow to a large stone building, or rather a group of buildings together in a square like a Danish steading, with the buildings at one end and a stone wall enclosing most of three sides. The wall was falling and the buildings' tile roofs had collapsed, but there was likely to be some kind of shelter there.

" 'Tis a *villa*—one of the farms of the old Romans," said Llary. As they spoke lightning struck a tree nearby and set it ablaze. They sprinted across the meadow under a roiling gray sky, wet to the skin.

They entered through the gateway and across the yard. They went under a pillared porch and inside one of the buildings. Llary and Elen set the cauldron down in a corner. With leaves and sticks gathered from the courtyard and the room itself they built a fire, lighting it with flint and steel. The floor was made of small squared stones, arranged in patterns.

"It makes a picture," said Llary, holding a flaming stick up to show him the floor. The small stones had been laid out to form a hunting scene, a group of men on horses with spears pursuing a wild boar.

"The Romans were great folk," said Llary. "We try to steward the things they taught us, especially the Faith. 'Tis what we fight for. That and vengeance."

He gestured and led them into an adjoining room. "There should be another such here," he said. But when he kicked the leaves and trash away with his toe, there was only plaster there. "It looks as if they covered this one over. I wonder why," he said.

They went back into the first room, and the two Britons brought cheese from their packs and they all ate.

"The day's far gone," said Amlodd. "We won't find better shelter for the night than this."

"We've but two blankets," said Llary. "We'll warm ourselves best if we huddle." And so they did that, in the light of the dying fire. Elen made sure she lay on Llary's other side, away from Amlodd.

Amlodd dreamed as he slept. He dreamed that a man in strange clothing, all black with a white band around the neck, stood over him, pointing to the next room, where the floor had been plastered over. He rose and went into it. In his dream he could see, in spite of the night. He did not see the man in black again.

He knelt on the floor and drew his belt knife. With it he jabbed at the plaster floor, chipping and making a small storm of bits that made him blink. Slowly the old plaster came to pieces. He uncovered a small section of the stone picture beneath, then larger sections came loose which he pried up and pulled away with his fingers. At last the entire picture was revealed, but he did not look at it. He went back to his sleeping place.

They all slumbered hard, but Amlodd woke again before the others, at the first light. Llary snored, over Elen's steady breathing. The brother and sister leaned together and Amlodd threw off his blanket end and crept away from them. The thought crossed his mind that he could cut their throats while they slept, but he did not entertain it.

He was mad to know what was inside the cauldron. It was dim in the room; the others would waken shortly.

Very, very slowly and carefully he crept toward the corner where the two had left the vessel. Very slowly he lifted the piece of silk that covered whatever was inside.

He saw a man's head there.

The head rolled its eyes up and looked at him.

He dropped the silk and fell back. An arm came around his neck like a snake. He felt the point of a knife at his throat.

Then the arm and the point were gone, and he swung around to see Llary struggling with Elen. Llary twisted her wrist and her knife clattered to the floor. She spat angry words and stomped into the next room.

"Be warned about my sister," said Llary, pointing at Amlodd. "She's a warrioress of the old Sisterhood. She's fast and she's strong, but not as strong as you. She knows this. Therefore she will not hesitate. If she thinks you threaten her, she will kill you in a moment."

"I did naught to threaten her."

"You profaned the treasure. She and I are sworn to protect it and bear it to its place. To hinder us is as much as to threaten."

"What magic's in that cauldron?" Amlodd cried. "The head looked at me."

Llary looked away. "You mistake," he said.

"I don't mistake. I saw it."

"The room is dark. I can scarce see your eyes now."

"I see your eyes well, when you've the honesty to look plain at me. And I saw his well enough."

"'Tis dark yet. You're weary."

"All I'm weary of is being lied to. But have it your way."

Elen's voice came from the next room. The two men went through the door to look at the stone picture, now revealed in a ruin of plaster shards.

"Who uncovered this?" asked Llary.

"I suppose 'twas me," said Amlodd, only now remembering.

"When was it done?"

"In the night. I dreamed I did this. I must have done it in truth." He drew his belt knife. "I spoiled the point."

"You did this without remembering?"

"I was weary."

"This is an evil thing," said Llary.

The picture showed a hill under a starry night sky. On its top was a ring of standing stones, about half the height of a man.

One stone was taller than the others, and on its top stood a man in a tunic with legs bare. He held a sickle in his right hand, raised high. He looked upward, toward the figure of a monstrous goat-headed man, who towered over him, filling a third of the sky.

" 'Tis only a man calling on his god," said Amlodd. "Gods are gods. There's no good or evil about them."

"You really believe this?" asked Llary, looking him in the eye. "This god is called Dublugh; he is a destroyer. Should you ever look on his face, you'll know what evil is."

Amlodd went out into the courtyard and walked by himself in the dew.

He did not speak of the thing that troubled him most.

He wanted Elen.

For some reason, from the moment she'd tried to kill him, he'd felt a stiffening in his manhood like the aching ones he'd had when he was fifteen. He did not want her to see this. He felt it would give her power.

Why should it excite him that a woman tried to cut his throat?

If it was so, then what he saw next should have brought him off then and there, for through the gate of the villa came a party of twenty women, all dressed in plaids kilted up over the knees, armed with spears and shields and bows and arrows. They stood in the yard looking about them, but their leader, a tall black-haired woman, stared directly at Amlodd.

Amlodd slipped back through the doorway and told Llary and Elen what he'd seen. Before he finished speaking, the warrioresses were upon them. Llary and Elen did their best to protect the treasure cauldron, but were soon overpowered. Their foes used the butt ends of their spears, and so took them without great injury.

Their hands were bound, and a single rope looped around their necks. The warrioresses marched them out of the villa and into the forest. They brought the cauldron without examining it, as if they already knew its contents.

"These are of the sisterhood," said Llary to Amlodd as they trudged under the trees.

"Like Elen? They didn't act as friends."

"Who said they were friends? Are you and I friends because we're both warriors? There are British sisters and Pictish sisters; Christian sisters and pagan. These are Picts, and pagan. Look for no kindness from them."

They stopped at last, for no reason Amlodd

could tell, and the sisters tied them to trees and left them there, taking the cauldron away. Only a woman with a spear guarded them. Amlodd did not fear to speak before her—he doubted she knew Danish.

"What do you suppose they're doing?" he asked.

"They've kept us living for some reason," said Llary. "I'd wager for sacrifice."

"Sacrifice?"

"These women live by blood, and worship the same."

Amlodd struggled harder. His was no mean strength, but the more he tugged and twisted, the tighter the ropes grew.

Hours passed and the captives grew hungry and thirsty, stung by insects they could not shoo away. The sun crossed the sky and waned, and the shadows reached eastward to bruise the day. As the first stars opened their eyes, six of the sisters returned and unbound them, prodding them with their spears along a path. The path took them uphill, and they emerged onto a bald summit.

Amlodd gasped. He knew this place.

"This is the hilltop in the stone picture I uncovered," he said to Llary.

"It stands to reason. 'Tis a holy place in the neighborhood," Llary replied. "The folk who made the picture were heathen as these. Heathen as you."

The tall dark leader of the sisters shouted commands, and her followers jumped to bind Amlodd and Llary hand and foot, pushing them off their feet to fall on the ground. Elen they bound only by the hands, leading her to a stone table at the center of the ring, made of a flat slab atop two short pillars. They made her lie on it.

"Oh, God," said Llary. " 'Tis the virgin sacrifice."

"Elen's a virgin?" asked Amlodd.

"Of course."

"What will they do?"

"They'll drain her blood for the captain to drink. They think there's power in a virgin's blood, to rouse a prophetic fit."

"We can't let that happen."

"No need to say that."

They both struggled till their wrists bled, but had no better luck than before.

The sisters bound Elen with long ropes, around and around her body and the table, fixing her to it. They laid a wooden pole under her shoulders and bound her hands to each end, so that her arms were stretched wide. The dying day bled red like a shirt about an arrow wound. The sisters built a bonfire.

Into the circle walked two young warrioresses, singing and carrying in four hands a spear longer than usual. It had been steeped in blood, which ran down the shaft and onto their hands. When they reached the stone table, they went silent a moment and stared at Amlodd and Llary. Amlodd felt as if something was expected from someone, but he had no idea what or whom.

The song resumed and the first pair was joined by two further warrioresses, who carried a platter. On it sat the head Amlodd had seen within the cauldron. Its eyes looked all about, sunken and miserable. The two bearers went to stand beside the spear bearers and set the platter on a low stone nearby. Again they went silent and stared at Llary and Amlodd.

Then came two more singing sisters, carrying Llary and Elen's cauldron. Another silence, another look, and the song began yet again.

At last came the dark captain. She approached the table and raised a bronze sickle. The singers ceased. She turned to Llary and Amlodd and stared at them, longer than the others. Seemingly disappointed, she beckoned to the women who bore the cauldron, and they set the vessel on the ground beneath Elen's outstretched right arm.

The captain took the sickle, and with it she slashed at Elen's arm. Elen cried out, and a flow of bright blood arced from her wrist into the cauldron.

The singers raised their voices once more.

"Damn these heathen, horse-eating, painted harlots!" cried Llary.

"Why did they stare at us?" asked Amlodd. "What did they want?"

"I've no idea. Can't you do anything to get free?"

"I'm trying no less than you."

One of the sisters noticed what they were

doing and gave each of them a whack with her spear butt.

Then the music rose and the women began to dance. When you think of women dancing, you think of something lovely and winsome, but this was nothing such. There was no grace in this dance, no beauty. They footed it hunched and howling, like madwomen.

And ever and anon, when the path of sight was clear between them, Amlodd saw Elen staring toward her brother from her last, hard bed, and the pain in her dimming eyes wrung his heart. He'd seen death enough in his time without fear or pity, but never like this. He struggled with his bonds—the guard paid no further mind, having joined the dance herself—but got no more than senseless hands and the warmth of blood where it soaked through his clothes.

He saw another face as well, from time to time. The head from the cauldron sat, as chance would have it, facing him. When the dancers parted a moment, he could see the two eyes of the unbodied man staring into his. He fancied the eyes were trying to tell him something, but he could not guess what.

Then the flow of blood from Elen's wrist dwindled and ceased. Elen lay still and pale, her eyes fixed. A groan went up from Llary and he ceased struggling.

The captain of the sisters emerged from the whirl of the dancers and came towards them, the sickle in her hand.

She stood over Llary and spoke shortly to him. Llary screamed and arched himself up on his heels and the back of his head, then went limp and lay whimpering. Amlodd wondered to see so brave a man broken by a word.

With a sneer the captain turned her back on them, and strode to the stone table. One of the sisters dipped a cup of blood out of the cauldron, and the captain drank it. Then she raised the sickle in the air and began to shout. Amlodd did not understand, but he thought she was making her prophecy.

There was a space between two of the sisters' bodies through which he could see again the head on the platter. The head was still turned toward him, but it had turned its eyes toward the captain. It stared at her with a force he could almost feel.

She shouted loudly, bringing howls and shouts from the sisters. She lowered her voice to a whisper, and all fell silent to listen closely. Then she shouted again, and her harangue became something like a song. She waved her hands, and her sickle went flying over the sisters' heads.

It landed with a whack not two spans from Amlodd's ear. Amlodd started at the sound, and his eyes met those of the bodiless head, now staring straight into his again.

He did not hesitate. While the captain prophesied, the sisters had their eyes fixed on her. Quickly Amlodd wriggled to the sickle, which stood upright, its point buried in earth. He held his wrist bonds to it and began to saw at them, caring not for any injury to skin or sinew.

He soon had his hands free. He fumbled to cut his ankle bonds with nerveless fingers. Then he scrambled to free Llary, who lay like a dead man and did naught to help.

"We must get away!" he whispered to Llary.

"Leave me," came the reply.

"I could do naught for your sister. I'll not leave you here."

"I stay to die. 'Tis all that's left for me."

"What's happened to you, man? Where's your spirit gone?"

"Gone with my sister," said Llary, and he turned his face away.

For one moment Amlodd thought of making his escape and leaving this wretch to his fate, but he knew that would be a shameful act.

He looked at the dancers. It would not be long before they noticed he was free.

He looked at the captain.

He looked at the ring of stones.

He looked at the starry night sky.

He looked at the sickle he held. Lances of pain were jabbing at his hand as the blood returned, but he ignored that.

In a flash he knew what he must do. He wasn't sure of his plan, but it was the only one he could muster.

He ran behind the nearest stone, then around the outside of the ring until he came to the tallest stone of all. Taking a deep breath, he clambered to its top and raised the sickle high.

"*Dublugh! God of this place!*" he shouted. "I stand here in your ring with the sickle, and I call on you by name as they did in times past! Hear me and show yourself!"

And before his eyes, and the eyes of the wondering sisterhood, a mist appeared, which thickened into the bright body of a naked man with a goat's head and glowing eyes, as tall as five men.

The warrioresses screamed, took up their arms, and began to fall upon one another. One half killed the other half within a few minutes; then those who remained fell on one another. Within half an hour only the captain yet stood, and she was wounded so that she fell and died soon.

There remained only Amlodd, Llary on the ground, the dead woman on the stone and the living head on the platter.

Now I've brought him, Amlodd thought, *what will I do with him?*

The apparition solved the problem by giving something like a smile and turning to stride away through the forest, like a man through a field of grain. Amlodd watched his glowing form until it disappeared over a hill.

"What have you done?" cried Llary, who had risen and stood now unsteadily.

"I did what I must to save our lives."

"At what price, heathen? Do you know what Dublugh is?"

"You said he was a destroyer."

"Yes. A destroyer of love. He turns all human loves to hate, so that we slay our dearest friends and kinfolk. You saw what the sisters did to one another. Foolish foreigner—you've unleashed fire upon all Britain to save our miserable lives. When you go home to Saxland, you can boast to your friends. You Saxons have long yearned to destroy us. You've done it on your own. But don't think Dublugh will be content with destroying us!"

"Why were you and I spared?"

"Because you and I care no more for each other than for dog's sweat. If Elen had lived, I've no doubt you'd have seen us at each other's throats."

Amlodd leaped down from the stone. "I knew not," he said. "What can I do? There must be something."

Llary walked to the stone table and looked down on his sister's corpse. He picked up one of several abandoned spears and cut her bonds with it. He smoothed her hair with a trembling hand.

"What did the captain say?" Amlodd asked. "What word struck you like an axe-hammer back there?"

"I could have saved my sister," said Llary. "All I need have done is to ask them what they were about. They stopped several times to give me the chance to make the question, but I knew not the ceremony."

"That was a great cruelty. I'm sorry for your

sister, and for you. I'd have saved her if I could. But if there's aught we can do to stop this Dublugh, you must help me."

"First we bury Elen."

"Have we time?"

"We'll make time. When all is over, I'll see her conveyed to holy ground. If I or anyone yet lives in the land then."

They used the dropped spears to scrape a shallow grave, and placed the woman in it.

"We must set the head in the cauldron again," said Llary. " 'Tis drooping a little, but my poor sister's blood will revive it. If we can finish our journey in time, perhaps Dublugh may be stopped."

He looked around him. The dawn was rising. "Look," he said.

Amlodd looked and through the red light he could see smoke rising in the distance.

"Dublugh has begun his work."

They shouldered each a spear, took the cauldron with the head between them, and set out through the forest.

Llary led the way without hesitating at forks in the path. They walked through the day, not stopping to eat, for they had no food with them and no time to seek it.

As evening fell they reached open fields and a broad lake. They approached the wattle hut of a fisherman.

"Perhaps we can sleep in this house, and set out across the water at dawn," said Amlodd.

"We'll cross tonight. There's moonlight enough, and our errand will not wait."

Llary pounded on the door, and a skinny bearded man opened to him. Llary spoke to him in British, and at first the man shook his head angrily. Then Llary spoke the word 'Dublugh,' and the man's eyes went wide and he crossed himself. He bowed and went inside to fetch something, then led them down to the water. They got into his boat.

The man rowed them in silence and darkness, and soon they were far out on the water. Amlodd, who knew something of boats, cared little for this one. It was roundish, and made of hides stretched over a framework. He sat as still as he could, lest he tip the thing.

"Hold!" cried Llary.

They all sat with backs to the bow, as one does in a boat, but Llary had turned to see what was in the way.

Before them stood an unnatural thing—a wall of water, black and glittering with starlight as with jewels, blocking their passage like a cliff face.

Before this wall stood a woman, upheld on the water itself. She had long golden hair that waved in the breeze, though there was no breeze. She wore a gown of green, or perhaps of blue—Amlodd was unsure because of the darkness.

"Is this a ghost?" Amlodd whispered.

"Would that it were," said Llary.

"Llary, son of Casnar Wledig!" cried the woman. "You hold a thing that belongs to me! Yield it up and save your life!"

"I've no time to parley with you, Morrigan," cried Llary. "Let us by, as you love this land."

"And does such as you command me now?" Amlodd could feel the witch's anger, and her eyes changed hue from green to gray.

"I do not command; I would not presume. But Dublugh is loose in the land. We need the head now, or the land will be laid waste like Sodom and Gomorrah."

Morrigan's eyes shifted again to green. "Is it true?" she asked. "How came it to be?"

"This Saxon, all in ignorance, called him up."

"You'll pay for that, foreigner, if there's justice in the world," said Morrigan.

"Time enough for that if we live," said Llary. "Now give us way to the king's camp."

Until that moment, Amlodd had not known their goal. It seemed a perilous one for a Dane, but he would not shrink from it.

"Why do I understand your speech of a sudden?" asked Amlodd, amazed.

"I did it by a tongue-spell," said the woman. "I don't care to waste time with word-changing."

Morrigan waved her arm, and the wall of water subsided. She led the way, walking on the surface, as their boatman rowed them the rest of the way to shore.

There was a guard at the jetty. He bowed at the sight of Morrigan and Llary and conducted

them through the tents of the Britons' camp.
They entered a large timbered hall, not so different from a Danish one. At the far end was a
carved camp chair on a dais, and on it sat a tall,
powerful man with a black beard and a circlet
of gold around his temples. He looked familiar to Amlodd.

Llary son of Casnar Wledig did not stop to
greet his king. Instead he strode to the dais,
seized a sword from one of the warriors seated
there, and with it struck the king's head off.

It had been done so quickly, and was so
unexpected, that no one had moved to stop him.
Now every man leaped to his feet, and a hundred points were directed toward Llary.

"*Hold!*" cried Morrigan. "The king is not
dead!"

"What mean you, not dead?" cried a tall,
clean-shaven man.

"Look there!" said Morrigan, pointing at the
king's chair. The king's body sat as before, erect.
The chest rose and fell with living breath. No
blood spurted.

"What means this?" the man asked.

"'Tis my work, Cai," said Morrigan. "I took
my brother's head to keep it safe, and left a perfectly good one of my own making in its place."

Cai's jaw dropped. "Why would you do such
a thing?"

"He's my brother. I wished to protect him."

"By taking his head?"

"If I took it first, no one else could."

Cai threw his arms out. "Impeccable logic!" he said, bitterly.

"Has the head I gave you done ill?" asked Morrigan. "Have you been losing battles?"

"No, the war has gone well. But I'd wondered why he took such a sudden interest in gardening."

"I thought he ought to have one civilized passtime."

"And what should we do now?"

"The true head is in that cauldron. Let us make the procession and I will put it back in its place."

Within minutes all was arranged. The king's chair and body were moved to one side of the dais. A table covered with cloth of gold was set as an altar, a golden and ivory crucifix upon it between two golden candlesticks.

All sat quietly on the benches as the procession entered. Amlodd sat beside Llary.

In strode two young women carrying a spear.

Then two young woman came bearing the king's head on a platter.

Then two more bearing the cauldron between them.

Then came a Christian priest swinging a censor with incense smoke. He was a middle-aged man, beardless, the front of his skull shaved ahead of the ears.

"How is this different from the heathen's procession?" Amlodd whispered to Llary.

"Ssh."

"How is it different?"

"For one thing, we're not going to sacrifice anyone," said Llary through clenched teeth, and Amlodd was sorry he'd asked.

At last came Morrigan, who wore a white linen cloth over her head for some reason, and she took the head from the platter (one of the girls holding it nearly fainted), and carried it to the king's body. She raised it over its proper neck—

And suddenly the hall was a woodland glade.

The pillars of the hall were oak trees.

Its roof was leafy branches, the sky bright and blue above.

And where the gable of the hall had been, behind the altar, stood goat-headed Dublugh, yellow eyes blazing even in sunlight.

A great crying and roaring went up from the assembled company. Half the company drew their weapons against the other half. Shouts of "Traitor!" "Liar!" "Backstabber!" filled the air with the clash of steel on steel.

"Whoreson!" cried one man as he laid on his best friend with an axe. "You took the last honey cake when you knew I wanted it!"

"Scoundrel!" cried another. "I've seen the way you look at my wife!"

"You sold me a spavined horse!" shouted another as he struck his brother-in-law's head off.

Dublugh, looking on, only laughed at them. The women ran in terror, and of the warriors only Amlodd stood unattacked, having no friend to fight, though he began to have hard thoughts about Llary.

Meanwhile the priest stood his ground, shouting in his strange tongue, holding up a small image of his god on a tree.

Dublugh stretched his hand toward the priest, mouthing words in a secret tongue of his own. The priest went pale, and blood began to gush from his nose. But he did not cease his words.

All around, men were falling at the hands of their friends and kinsmen.

Dublugh's eyes widened, and he roared even more loudly at the priest. His outstretched hand became a kind of tentacle, like a squid's.

Blood began to gout from the priest's ears. His voice faltered, but he stood firm and spoke on.

Dublugh's body began to sprout more tentacles, and scales appeared all over him. He waved the tentacles wildly, and the earth shook with his raging.

Blood began to well from the priest's fingernails, and from the places where he'd cut himself shaving his face and head.

The men who had killed their friends and brothers turned now on others who had killed friends of their own.

Amlodd thought he saw something genuinely like fear in the god's eyes.

"*Llary, son of Casnar Wledig!*" roared Dublugh.

Llary struck down a fellow Briton and turned to face the god.

"Behold!" said Dublugh.

And there, before them all, stood Elen, Llary's sister.

"I've the power to raise the dead," said Dublugh. "Call off the god man and I'll give her back to you."

For one moment Llary stood considering, staring at his sister. Even the priest went quiet for that moment.

Llary's eyes were mad. "I'd only have to kill her!" he cried. "Priest, say on!"

The priest, holding his image in bloody hands, took up his words again, and Dublugh vanished with a cataract of sound that shook every one of them off his feet.

Then all was silent, and those who lived looked about them. They were in the shadowed hall once again. Amlodd and Llary stood. The priest lay dead, white as Elen's corpse. About a dozen other men stood, realizing in a cold awakening what they had done under Dublugh's power.

At last came Morrigan, her brother's head under her arm. Without ceremony she set the head on her brother's shoulders, and the king rose to take possession of what remained of his court.

And so it was that Amlodd Orvendilsson broke the power of the Britons and cut off their battle strength in a single day.

❧ CHAPTER XVI ❧

Sean entered the great hall with his shoulders slumped, the picture of a man who knows himself condemned. He went to sit on one of the chairs at the table.

"Don't sit on that side; I want you all on this side," Eric said to him. Eric was still dressed like a Sunday School-book Jesus. He took his seat at the center, and the rest of the troupe sat up and down from him.

"Let's get this show on the road," said Howie.

"Why the hurry?" asked Eric. "Have a drink, everyone."

They all dutifully sipped from the goblets set at their places.

"Water?" asked Bess. "Is this in memory of Peter?"

"Drink again."

"Wine," said Diane. "Cute."

Sean took the liquid down the wrong pipe, and Bess had to pound his back to stop him coughing.

"Why are you playing with me?" Sean asked Eric when his fit was over.

"Playing with you?"

"You're going to kill me for sentencing your father to death. Well do it, damn you to Hell, and get it over with. I'm a king. At least let me go with a little dignity."

"What makes you think I'm going to kill you?"

"You're trying to change the end of the play. I die at the very end in Shakespeare. Killing me now would break the play."

"Not killing you at all would do the same."

A little flame of hope lit in Sean's eyes. "That's true," he said.

"He wanted to kill me!" said Howie.

"Can't hardly blame him for that," said Eric.

"What do you mean?"

"I mean I've wanted to kill you for a long time myself. I might still do it. Sean here hasn't done me any harm. But you have."

Howie went pale. "When did I ever do you any harm?"

Eric's eyes went soft for a moment. "Do you remember the day I smashed the dishes?"

"Yes . . ."

"Mom's good china, the ones she inherited from Grandma?"

"You were . . . very upset that day."

"I sure was. And you know why?"

"We were never sure."

"Because you didn't stop me."

"What?"

"I broke one plate by accident. Nothing happened. I broke another plate on purpose, just to see if anything would happen then.

"I wanted to know you'd protect me from myself. I wanted to know you wouldn't let me do everything I was able to do. I was afraid of what I was able to do. But you wouldn't stop me. I broke every dish and cup and saucer, one after another, praying all the time you'd do something about it. But you stood there like morons. It was then I knew I didn't have anybody to protect me. I knew I was all alone in the world."

"Did you want us to spank you?"

"It would have made me feel better."

"You're talking crap."

Eric's eyes blazed and thunder blasted somewhere outside. "You don't get to talk to me that way," he said. "You had your chance to pull me up short, but that's over now. Now I'm in charge."

"Of—of course. But you were joking. I know you were joking."

"Joking about what?"

"About killing me."

"Why do you think I'm joking? Didn't I kill Mom?"

Howie nearly fell off his chair. "Don't say that, Eric. Not even to be funny."

"Nothing funny about it. I killed her."

Howie sat with his mouth open.

"She was taking one of her vodka naps. I got one of those thin plastic bags—you know, the ones you're not supposed to let kids play with— and I put it over her head and sealed it down with duct tape around her neck. I thought I might have to tape her wrists, but no. She just lay there and suffocated real nice for me.

"Then I had to figure out what to do with the body. I remembered the Flattenbagger, that thing that sucks the air out of a bag so you can pack things small. I put her in the biggest size bag and attached the vacuum cleaner. I sealed it up good and stored her under my bed. She's still there."

"Under your bed . . ." said Howie.

"Yeah. Funny, ain't it? Everybody looking for the body all over the state, and she's under my bed all the time."

"But—why?"

"She was gonna leave us."

"Leave us? No, you're wrong—"

"What the hell did you know? You were never home. She had plane reservations. She was running to Mexico with her boyfriend."

"Boyfriend?"

"Do you know what a clue is? Ever have one?"

Howie sat staring at his hands in front of him. "I thought you loved your mother," he said tonelessly.

"I did. I loved her more than anybody. That's why I couldn't let her leave. If she'd left, I'd have had to hate her. But dead, I can still love her. Love's the important thing. You always told me that."

Howie said, "My god. My god."

"You're my father. You're supposed to be in charge and you're supposed to be smarter than me. You kind of screwed up, didn't you?"

Howie said nothing.

"I'm glad I didn't kill you. This is better."

Everyone was staring at Eric. "What you lookin' at?" he asked, and everyone looked away.

"Listen, I'm a pretty cool god," he said. "I'm not gonna lay a whole bunch of Ten Commandments on you. You want to have fun, have fun—it's cool by me. But you don't get to judge me either. I killed my mom—so what? Maybe that ain't right for you, that's cool. But don't go telling me what's right for me. Here's Rule One—I'm God."

"And if we don't please you, you'll do the same to us as you did to your mother," said Bess. Her face was pale but her voice didn't quiver.

In reply Eric stretched a hand out, palm down, fingers extended toward her. Bess's hands went around her throat in a choking gesture. She rose in the air, feet kicking like a person hanging.

She hung in the air a moment, then dropped as Eric opened his hand.

"I'll kill you later," he said as Bess got up from the floor, groaning. "Right now I've got other things planned.

"I've been thinking a lot about what kind of god I want to be.

"I saw a movie once about old religions. They had some really cool ones, where everybody screwed during church. That's the kind of god I want to be. I want to be a party god.

"You people ever try an orgy?"

They all looked at each other, and Diane went red in the face.

"I'd rather not," said Diane.

"I don't give a flying fart what you'd rather not," said Eric with a smile. "Rosey, mosey on over here by me."

When it was all over, Rosey Schmitt stumbled out of the castle and into the clean air. The sea smelled fresh and wholesome, and she thought she was polluting it all with her presence.

She tried to forget what had just happened. She had found herself the center of a lot of attention, and had vague recollections of various body parts rubbing on and in her—mostly male but not exclusively. She even thought that at one point she'd felt a tentacle along her leg.

She'd had bad sex before. She'd never had horrific sex. She had a sudden, vivid recollection of a boy named Georgie, a boy who'd loved her and touched her gently. She'd hurt Georgie, and her throat twisted in a sob to think of it.

As if in response to her memory, there was a soft touch on her shoulder and she turned to look into Georgie's face.

"It can't be," she said.

"It isn't," said the figure. "I'm one of the servants. But I pitied you, and took this form to give you comfort."

Almost without intending to, she threw herself into the familiar arms. "It's so horrible here!" she sobbed.

"I know, I know."

"Nobody cares about me here. I'm just a playtoy. And I'm next in line to die!"

"No, no, baby."

"Oh, Georgie, I need you so bad. Will you hold me awhile?"

Together they sank into the heather. It was soft and smelled fresh. "Georgie" held her awhile, then began to caress her. She responded hungrily. They coupled in the heather and she slept, comforted.

When she woke it was late in the afternoon. She looked at the face of the man who held her in his arms.

"Randy!" she said. "Where did you come from? Where is—"

"Sweet, sissy little Georgie? He was never here. It was me all the time."

"Why?"

"You're a stupid, ugly cow. And you're a lousy lay." He slapped her and vanished.

Rosey wailed as her soul hemorrhaged. She stumbled to her feet.

She took the path to the sea cliff.

❖ CHAPTER XVII ❖

A party of people waited at the jetty when the ship sailed in from its voyage to Britain. Will recalled reading that the Norse had not perfected sailing navigation until sometime in the eighth century, but the ship he was in seemed to have managed just fine. *Well, we knew they invaded Britain,* he thought. *How did we think they got there? On foot?*

Chief among the greeters was Gerda, Amlodd's mother. Gerda gave Will the first drink from a huge horn of ale she (or technically the thralls) had brought. There was actually a chorus of young girls there to serenade them.

After his drink Will hugged Gerda hard. He never wanted to let her go. This woman loved him—wholeheartedly and without stint. He had missed her badly in Britain. It flashed in his mind that he would never go back to his own time, even if he got the chance. There was nothing for him in the twenty-first century compared to this.

"It will be tonight," whispered Gerda. "Everyone will be drinking deeply, and I've seen to it that the ale is specially strong."

When he finally disengaged, he saw Katla standing by herself. He went and hugged her too, and the look in her eyes washed his soul like a bath of clean water. "I missed you, brother," she whispered.

"And I you, I you," Will answered. Afterwards he had to rub his eyes to be rid of the tears. He dared not let the men see them.

Ponies waited to carry them to the village. They entered the great hall to shouts and laughter, and Amlodd thought Feng greeted him with the look of a man who'd eaten bad shellfish.

There was much food and much to drink. Will was not very hungry, and he had too much sense to drink heavily in the presence of his enemies.

But he had to hide that good sense, especially while Feng watched him.

He called for a thrall boy and asked him to fetch him sticks from the woods. "Fresh sticks," he said. "Shortish ones. As many as you can find. A sackful."

When the boy brought them, Will took his belt knife and began to carve, cutting out a section in the center so that he had long "C"-shaped pieces, with sharp ends pointing inwards towards the cutout.

When he'd cut about a hundred, he got up and walked between tables down to the hearthway, where he sat in front of the long-fire. He held the sticks, one by one, in the fire, to char them black and harden them.

"Not eating and drinking, nephew?" Feng called to him.

"The food tastes of blood. The ale tastes of iron," said Will.

"What are you doing with those sticks?"

"I'm making fishhooks."

"For what purpose?"

"To catch a murder-fish."

"What's a murder-fish?"

"*A man may fish with the worm that hath eat of a king, and eat of the fish that hath fed of that worm.*"

This would be a hard thing, he thought. *But it must be done.* He'd found a home, and here he would stay. But he must be rid of his enemies. It was him or them, to live or die. The real Amlodd's way would be as good as any.

This was not something Will Sverdrup would have been able to do. But he was no longer Will Sverdrup. He had Will's knowledge and memories, but he wore Amlodd's body, and the body has its own memory. He wondered what it was that made a person a person. It didn't seem to be the mind alone, or the body alone. He remembered a phrase from somewhere—"*neither dividing the essence nor confusing the persons*"—or something like that. What was that from? Not

Shakespeare. He wondered if he wasn't losing Will Sverdrup bit by bit—if Will would be subsumed under Amlodd in time. Well, what of it? Amlodd was a simpler and happier man than Will had ever been.

He grew aware of someone standing near him and looked up to see Katla there.

"May I sleep in your bed tonight?" she asked.

"You know we mustn't do that."

"I don't mean sleep with you. You'll be feasting through the night with the household, of course. I just want to sleep in your bed. I slept there all the time you were gone. It made me feel close to you."

"Surely, if it means so much to you."

"Thank you, brother. I love you." Katla stooped to kiss him, then ran off.

It took him some time to char the hooks to his satisfaction. Through the night there were stories and songs, and more songs and stories in the hall. The roar of the feasters grew louder as they drank, then softer as one by one they passed out, snoring. Gerda had been right about the ale. He'd seen this crowd feast before, and had never seen them knocked out so quickly.

Even Feng lolled in his high seat, in spite of his famous endurance.

They all slept.

Every one of them.

It was frightening being the only one awake in the room. It reminded him of when he was a boy, tiptoeing around the house while his mother slept off one of her binges.

The memory worked inside him like a strong drink of his own. He shivered from head to foot, and was afraid he'd fall into the fire. He looked at Feng. He looked at the sleeping warriors.

I can't do this, he thought. *I'm Mrs. Sverdrup's boy.*

He trudged heavily out of the hall, through the entryway, and into the yard.

Gerda stood there, wrapped in a shawl. Silently she took him by the arm and led him into a shadowed place under a roof overhang.

"Is it done, my son?" she asked. "Can we go ahead?"

He stood facing her. His arms hung at his sides.

"I can't do it," he said. "I'm sorry."

"They killed your father!"

"I'm sorry." He turned away without daring to look at her, and headed for his house.

He thought he heard a voice cry out. He thought he saw a shadowed figure running from his house.

The moment he entered the door he smelled the blood.

But he couldn't see anything inside.

He needed to see. He would not search that house with his hands.

He went back to the hall. Gerda was gone. He entered and seized one of the hanging oil lamps spiked to the pillars.

He carried the lamp, a bronze bowl on three chains, out and back to his house. He held it high.

Katla lay in his bed. She lay motionless, her eyes open. A pool of blood spread all around her. A wound under her heart hung open like a drunkard's mouth. There was another in her stomach.

For a long time he stood there, unmanned by the horror. A single thought ran through his mind in an endless loop—*For the rest of my life, I must see this sight whenever I close my eyes.*

As his reason returned, he asked himself, "Who could have done this? Why?"

He knew the answer at once—someone had been sent by Feng. It was his bed. He had been the target. He did not know how the mistake had been made, but the killer had come to do his job at the wrong time.

"Revenge" had always for him been a technical word—a description of a stock motive in a stock theatrical form. He had understood, vaguely, how one could want to kill someone who had killed someone he loved, but it had been theoretical to him. He'd honestly never cared enough for anyone to feel anger at losing them.

Until now.

Now revenge was a beast with particular scales and claws that lodged fishbone-wise in his gullet, fidgeting to escape by one outlet or another. He could no more hold his revenge in forever than an expectant mother could keep her baby in. It must come out. It would come out.

Why had he thought it impossible to do this thing? Nothing could be easier, more natural.

His hand went to his sword hilt. This was not the weapon he meant to use tonight, but it comforted him to touch it. *A man unarmed is no man at all,* he thought. He strode with sure steps toward the hall.

With all asleep, the thralls had cleared the tables away, leaving the warriors sprawled on the benches.

First of all he went to where Guttorm lay, propped against the wall. "You were ever my friend," he said. He took the big man under the armpits and lugged him outside, his heels dragging in the rushes. He lay him on a patch of grass some yards off, then went back in.

He climbed up on a bench and pulled down one of the woven tapestries that covered the walls. It ripped as it came loose from its hooks, but that was no matter.

He lay the first tapestry on top of one of Feng's bodyguards, one of those who'd tried to drown him at the seashore. He rolled the man up in the cloth. Then he went for his sack of hooks, which lay still by the fire, and used three of them to secure the loose end, making the roll a tight package.

He could see he wouldn't have enough tapestries for everyone. It would have to be the chief men, the most evil.

Feng himself, for starters.

He took a step toward the high seat, then noticed that the seat was empty.

"Looking for me, brother-son?" asked a voice from behind him.

Amlodd's instincts sent him leaping over the long-fire, away from the sweep of Feng's sword.

"Troll!" cried Feng. "Are you never where you're struck at?"

"You killed Katla!" Will shouted, fetching up against a pillar, whirling off it and drawing his sword.

"She was in your bed! Now you've brought the crime of killing a madwoman on me!" There was blood on his blade. Feng had killed already tonight.

"For one who's killed a brother, that ought to weigh but little," said Will. They faced each other from opposite ends of the fire—about eight feet apart. "But fear not. You'll not have to bear that burden long."

"You were never mad, were you?" asked Feng. He leaped up on the bench and took a spear and a shield from their brackets on the wall. He cast the spear at Will, who avoided it, but it gave him time to rush to Will's end of the hearth.

Feng having the shield advantage, Will retreated rapidly, looking from side to side for something with which to defend himself. He caught up a hand axe that lay beside a warrior. He could use its haft to ward sword blows—until it got chopped through. It left his fingers exposed, but it was the best he could find close by.

"It did not need to end like this," said Feng, striking out. "You could have been jarl after me."

"You should have made up your mind. Kill me or embrace me. You kept shifting your course." Will made a sweep at Feng's legs, but Feng leaped over it. He was doing well for an old man who'd drunk too much. As he came down he aimed a chopping blow at Will's head, which Will fended at the cost of a big chunk of axe haft.

At the risk of exposing his back, Will leaped to the bench and took a shield of his own from the wall. He sensed Feng close behind him, and swung the shield over his back by its shoulder strap, feeling the shock as Feng's sword hammered it.

He leaped, planted his feet against the wall and pushed off, bulling into Feng with the shield and falling atop him. Feng fell onto the bench; Will tumbled over him and came up on his feet in the hearthway. He spun and struck at Feng, who rolled out of the way.

Feng swept at his legs from that position, and Will jumped backward, which gave Feng a chance to get up. Now he was above Will, and he aimed a downward blow, which Will caught on his shield.

Will swung back, then hopped up on the bench. The bodies and sitting benches left them little room to maneuver, and soon they were both back down in the hearthway.

Feng swung a mighty blow, and instead of warding with his shield, Will ducked under it. He was standing in front of one of the high seat posts, and Feng's sword bit deeply into the carved belly of the god Njord. The sword stuck there and Feng let go of it, his hand numbed by the shock.

Will struck at him, but Feng still had his shield. Will's sword glanced off it, and as its momentum swung him around, Feng leaped onto the bench to seize a sword that hung near the high seat.

As Will followed him up, Feng turned to face him and made to draw the sword.

He could not draw it.

It was Amlodd's father's sword, riveted in its sheath.

He had no time to raise his shield again before Will's blade fell on his head.

As the death blow fell, Feng said, *"Orvendil."*

Will stood over him, chest heaving. He wondered whether this was how it should feel. He was uncertain how he did feel.

No time to worry about that.

He left Feng lying in his blood. One by one he rolled the cruelest of the warriors in tapestries and secured them with his blackened hooks.

Then he pulled faggots from the long-fire and threw them into the rushes on the floor. That done, he walked outside.

He stood in the yard watching. It took a few

minutes. Smoke more than usual began to billow from the smokeholes at the gable peaks. Then smoke began to come from the door, and at last flames appeared.

"You have made me proud, my son," said a voice beside him and he turned his head to see Gerda.

"Are you satisfied, Mother?"

"Only one thing remains." She began to walk toward the building.

Will rushed to grasp her sleeve and stop her. "What are you doing?" he cried.

"I married my husband's murderer," said Gerda. "The shame of it is not to be borne. I suffered that life long enough to finish our vengeance. Now I go to our ancestors."

"You mean to die?"

"You knew this, Amlodd. I told you what I purposed when first we spoke of vengeance."

"I—I did not remember."

She kissed him. "Goodbye my son," she said. "You have been all I could have wished, and you will be a great jarl."

"I did it all for you—so we could be together!"

"You did it for your honor! I am proud and our ancestors are proud! Do not act the weakling, sobbing for your mama! I raised you better than that!"

Will wrapped his arms around her and clung tight. "No!" he shouted. "I cannot bear this again!"

Gerda freed herself and slapped his face. "You

shame me with your tears! Play the man, or bear my curse!" Will put his hand to his burning cheek, too shocked to do anything as he watched her walk into the blazing hall.

One or two men ran out, coughing and blinded, falling on their hands and knees and gasping at the clean air.

The house burned and the roof fell. Will's dreams collapsed with it, dissolved into their several elements, spirit and matter the same.

"All finished here?" asked a voice, and Will turned to see the red-eyed dead pastor.

"Nothing is left," said Will. "This whole country can burn for me."

"Then bear me company, and I'll show you your way home." He turned and walked toward Will's house, and Will followed. Will's house? Will's cell. No one lived by themselves in this time and place, save madmen and prisoners. Hamlet had been mad after all.

It was very dark through the open door, and Will was afraid to go inside where Katla yet lay. But when he was through he knew he was not in that same house. He was in no house at all. He felt around him and touched what seemed to be cold stone.

"Where am I?" he asked.

The ghost's voice said, *"But that I am forbid*
    To tell the secrets of my prison-house,
    I could a tale unfold whose lightest word

> *Would harrow up thy soul, freeze thy*
> *young blood,*
> *Make thy two eyes, like stars, to start*
> *from their spheres,*
> *Thy knotted and combined locks to part*
> *And each particular hair to stand on end,*
> *Like quills upon the fretful porpentine. . . ."*

"What is that supposed to mean?" Will scrabbled at the wall, trying to find his way back where he had come. There was no such way.

"I am Hamlet's father!" said the ghost. "With your help I have altered the past! The true Hamlet's spirit is trapped in another world. His body is trapped here, with you, separate from the spirit forever! For all any man can say, Hamlet died in the fire on the night of his vengeance, not so differently from the play!

"Do you see my triumph? I have reshaped history to Shakespeare's pattern! If you were to return to the future—which you shall not—you would find there was no Shakespeare at all— his ancestors died in the great death let loose by Dublugh. Thus I have fulfilled Shakespeare and destroyed him at a stroke, making his plot mine!

"In the new future I have made, instead of Shakespeare the great playwright, there is another master—one named Thomas Kyd—who wrote the great historical play of Hamlet."

"Kyd's a great author?"

"Someone has to be."

"And from that alternate future you stole a book, which you placed in my attic," said Will.

"My confederate Randy did the actual physical work, but the idea was mine," said the ghost.

"And I was right in my lectures. Hamlet's father was a demon."

"If you will."

"What's to become of me?"

"You are in the labyrinth of worlds. These passages contain doors opening onto a billion billion universes, some much like yours, some different, some unlike anything you can imagine.

"Spirits such as I, and the Old Ones, may pass through the doors and traverse the universes. You, of course, being mortal, cannot. You shall wander the passages for the rest of your natural life—which shall not be long, for there's nothing here for you to eat or drink. When you die, your soul may flit from world to world, and perhaps you can find one you'll be pleased to haunt."

"What have I ever done to you?"

"You flatter yourself. It's nothing personal. You happened to be the right tool in the right place; though you did make it easy for me by being a self-centered bastard with no ties of love to any human soul. Amlodd was more difficult to pry loose, but once you were out of your world, the Great Balances themselves helped pull him the opposite way."

"Wait—please, don't leave me here—I almost learned—"

The ghost was gone, and Will stood alone in the darkness.

He'd heard that the devil was a liar. Perhaps if he went . . . somewhere, did . . . something he could find an escape—if not to his own time and place, at least to somewhere where he could live.

A line of Horatio's went through his head:

> "What if it tempt you toward the flood,
>   my lord,
> Or to the dreadful summit of the cliff
> That beetles o'er his base into the sea,
> And there assume some other horrible
>   form,
> Which might deprive your sovereignty
>   of reason
> And draw you into madness? think of it:
> The very place puts toys of desperation,
> Without more motive, into every
>   brain . . ."

Well, what of it? Madness might wait further on; it could as well be waiting here. Madness might be rather welcome if it came to that. The less he understood at the end, perhaps, the better.

He set out and walked down the stone corridor, feeling his way, utterly blind in the perfect darkness. He walked carefully at first, alert for unexpected steps or pits or the dreadful summit of a cliff, but the passage only seemed to go on. It occurred to him that perhaps it was circular, and he was going around and around it. He almost stopped at that thought.

But what of it? It was something to do. Will Sverdrup might have curled up in a corner (if a corner had been available) and died, but Amlodd's body was conditioned for action.

So he walked. The passage was wide enough so that he could not quite touch both walls at once, and high enough so he could just reach the ceiling with his hand. The proportions did not change as he proceeded.

"Well, Sverdrup," he said to himself. "You've always wanted your own space."

He had no sense of time. He had no sense of progress. He imagined a foursquare treadmill, the walls and ceiling moving at the same speed as the floor, giving him the illusion of going somewhere when in fact he trod hamster-like in one place.

After minutes or hours he thought he saw a glowing ahead of him, to his right. He thought it might be only phosphors on his eyeball, but he broke into a run and found to his joy that the glowing enlarged as he approached. He came to what looked like a window in the wall, though to his touch it felt like the same cold stone. It was oval and about his own (or Amlodd's) height. He looked through it into the blessed light (which hurt his eyes at first) to see a party of Asians in conical straw hats toiling in a rice paddy.

He had never seen such beautiful humans. He

pounded on the "window" and tried to get the people's attention, but they showed no sign of hearing him.

He remembered something someone had said once, as a joke—"Statistically speaking, chances are you're Chinese." Which didn't hold anymore, since the Indians had overtaken them.

That reminded him of a talk he'd had with Peter Nilsson once, where he'd used the statistical quotation, and Peter had said, "Of course, statistically speaking, you're probably also Christian. It's the largest religion in the world, and the single belief system believed by more people throughout history than any other." That hadn't sounded right, but it turned out to be true, if you didn't consider paganism in general a coherent belief system, which Will didn't.

He could have stood and watched the rice pickers for the rest of his life—they were so human, so comforting, but he happened to look down the passage and see another glowing window. With reluctance he pulled himself away and went toward it.

This window was a disappointment. It showed open space, as it might be seen from a starship. It was pretty in a cold sort of way, but he was hungry to look at people. He looked back toward the last window, but before he went back there he turned to check further down the passage. Yes, it looked as if there were more windows. He'd try them.

One by one the windows led him further on.

Some were disappointments—empty landscapes or underwater views, without form, and void.

But others showed people—black people, white people, brown people of various cultures and, apparently, various historical periods. He saw what he thought were ancient Sumerians through one window, and another showed a nineteeth-century war, though he couldn't make out who was fighting. He didn't linger long at that window. How could anyone kill something so precious as a human being? "Don't waste them!" he cried. "Send them to me! Even the ugliest, the dullest and most exasperating! Just let me have some human company!"

But they did not hear. They continued their mindless vandalism of flesh, and he turned dejected to see what the next window offered.

This one was a shock. He saw himself, talking to Ginnie in the parking lot.

"Don't let her go, you cretin!" he shouted to himself. "Do you understand what it means to be alone? Why would anyone *choose* to be alone?"

But nothing changed from what he remembered, and Ginnie turned and walked away. Will turned too, and went to the next window.

This one showed what seemed to be ancient Aztecs at work in a cornfield.

Then there was a Russian family, slowly eating a meager meal in a cold house. It looked beautiful to him.

Next came another scene from his own life. It was another scene with a girlfriend. She was someone he'd dated in college. He couldn't remember her name.

"Something's going on here," he said. "Two scenes from my life out of an infinite cosmic timeline—the chances against that are off the chart. Someone is selecting these scenes for me.

"That means I'm not really alone."

The thought was like food and drink. He felt strong and hopeful for the first time. He rushed to the next window.

This was an ugly scene. A man in an old-fashioned bedroom was beating a little girl with a razor strop. Will could not hear anything, but he could imagine the girl's screams as the man, red-faced and probably drunken, struck her again and again on her bare bottom, raising welts and blisters and blood at last. Finally he finished and stumbled out, leaving the girl to weep facedown on her bed.

Will found himself weeping too.

"Terrible, isn't it?" said a voice, and Will turned to see a tall man dressed in the Danish style. He had a long white beard but a strangely young face.

Without thinking about it, he fell to his knees and embraced the old man's waist. "God bless you!" he sobbed. "God bless you for being here. Please don't leave me alone again."

"I will not leave you alone. Be easy, lad. Now listen and answer me. What do you think of what you've just seen?"

"The man and the girl?"

"Yes."

"It's terrible. How can anyone treat a child like that?" Will got to his feet again, trembling.

"What would you think if I told you the child was your mother?"

Will shivered. "That's not true. My grandfather was the kindest man who ever lived."

"Who told you this?"

"It's just the truth."

"Did you ever meet your grandfather?"

"No. He died before I was born."

"So who told you he was kind?"

"My . . . mother, I guess."

"And did your mother never tell a lie?"

Will shook his head. "I can't believe this."

"This little girl you see crying here—she was made to lie all the time she was growing up— to pretend that her father was not a drunk; to pretend that her family was happy. She learned that that was how you kept the peace and made a family work. She learned that you dealt with your own pain by hurting those weaker than you."

Will leaned against the window and stared at the weeping girl.

"What would you do if you could pass through that window?" the old man asked.

"I think I'd kill that old man."

"That is the wrong answer. I could show you another window where he is beaten by his own father. Anger is like a snowball that rolls down a hill, growing larger and larger as it goes."

"So everyone is innocent."

"No, not at all. Everyone is guilty. Left to ourselves we will pass the evil along forever."

"How do we stop it then?"

"Not by killing. Killing is sometimes necessary, to protect the weak, but it does nothing to stop the evil. Rather, it makes it worse."

"How then?"

"Someone must place his body before the snowball, and take its shock, saying 'It stops here, with me.'"

"Such a man could easily die."

"As often as not, yes."

"I don't know if I could forgive some people. It goes beyond human power."

"What were you saying a few minutes ago? 'Send them to me! Even the ugliest, the dullest and most exasperating! Just let me have some human company!' At the time you thought all people were precious."

"You just said we were all evil."

"I did not say we were not precious."

"Cognitive dissonance. We hold two opposite opinions at once."

"Yours are opposite. Mine are only difficult. You will have to make up your mind how you feel about your fellow man."

"It's possible to know the right thing and yet not do it."

"More than possible. Common. Common as evil."

"Everybody lives with opposites, dissonance.

We keep one foot on one side, one foot on the other. I've always run from taking a stand on one side or the other. If I was going to choose a religion, I'd lean toward one of those Eastern ones, where they say nothing is 'either-or,' only 'both-and.' "

"That's not entirely true, you know," said the old man. "Those religions come down strong on one side in at least one of the great questions."

"What question?"

"The question of body and soul. Flesh and spirit. From the beginning, men have struggled to find a balance between the two, to reconcile their conflicting needs. The religions of which you speak deal with that struggle by coming down strong on the side of the spirit, claiming the flesh does not exist at all.

"Christianity, on the other hand, says 'both-and' to that particular question. Body is real, soul is real. God became man. The Word became flesh."

"No, no," said Will. "Christian belief goes against everything I've learned. There are many worlds. Every fork in time creates a new universe. Even strongly held fantasies, like Shakespeare's *Hamlet*, can become reality. What does that mean, if not that everybody's equally right in the end? Believing makes it so. You can't deny that."

The old man smiled. "You've worked out a broader view? Learned to see the larger picture?"

"Yes."

"There's a larger picture than that. Are you prepared to see some unpleasant things?"

"I saw my mother try to kill me. I saw Katla bloody and dead. I saw Gerda walk into the blazing hall. I think I can handle nearly anything now."

"Very well. Follow me." The old man turned and led him down the corridor to another window. He gestured for Will to look through it.

Will saw what appeared to be a hotel room, with most of the lights off. There was a bed there, somewhat rumpled. A tiny speck, like a flea, leaped about on the bedsheets. Will wouldn't have noticed it if it hadn't moved. In front of the bed a television stood. The light it emitted told Will that it was turned on, but he could not see what the screen showed. On the bedtables were many boxes of paper tissues. Used tissues lay scattered around the floor.

"What's this?" asked Will.

"Do you remember the story of a rich man— a very rich man from your time? One who ended as a hermit, living in a room like this, watching the same drama on that box again and again?"

"Yeah. He went crazy."

"What was the difference between him and you?"

"A few billion dollars."

"The wealth is nothing in itself. It's what the wealth buys that matters. What does wealth buy?"

"Most anything."

"Correct. So how is this man different from you?"

"He can get almost anything he wants."

"Very good. What does that mean for the kind of life he lives?"

"He can live any way he wants to."

"Excellent, excellent. And how did he choose to live?"

"He turned away from the world and from other people. He built his own prison and spent the rest of his life in it."

"Yes. And why?"

"Why? There were lots of reasons, I suppose— his childhood, his experiences, his disappoint-ments—"

"I'm looking for a simple answer."

"What simple answer?"

"He did it because he *could*."

"Because he could?"

"God is merciful to most people in this—He does not allow them to do everything they would wish. But a few unlucky ones get the power to shape their own lives according to their deep-est desires."

"Ultimate power corrupts absolutely."

"The words of a man who knew something of the world."

"What's your point?"

"What if all men had unlimited power to choose how they lived? Do you think they'd do better than this man?"

"I don't know. It's academic, isn't it?"

"It is not. It is the fate of every human. In life, there is hope of salvation, in that all, even the very rich like this man, are to some extent frustrated in their wants. Thus they have the chance to surrender their own ways to God's.

"In death, it is as you said—whatever you believe becomes real for you. But having one's own way is not the same thing as happiness. What do you think you are seeing through this window?"

"What you said. That billionaire in his hotel room. He must have gone to the bathroom or something."

"No. He's still there."

"I don't see him."

"Do you see that speck on the bedclothes?"

"Yes. . . ."

"That is he. This is not his earthly life. This is his eternity. He chose it while he lived, as all men do in one way or another; only because of his wealth he was able to purchase an installment on his eternity early. Why should it change once he died?

"That speck is what remains of him. In life he grew smaller and smaller, as he turned more and more from great concerns to selfish ones. In eternity he grows smaller yet, forever and ever.

"In his universe there is no love. There is no one to love. There is nothing but himself, and he grows more miserable as time goes on."

"Until he becomes nothing."

"He never becomes nothing. Nothing ever becomes nothing. Everything under God becomes more and more what it is, eternally. Every length can be halved, given a sharp enough knife. The knives of eternity are very sharp indeed."

"But at least it's what he wanted—" said Will. "It's not like fire and brimstone or devils with pitchforks—"

"He endured this life while he lived because he succumbed to fear and deadened himself with drugs. There are no drugs here, and no self-delusion. The one thing denied souls in eternity is the comfort of a lie. This man knows who he is, and what he might have been. He knows what was given to him, and how much is required of him. He knows where he could be now if he had been braver."

"Wait a minute, wait a minute," said Will. "Not everybody's like this guy. Some people sin out of love. If they get what they've chosen in eternity, they'll have love forever."

"Come and see," said the old man. He led the way to another window.

Through that window there was only darkness.

"There's nothing there," said Will.

"There's no light there at least," said the old man. "We need to shine some in."

He set the palm of his hand to the window, fingers spread. From the hand a cone of light stretched into the space, like a very wide flashlight beam.

"I still don't see anything," said Will. "It's just a black stone room. It's empty."

"Not quite. Look."

As the old man spoke, a small pink round thing, like a striated ball, bounced across the light beam.

"What's that?" asked Will.

"Better to ask, 'What are *they*?' although it's hard to know whether to say 'it' or 'they' at this point."

"So what is it? They?"

"That is a pair of lovers. They loved each other with a passion that would not be quenched. They left their homes, their families, their responsibilities. They defied convention and God Himself, to be together. They have what they wished. They are together forever now, inseparable. They were all the world to each other. Now each is the only world the other has, for all time."

Will watched for a while, as the ball rolled and caromed and bounced about the cell. "Still, if they love each other . . ." he said. "And eternal sex can't be too bad."

"Would you like to hear what they say to one another?"

"They talk?"

"For now. A time will come when they dwindle to a point where they can't speak—or rather they can, but they won't. But at this point we may listen."

He set his other hand against the window, and

the voices came. They were high-pitched voices, as if insects had speech.

"*You never loved me like I loved you!*"

"*Like you loved me? You know what I gave up for you? And for what?*"

"*I gave you the best years of my life!*"

"*You never understood me!*"

"*As if you understood me? Do you know how much you hurt me with your sarcasm and your sulky moods?*"

"*If you'd have really loved me, I wouldn't have had any sulky moods!*"

"*That's just like you! You want me to make everything right for you, and my needs can take care of themselves!*"

"*I did everything I could to meet your needs! Was it my fault you were neurotic?*"

"*Yes! If you'd really loved me, I wouldn't have been neurotic!*"

"*And if you'd loved me you, wouldn't have demanded the moon and stars!*"

"*You promised me the moon and stars!*"

"*And you promised me we'd always be happy if we had each other!*"

"*We would have been happy if you'd really loved me!*"

"*Loved you? You never loved me!*"

The old man took his hand away.

"It just goes on like that," he said. "You get the idea."

"They got what they wanted?"

"'*Where your treasure is, there will your heart*

be also.' You may have whatever you wish, but if you wish for that which is not food, you must bear to be forever hungry."

"And for a man like me—one who flees other people, and love, and God, for fear of being hurt—what kind of Hell would there be for me?"

"Would you care to see?"

Will shivered. "I told you I could bear to see anything. I was wrong. That I cannot face."

"As you will."

Will hugged himself. "Who are you, old man? Why have you come to me here?"

"Do you remember a boy to whom you gave a piece of amber?"

"No. Yes. At the whale slaughter?"

"Just then, yes. The boy gave the amber to his father, who had been saving to buy his freedom and his family's. It gave him what he needed to accomplish this."

Will fell back against the window. "I've never heard such welcome words," he said. "You mean this is one of those situations where one good deed redeems a whole life? I didn't know I'd done enough good for that."

"And you haven't. This is not a reward for your virtue, such as it is. This was a mercy to me, because I wished to do it for you."

"Well . . . thank you."

"If I could show you a way back to your friends from the theater, what would you do?"

"I'd hold—I'd do—I wouldn't do—oh damn. You want me to tell the truth, don't you?"

"Very much."

"I don't know what I'd do. I want to say I'd be a different man; that I'd care for people and keep them close and keep Christmas in my heart every day of the year. I want to do that. But I'm not sure I can. I'm still Will Sverdrup, who's terrified of commitment."

"That is the right answer. If you'd made promises you couldn't keep, you'd have stayed in this passage for a very long time."

"I can promise even less if you like."

"The point is to recognize that you cannot rescue yourself."

"I can't."

"Then you must turn to One who can rescue you."

"Where is he? She? Whoever?"

"Look through that window."

It was another ugly scene there. It was an execution of the most brutal kind.

Will thought it was the most beautiful thing he had ever seen.

❊ CHAPTER XVIII ❊

There was a small church outside the castle wall. It hadn't been there the last time Amlodd had been in the neighborhood, but he'd grown used to buildings sprouting like flowers. He didn't recognize the building as a church—churches were outside his experience in Denmark—but he recognized it as an important building.

The building was surrounded by a low stone wall. From behind the wall he heard a noise as of digging. He went closer to investigate.

He entered through the churchyard gate and was surprised to see, through a low forest of tombstones, Bess Borglum digging a grave. He guessed it was a grave. This was not how they did graves in Jutland.

"Is this a grave?" he asked, going closer.

"Well, there you are," said Bess, taking a breather. "Where have you been?"

"Sleeping rough, in the forest," said Amlodd. "I never knew how uncomfortable it is for weaklings. I thought I'd freeze to death."

"It's good you're back."

"I thought you'd all be hunting me for killing Peter."

"With all the crap that's been going on here, one murder more or less seems forgivable. Assuming you were fooled. You *were* fooled, weren't you?"

"Do you think I've lied to you?"

"That's what I don't know."

"There was a time when I'd have struck you for saying that. But weak men must live another way. So I ask you to explain what you mean before I strike you."

"After you killed Peter, you spoke some lines straight out of the Hamlet play. How did you know them?"

"What lines?"

" *'Thou wretched, rash, intruding fool, farewell—'* Don't you know it's from the play?"

"I only spoke what came to my mind."

"It's from the play."

"Did this man whose skin I wear—you call him Will?"

"Yes."

"Did he know these words?"

"Yes. He knew them very well."

"Then I must have got them from his mind. I often find words in my mouth that seem to have been left behind with the body, as a man might leave an old, broken knife or a cloak pin in a house when he moves elsewhere. I think the body has memories of its own. Sometimes I dream of a world I've never seen. The colors are too bright, and there's too much noise."

"Sounds like our world."

"Did you really think I was your friend, playing some terrible joke?"

"It got pretty nasty when you killed Peter."

"I was deceived. I wanted my strength back so badly."

"It's hard to figure the rules in this world."

"Have you waited so long to bury Peter?"

"This isn't Peter's grave."

"Whose grave is it?"

"'*Mine, sir.*'" Bess looked closely at him as she spoke.

"'*I think it be thine indeed, for thou liest in't.*'"

"There! You did it again!" cried Bess, pointing at him.

"Was that from the play?"

"Word for word."

"I did not know. Whom is the grave for?"

"'*For no man—*' Forget it. It's Rosey's grave."

"Rosey?"

"She killed herself. Threw herself from the cliff into the sea."

"Gods. Why?"

"Nobody knows. But it's how she died in the play. In the play she did it in a river, but she drowned. All of us are dying in the order we do in the play, and pretty much in the same way.

And we're getting close to the bloodbath at the end."

"When do you die?"

"Technically I'm not in the play at all. But I guess I'm the gravedigger now. Fortunately for me, the gravedigger isn't important enough to get killed. He comes on, does a couple jokes, and then disappears."

"What happens now?"

"They bring in Ophelia's coffin—that's Rosey's coffin. Laertes—that's Randy, who's also disappeared—goes into hysterics, and then Hamlet comes out of hiding and says, 'Hey, I loved her more than you did,' and then Laertes says, 'You're the reason she killed herself,' and they go for each other's throats and the congregation has to separate them. That's what sets up the sword duel at the end where Hamlet and Laertes manage to kill each other and everybody else too."

"This is my story?"

"It was simpler in real life. You killed your uncle and burned his warriors in the hall. And you survived."

"I like that version much better."

"Unfortunately, you're stuck in this version."

"I call that unjust. Unless my body fell dead when I came here, I have to suppose your friend Will is living my life. How good is he at avenging blood?"

"I . . . wouldn't say it was his strong suit."

"I expected no better from a man with a body

like this. Tell me, why do you dig this grave? I know you folk have no inkling of what's proper to men and women, but surely a man could do this job more easily."

"We're running a little short of able-bodied men. Randy's run off; Peter's dead; Sean's too high and mighty to work with his hands, and Howie's a prophet, which is even worse than a king."

"Well, let me take the shovel. It's hardly proper work for a warrior, but it would be shameful to stand and let a woman wear herself out."

"I ought to take offense at that, I suppose," said Bess, "but the fact is I'm getting blisters here. Take the spade and welcome."

They traded places and Amlodd dug down to the six-foot level. "I could have done this much faster with my own arms," he said.

"Do you know, Amlodd, we're all getting a little tired of hearing how strong you used to be. It's almost as bad as Sean's stories about the famous actors he almost worked with."

"That bad?"

"I'm the director. It's my job to share hard truths with the cast."

"I really was very strong."

"Not much use now, is it?"

"I suppose not." Amlodd threw the shovel up and hoisted himself out of the hole. He walked away toward the cliffs, his head bowed.

"Wait! Amlodd! Where are you going?" Bess ran after him.

"To die, perhaps. There's no more cause to live."

"I didn't mean to hurt your feelings."

"I've lost all that made me a man. I have no strength. I have no honor."

"Every man can't be strong. They can all have honor."

"A weakling is worth nothing."

"You're wrong. Listen—how does a hero end?"

"End?"

"How does a hero end his life?"

"By dying bravely, in the face of his enemies."

"Not in victory?"

"No man can be victorious forever."

"So couldn't a weak man die the same way? Wouldn't he be even more heroic, since his enemies must always be overwhelming—not only at the end but all his life?"

Amlodd put his hands on either side of his head. "I cannot hold these thoughts. There is no peg in my mind where they can hang."

"Your mind's okay. It takes time for anyone to get used to a new idea. New ideas come so fast in our time that we don't dare let ourselves love any of them, because we assume we'll have to throw them away soon. Then we move on to new ideas we don't love either. It hardly seems worth the trouble, but it makes us feel important."

"In my time I could go my whole life without stubbing my toe against a new idea."

"Who am I to say our way is better? But give things time at least. Don't die. There's been dying enough here."

"What's that?"

A sound of singing came from the direction of the castle. As they turned to watch, a line of figures emerged from the keep. Six of them carried a coffin, but they did not look like a conventional funeral party. As they sang, the processionors walked in a strange, stilted fashion, making small hops and waving their arms in a jerky fashion.

As the procession neared, Amlodd and Bess could recognize that the hoppers were their friends, Diane and Sean and Howie. Servants carried the coffin. And behind them, leaping and whirling, white-robed, came Eric.

Amlodd and Bess walked to meet them. They came together at the grave. The servants set the coffin down by its side.

"What's with the chorus line?" asked Bess.

Everyone looked around them, and no one spoke.

"My idea," said Eric with a smile. "A funeral dance. I want my worshipers happy. I don't think people should get all bent out of shape just because somebody croaked. Hey, my mother died and I didn't go all weepy."

No one spoke the obvious response aloud.

"You're all afraid of this troll?" asked Amlodd.

No one answered.

"You're letting him rule you?"

Bess said, "Yes, he's decided he's God."

Amlodd frowned. "The true gods will not stand for this."

"True gods?" cried Eric. "Look at me! What do you want in a god? You want big? I can be big!" Before their eyes he transformed into Yggxvthwul and towered over them, tentacles waving.

"You want powerful?" he roared. He opened his maw and a rumbling issued forth. The earth shook beneath their feet, and all the headstones in the graveyard flew into the air like leaves in wind and sailed into the sea.

"You want something more familiar?" Eric thundered. His figure changed again, and he became a gigantic man with a red beard and a hammer in his hand.

"You should have showed me that one sooner," said Amlodd. "You might have fooled me with that."

Eric went back to his Yggxvthwul guise. "Let me explain this in little words you can understand," he said. "There are no gods. Not in the way you're thinking. The only thing there is, is power. If you've got power enough to make people worship you, you get to be a god. That's what I am, because I've got the power."

Amlodd turned to Bess. "Even you?" he asked.

"I'm not gonna be a martyr over a religious issue," she said.

"What about your freedom?"

"Eric's pretty easygoing about morals."

"There's more to freedom than sleeping with whomever or whatever you like. I was thinking of your freedom to hold your head high and bow to no man."

"I prefer the freedom to go on living."

Amlodd sneered. "Such as you will always lose your freedom. I might bow to a worthy god, but not to a troll boy with the face of a thrall."

Eric asked, "And what are you gonna do about it?"

Amlodd drew his sword. "Someone who does not live by her own words told me not long ago that even a weak man can die. This I can do— I can spit in your troll face and defy you!"

"Okay, have it your way," said Eric. He reached a tentacle out and seized on Amlodd's sword, wrenching it away and tossing it outside the churchyard wall, where it stuck pointfirst in a tree trunk.

Amlodd cursed and ran to leap the wall. He seized the sword by its grip and tried to pull it out. He could not.

A tentacle wrapped itself around his neck and lifted him off the ground. He hung strangling until Eric let him go. He dropped about eight feet and lay on the grass, his chest heaving.

"Poor little barbarian," said Eric. "Poor little bones broken? Poor little muscles tired? Are you gonna tell us about how strong you used to be now?"

"Is that—the best you've got, troll?" Amlodd panted.

"That's nothin'," said Eric. "Ever hear of golf? I'm gonna show you a hole in one."

With one tentacle he struck Amlodd a swinging blow that threw him high in the air and dropped him neatly into Rosey's grave.

Eric's laughter boomed in waves that could be felt on the skin as much as heard.

Amlodd lay in the grave, unable to move. The sky above looked like a small open door, far away. He knew he would die in this hole, and no man would ever know how his saga ended. He hated the thought, but this body was done. It had no more to give. He thought his arm was broken.

Then he felt a small wind, like the draft when a door opens. He looked up at a man who towered over him. The man was dressed like a Dane, with red-gold hair and beard and a sword at his side.

"I know you," said the man, in the Danish tongue. "What happens if we touch?"

The man bent and put his hand on Amlodd's shoulder.

Amlodd spun as if in a maelstrom at sea. He felt helpless, as he had when Yggxvthwul had been tossing him about.

Only now he felt stronger every moment.

When his vision cleared he stood in the grave. At his feet lay a brown-haired man in clothing like the actors'.

He looked down at himself.

His clothes were Danish.

He was strong and tall.

He was himself again.

"I lend you my body and look what you do with it," moaned the man at his feet.

"I beg your pardon," said Amlodd. He found that he remembered the new tongue he'd learned. "But I think I can do this thing now. You rest."

"I'm not going anywhere."

Amlodd reached a hand up out of the grave, grasped the turf, and pulled himself up and out.

"Who are you?" roared Yggxvthwul.

"I am Amlodd Orvendilsson. I am the death of trolls."

"Where did you come from?"

"I've been here all the time. But I have my body back now. You're all tired of hearing me talk about it. Now I'll show you what it can do."

"It'll be a quick demonstration," said Yggxvthwul, stretching out a whiplike tentacle.

Faster than sight, Amlodd drew his sword and flicked the tip of the tentacle off.

Yggxvthwul roared in pain, drawing the tentacle back and tucking it into his mouth.

"You hurt me!" he screamed in Eric's voice.

"About time you found out how it felt," said Amlodd.

"You hurt me! I'm gonna hurt you!"

Yggxvthwul struck out with four other tentacles. Amlodd wielded his sword two-handed,
whirling and ducking as he sliced off two more
ends.

Yggxvthwul erupted in a shriek of agony, waving his tentacles as green ichor spouted from
three of them. He hopped around like a child
with burned fingers.

"Daddy!" he cried. "Daddy! Daddy!"

As he danced about he grew smaller and
smaller before them, and he changed from green
to flesh, and became Eric Smedhammer, hopp-
ing up and down naked.

When he was small enough to handle, his
father held him in his arms, and looked at the
three fingers which had been cut off at the tips
or first knuckles.

"I'll sue your ass, you bastard!" Howie shouted
to Amlodd.

Amlodd only laughed. "I'll miss you people
when I'm gone."

Howie ripped strips from his shirttail to tour-
niquet and bandage his son's fingers, and sent
a servant for something for him to wear.

A voice emerged from the grave. "If the fight's
over, could somebody help me out of here? I
think I've got a broken arm."

With a little trouble, and a rope the servants
brought under his armpits, they managed to get
Will out of the grave without too much pain to
him. Howie called for splints from the servants
and set the limb with ill grace. It was a break

above the wrist, and Howie rigged a sling. Will groaned. One of the servants brought Will the sword Amlodd had lost. When Will looked at it without recognition, the servant slipped it into the scabbard for him.

"We still have a funeral to do," said Bess.

"I suppose someone ought to say a prayer or something," said Sean.

"I'll pray," said Will.

"You?" asked Diane.

"I've been going through some changes."

Pale and a little unsteady, Will made a prayer over the grave, and the servants lowered the coffin in. The cast left them to fill the grave as they took the road back to the castle. Eric leaned on his father, and Will leaned on Amlodd. It seemed strange to borrow strength from what had been his own body until a few minutes ago.

It took them some time, during the walk and sitting in the hall over flagons of ale, to compare stories.

"Just like in the play?" asked Will. "Peter and Rosey, by stabbing and drowning? And Del, too?"

"Of course Del wasn't in the script," said Bess, "but we've learned a whole new meaning for the phrase 'the power of great literature.'"

"And it's got us pretty darn nervous," said Diane. Will was surprised to hear her use such a bland adjective.

"I don't think it can run through to Shakespeare's end," said Will.

"Why not?" asked Sean.

"Somebody explained it to me in Amlodd's time. They might have been lying, but I don't think so. This whole thing was set up by Randy. He's not a human being. He's . . . what we'd call an elf. I don't mean a short guy who lives in a tree and makes cookies. I mean a different kind of being, like an alien. I know it's hard to believe."

"Not so hard," said Bess. "We saw him disappear before our eyes."

"Jeeze. Well, from what I was told, Randy's people know the way between alternate universes. You understand about alternate universes—?"

"Been there, discussed that," said Sean. "Skip ahead, skip ahead."

"And since Randy's the only one of his kind in the cast—as far as we know—this must be his setup. He's playing with us. He didn't expect Amlodd and me to change places though."

"Why would he do that?" asked Diane.

"Hard to say. But according to my source, these people have no pain and never die, so they crave our sensations."

"That goes with what Randy told us," said Bess.

"Anyway, the thing is, if Randy can't die, the play can't end the way Shakespeare wrote it. He must have something else in mind."

"*We* can die though," said Sean.

They sat silent a moment.

"Tell me about Jutland—home," said Amlodd. Will told the story. As he related Katla's death and the burning of the hall, Amlodd stood up and began pacing.

"You took my vengeance!" he said when the story was done.

"I didn't have a choice."

"Katla died. If I'd been there I'd have done the job before the England voyage, and she'd have come to no harm. And I'd have had a chance to say goodbye to my mother."

"You're probably right. I did the best I could."

"I guess we know the reason for Hamlet's famous hesitation now," said Sean mildly.

"I ought to kill you for Katla's sake," said Amlodd to Will.

"Let's not forget you killed my friend Peter,"said Will.

Amlodd mulled that over. "I suppose the one balances the other," he said, frowning. "I was deceived by one I took for a god and did a shameful deed. I shall ask more of gods than mere power in future."

"This is all very interesting, but what I want to know is what you're going to do about it, Will," said Sean.

"Do about it?" asked Will.

"It seems to me it all goes back to that damn book you found. So you're responsible. This thing has gotten out of control, so I want you to do something about it."

"What did you have in mind?"

"Just because I'm the king doesn't mean I have to think of everything. Show some initiative."

"Shut up, Sean," said Bess.

"I *am* your king, remember."

"You're an old lush, Sean. You lost control of the situation some time ago. Don't push it."

Sean's bubble was no longer a robust one. He subsided with a look something like relief and poured himself a drink. He emptied the pot doing it, and called, "Servants! More wine!"

For the first time anyone could recall, no one came in response.

"What the hell is going on?" asked Bess.

"Look at the tapestries," said Diane.

"They're losing color, going black and gold again," said Bess.

Amlodd walked to the wall and pulled a tapestry aside to feel the stone. "No joints," he said.

"Everything's devolving," said Diane. "Maybe this whole world will dissolve to atoms under our feet."

The hall grew darker as she spoke. Even the torchlight dimmed.

"I think Will's coming back messed up the play," said Howie, who sat with an arm around the whimpering Eric's shoulder. "Without the play, this experiment is over."

"It's not so bad as that," said Randy, and they all turned to see him emerge from the shadows, dressed like a hero on the cover of a romance novel in tight black trousers, high black boots and a shirt trimmed with lace. His hair moved in a breeze that nobody could feel.

"It's not the end, it's the climax," said Randy.

"Time to cap the rising action and ring the curtain down."

"Tired of playing with us?" asked Diane. "Ready to find yourself other toys?"

"You'd be well advised to speak politely to me."

"I'll do anything you want," said Sean. "Just say the word."

"Heel boy, heel," said Bess.

"If you're actually behind all this nonsense," said Howie, "I demand you send us home again now. It stopped being funny a long time ago."

"How would I know?" asked Randy. "How would such as I know when anything stopped being funny?

"I don't understand about humor. I can make a joke, but not laugh at one. I know what's funny in theory. I know what's tragic, in theory. But they do not touch me.

"Tragedy is the greatest mystery of all. We know how you fear death. Yet you enjoy stories about death. Where could the pleasure be in that?

"So I took the greatest tragedy of all and built a laboratory for it. I had more than one reason for doing this, but I wanted to see if you could get the same things out of the story in real experience as you do on the stage."

"And what did you conclude?" asked Bess.

"The jury's still out. I'm afraid I'll have to run the process through to the end."

"I'm not gonna drink poison," said Diane.

"I'll give it to her, if you want me to!" said Sean.

"Shut up, Sean," said Bess.

"Oh, it won't end like the play for you," said Randy. "Hard to stage-manage that. All I need is to see the significant death."

"Significant death," said Will. "What do you mean by that?"

Amlodd spoke up. "A man's death is the last and best gift he can offer the gods." He stood a little apart from the rest of the party, an alien. "Each man should live each day in preparation for his death, so as to have a fine one to offer, as a token of entry to Valhalla."

"Quaint," said Randy. He waved a hand and a door opened in the stone wall. " '*Goodnight, sweet prince,*' " he said. "There's your way home."

"To Jutland?"

"Where else? Farewell, '*and flights of angels sing thee to thy rest.*' "

Amlodd hesitated. "I almost wish I could stay, to see the end."

"You've got your own ending to work out."

Amlodd squared his shoulders. "Farewell then, all of you. You've been . . . amusing. I'll not forget you." He turned toward the door.

Eric made a sudden jump and ran toward him. Amlodd whirled and drew his sword to defend himself, but Eric fell to his knees and grasped Amlodd's legs with bandaged hands.

"Take me with you!" he cried, tears coursing down his cheeks.

"Take you with me?" said Amlodd. "Why would you want to come with me?"

"I want to know how to be a man. Nobody'll show me how to be a man back home. I wanna be like you!"

"You'll never be like me," said Amlodd. "You slew your mother."

"I didn't know any better!"

"You knew. No man ever born was ignorant of that law."

"Don't make me go home to my own time! It's terrible there! I do terrible things there, and nobody stops me! I don't want to do them anymore, but I know I will!"

Amlodd said, "That's true. It would be a vile deed to let such a thing happen."

He stepped back quickly, drawing his sword, and struck off Eric's head. Then he stepped back again to keep his clothes from being soaked in the fountain of blood that shot up and ebbed.

Howie ran toward him, but stopped well clear of sword-length. "You bastard! You son-of-a-bitch! You killed my son!"

"I? It was you slew him. I only ended his misery."

He turned and went out through the door, which vanished once he'd passed through.

Howie fell to his knees, his face in his hands. Diane went to him, knelt, and put her arms around him.

"Amlodd *does* go home?" asked Will.

"Don't fret, said Randy I sent him back

whence he came. He's no further use to me. He'll be king of Denmark, and marry a queen of Scotland, and be killed in battle as he wished, if I recall my Saxo correctly. And if Saxo remembered correctly."

"So you need a significant death," said Will. "Someone has to die."

"Significantly. Someone has to lay down his life in the tragic way."

"You should have kept Amlodd around," said Howie. "That's his meat."

"Exactly why I got rid of him. Amlodd came from a culture that was gaga over significant death. So he's prejudiced. I want to see if a modern person can die the same way. You moderns are so superior. You're past the need to grow your own food. You're past the need to hunt. You're past the need to pray. You think all the necessities of your past are part of an evolutionary stage you've outgrown.

"I want to know if you've outgrown tragedy."

The actors looked at one another.

"I know I have," said Howie.

"I've always been more of a comedic actor," said Sean.

"I object to this whole thing," said Bess.

"It's not a real thing," said Diane. "If it were about some real situation, it would make a difference. But this is just a game you set up."

"Isn't all of life just a game God set up?" asked Randy.

"No, it's just a game," said Howie.

"That's what I want to see," Randy answered. "I want to know if tragedy was just a fashion of an age past, or whether it's something that still holds true. I want to know whether a human being's death can still matter."

"And why should we help you with this experiment?" asked Bess.

"Because if one of you stays, the others may go home."

They all looked at each other.

"I suppose I'm the most expendable of the group; no family, no career to speak of and all that," said Sean. He mused a moment. "I won't do it though."

Will stepped forward. "*'I'll be your foil, Laertes. In mine ignorance your skill shall, like a star i' th' darkest night, stick fiery off indeed.'*" He drew the sword that hung at his side.

Randy smiled. "I knew it would be you, Will."

"You're injured, Will," said Diane. "You've got a broken arm. You can't fight."

"*'I have been in continual practice. I shall win at the odds.'*"

"This is crazy," said Bess. "Don't do this, Will. There's got to be another way."

"No. I've been Hamlet. I've *been* Hamlet. I've lived a life that meant something. I learned things in the ways between the worlds. If I went back with you, and let 'Hamlet' be destroyed, I'd live the rest of my life in a cloud and probably jump off a bridge." He went on guard and said, '*Come on, sir.*'"

"'*Come, my lord,*'" said Randy.

It was awkward fencing with one arm in a sling, but Will was surprised at how well he managed. He'd learned a thing or two in the sixth century, and Amlodd had clearly been training this body.

Still, he was slow and weak compared to what he'd been used to up till a few minutes ago. Randy's point danced before him. He could feel its sharpness, its taper, the geometric angle of its reverse perspective, growing smaller as it approached.

"The point isn't envenomed, like in the play," said Randy. "Or perhaps it is. I forget."

"I don't think you forget anything," said Will.

Randy had the advantage. He fought aggressively; he did not seem to tire. Will parried and attacked, but found himself going on defense more and more, as his strength drained off.

"You know what this is, don't you?" asked Randy, making a feint and coming at Will from below with a move he barely parried.

"I think it's called a swordfight," said Will, making an attempt at a strong lunge and getting it turned away.

Randy pressed his attack in a flurry of steel. "This is the thing you've fled all your life. This is a commitment."

Will retreated, defending himself desperately. "Fear of commitment. That's a very Oprah thing to say."

"I don't just mean with women, though you have quite a record in that department. What do you fear most in the whole world?"

Will felt an agonizing jab as Randy's point pierced his injured arm. He jerked in response, and got a second jab in the chest muscles. He realized Randy might have killed him, and raised his guard in spite of the pain.

"What would you say, *'a palpable hit'*?" asked Randy.

"*'A touch, a touch; I do confess't,'*" said Will. "But it's not about points, is it?"

"You know a hawk from a handsaw," said Randy, and he attacked again. Will fought backwards, defending himself.

"You're running from me, Will," said Randy from behind a wasp's swarm of steel flourishes. "Just like you ran from your mother. Just like you've run from everything in your life that looked like it might have some permanence. Well this is death. You don't get more permanent than that."

"I know," said Will, still retreating.

Randy said, "I don't think you'll hold out to the point of death. I think you'll run away."

"So you're not just out to kill me. You're going to hurt me, again and again, until I can't take it anymore, so you can tell . . . whatever passes for friends in your world—"

Randy drove his point into Will's right upper thigh. Will dropped to one knee, then struggled onto both feet again.

"Friends," said Randy. "Another story you humans tell yourselves. Like love and loyalty and tragedy. All lies you've invented to make your meaningless lives bearable."

"So I'm here to defend the honor of the whole human race?"

"There is no honor. Run away. I'll send you home, and only you and I will know what we proved."

"If I did run away, it wouldn't prove anything."

"It would prove it to me, and to you. That's enough for me. It comes down to blood and judgment. It's always blood and judgment.

"Your human blood is all sweet and sentimental and needy. Your blood tells you, *I need love. I need people. I need to trade my personal freedom for the warmth and security of a family.*

"But your judgment says, *stay free. Keep your autonomy. Don't let yourself get trapped in something that might get uncomfortable.*

"If you listen to your blood, you regret it the rest of your life—you're trapped. If you listen to your judgment, you regret it the rest of your life—you're alone.

"Whatever you do, you lose. And that, my friends, is the meaning of life."

He lunged and set the point of his rapier to Will's throat.

Will stood his ground, and looked him in the eye.

"Yes, it's blood and judgment," he said, smiling.

"But it's not just the blood that wants love. The judgment knows we need it too. And as often as not it's the blood that's hurt and frightened, and running away from love.

"It's not one on one side and one on the other. The line runs right down the middle of both parts. It's physical and it's spiritual, and they're both broken.

"So I had to find something that wasn't broken—blood that was whole blood; judgment that was whole judgment.

"I found it. I found it hiding in plain sight, right where everybody said it was. Blood and judgment; flesh and spirit; God and man; death and resurrection. I learned there was such a thing as love; after that it all came together."

"How very touching."

"If I don't impress you, I apologize. But I can do one thing to beat any trick you've got. I can die."

He braced himself for the thrust he expected. Instead the point fell away. He saw Randy step back.

"It's all academic," Randy said, raising his arm in a dramatic gesture.

The floor began to shake and the shaking rose to a rumble. A crack appeared in the stone floor, separating Will and Randy from the others by a crevice about three feet wide.

"We spoke of a vacuum which sucked you all into this world," said Randy. "To let you all go would create another such vacuum. This vacuum would destroy the story of Hamlet forever. You were right. This is Hamlet's world. My placing the Kyd book in your world destroyed it, and created the vacuum that drew you all here.

"If any of you were to stay, save one, it would not be enough to hold this world together. Only Hamlet will do. Only Hamlet's presence will save the play.

"I will not kill you, Will. I need you, here.

"Somewhere in history we will find new actors to play the drama out. This rehearsal—this adventure with these people—was a good start, but it was not enough. We followed the outline of the story, but we improvised the lines.

"The next run-through will be better. It will be closer to the script.

"Then there will be another run-through and another, each with a new set of actors, save only you and me. Each time the actors will come closer to Shakespeare's script, not through memorization and rehearsal, but through the power of the story itself, winding about itself again and again in time like an electrical transformer.

"In the end—perhaps years, perhaps centuries hence—the play will be re-created word for word.

"Then you and I will fight in earnest.

"Then we shall slay one another."

"I thought you could not die," said Will.

"One thing is more powerful than the curse of Cain," said Randy. "I believe that the power of a tragedy can grant me the death I crave; the death I deserve. If I stand in Laertes' shoes, and the inexorable force of the story demands my death, then I *must* die."

Will said, "But you'll let these others go."

"*'You cannot, sir, take from me anything that I will more willingly part withal—except my life.'*"

"I'm not going without Will," said Diane from across the rift.

"You don't get a say," said Randy. He waved and there was a stone wall where the rift had been.

"They're back safe and sound?" asked Will.

"Safe as houses. Safe as prisons. Safe as the miserable little lives they're mired in. Epsom, Minnesota will not lose its entire artistic soul.

"But you stay here with me. You and I shall do a thousand performances or more of Hamlet. They tell me Hell's a lot like that—the same mistake repeated over and over."

"So I've heard. Do I get a chance to recover from my wounds? I'm bleeding here. If I bleed to death or die of infection, you'll have to find another Hamlet."

"Yes, all right." Randy waved his hand and Will felt a prickly warmth course through his body. He knew at once that his injuries were gone. His arm didn't hurt anymore, and he unbound his splints. He flexed the hand. It felt good.

"You should have been a doctor," he said. "You might have learned that it's pleasant to help people."

"Relieve pain and death? The very things I long to experience?"

"You could experience them vicariously."

"I'm not a voyeur, thank you very much."

"You? I'd call you the most intense form of voyeur."

"You're stretching the definition. 'Tacteur' might be a better word, if it is a word."

"It really is all academic to you, isn't it?"

"That's what I've been telling you."

"I can't say I honestly look forward to spending the next few centuries in your company."

"Already the commitment anxiety?"

Will sighed. "I guess so. Not much to be done about it now."

"Well, if you want to be alone, like Greta Garbo, I have some good news for you. I have to go locate a new cast."

"How long will that take?"

"Hard to say. You think Time's relative in your home universe? You ain't seen nothin' compared to this one."

Randy vanished.

Will sat alone in the dim hall.

Of a sudden he missed Randy.

"Why should it bother me?" he asked himself aloud. "This is what I've labored for all my life. This is the treasure I laid up for myself in eternity."

It had been a mercy, he thought, to learn now what a bad course he'd been on. Some people never learned it till they were too old to try anything else.

The half-darkness did not change. He sat with his back against a wall, lost in thought. Occasionally he imagined being left here permanently alone, duped by one final trick of Randy's. He fought down the feeling and prayed for peace.

The sound, when he grew aware of it, had already been in his ears for some time. It was something like voices, and something like music. It was, in fact, both voices and music.

Will rose and followed the sound. It was loudest at a point where he found a door in the wall—one he hadn't noticed before. He put his hand on the latch and pulled it open.

The door opened to a courtyard under the sky. There was nothing unfinished or devolved about any of it. The courtyard was of dressed stone, surrounded by high windows through which women and children watched.

Through the yard paraded a motley congregation of men, old and young. They wore jerkins and galligaskins and hose, many sporting soft caps with feathers in them. Some of their clothing was ragged, most of it was patched, but the colors were bright, reds and yellows and greens, and the wearers danced and leaped and walked on their hands. Some of them wore ribbons and some of them wore bells. Some of them played tamborines or wooden rattles.

Will knew them right away. He could not mistake them. They were his brothers, though he was much their junior.

They were actors.

In a moment he was in the midst of them, and they seemed to know him too, for they smiled and laughed with him, and somebody clapped him on the shoulder.

He turned to see a smiling face with a wine-red birthmark covering the left cheek. "Welcome, brother!" the man said. He offered him a skin of wine, and Will took a pull from it.

"Where are we going?" Will asked.

"We're going to see the king!"

"What fun! Is the king expecting us?"

"Not that I know of. But his nephew loves plays."

"So you think we'll be welcome?"

"Who knows? Sometimes they welcome us with hot food and purses of silver. Sometimes they drive us out with brickbats and offal. That's what makes it interesting!"

Will laughed.

They turned a corner and approached the entrance to the great hall, where four men stood talking to one another at the top of the great stairway.

One of the men was old with a long beard. The other three were young men. Tallest of them was a fair-haired man with a small beard, dressed all in black. He looked a little like Kenneth Branagh, a little like Richard Burton, a little like Laurence Olivier and John Gielgud, a little like John Barrymore and a little like Edwin Booth.

The old man was saying,

"The best actors in the world, either for tragedy, comedy, history, pastoral, pastoral-comical, historical-pastoral, tragical-historical, tragical-comical-historical-pastoral, scene individable, or poem unlimited. Seneca cannot be too heavy, nor Plautus too light. For the law of writ and the liberty, these are the only men."

❧ CHAPTER XIX ❧

They bundled Will in a thick gray blanket to protect him from the cold wind and opened the door of a big van for him. Inside the van he saw Bess, Diane, Sean and Howie, wrapped in blankets like his. It was warm inside when they shut the door. It felt good. There was no one else in the van to hear what they said.

"Is this . . . everybody?" Will asked.

"The others didn't come back with us," said Bess. "I guess they're lost in the fire."

Will could hear Howie sobbing.

"What did you think?" asked Sean. "Did you think we'd wake up like at the end of *The Wizard of Oz*, and find out it was all a dream?"

"I had hopes. My wounds went away."

No one said anything for a minute.

"What happened with you?" asked Diane.

Will explained about Randy's grand plan.

"So what?" asked Sean. "Is *Hamlet* destroyed now? I still remember it."

"No. Randy was wrong. Hamlet didn't need Randy to have his own universe. I saw him myself.

"Randy said it—a story is more powerful than almost anything there is. A little thing like Kyd's book couldn't destroy it."

"So what do they do there?" asked Sean. "Just do the play over and over again forever? Like the myth of Sisyphus or something?"

"I don't think so. I didn't get the impression anybody was bored with repetition. Just the opposite, in fact. I think it was what a theologian might call an 'eternal moment.' One event that's so large it fills a whole eternity. I think in a real sense I'm still there, with the players, and always will be." He smiled.

After a time a rescue worker got into the driver's seat and drove them to the hospital. They spent a couple hours being checked over, and then were taken to the police station, where they gave their reports. All the reports tallied. They'd agreed in the van what they should say.

It was after 4:00 A.M. when a deputy drove them back to the theater to get their cars and go home. As he approached his Cherokee in a borrowed parka, Will found Bess walking beside him.

"Where's the Kyd book now?" she asked.

"At my place. I'll destroy it if it's still there, but I'll bet it's not."

"Book-burning already? You're not wasting any time."

Will stopped and looked at her. "What does that mean?"

"You said you'd got Peter's religion."

"Well, yes I did."

"So I'm bitter. I get hurt when I lose a friend."

"I'm your friend."

"You've gone over to the other side. You're the enemy."

"I'm not your enemy. Neither was Peter. You never spoke badly of Peter."

"No. And I won't speak badly of you either. I respect you, and I'll go on casting you. But I choose my friends."

"I *am* your friend. I mean to be your friend."

"Don't knock yourself out." She walked away from him.

Will followed quickly. "You're not gonna pull this gay paranoia thing about how everyone who disagrees with you must hate you, are you? I thought you were bigger than that, Bess."

"Well, I'm not. Now just go to hell, will you?"

It was about 5:00 A.M. when Will got home. He let Abelard out (he went like a shot) and looked in the dresser drawer where he'd left the Kyd volume.

It was gone as if it had never been there.

Will nodded and made some instant cocoa. He'd take a personal day today. Soon it would be a reasonable hour to call people on the phone.

He looked up Ginnie's number. At worst he'd be able to ask forgiveness.

He was as afraid as he'd ever been, in any world.

Good.

THE
END